## DAMN YOU. . . . DAMN . . .

Those were the last words he remembered. They were the only words he remembered. The man came to lying on his chest, knowing nothing more except that he was alive.

That much was plain anyway. It was not memory.

As he became dimly aware of his surroundings, and the thick black night in his head became too bright day, he realized he did not actually remember anything more than those words. He did try to answer the involuntary first question, *Where am I?* He knit his forehead. As his mind struggled to get its footing, he found himself wondering: *What am I doing here?*

# RALPH COMPTON

## DEATH VALLEY DRIFTER

**A Ralph Compton Western by**

## JEFF ROVIN

BERKLEY
New York

BERKLEY
An imprint of Penguin Random House LLC
penguinrandomhouse.com

Copyright © 2020 by The Estate of Ralph Compton
Penguin Random House supports copyright. Copyright fuels creativity, encourages
diverse voices, promotes free speech, and creates a vibrant culture. Thank you for buying
an authorized edition of this book and for complying with copyright laws by not
reproducing, scanning, or distributing any part of it in any form without permission.
You are supporting writers and allowing Penguin Random House to continue to
publish books for every reader.

BERKLEY and the BERKLEY & B colophon are registered trademarks of
Penguin Random House LLC.

ISBN: 9780593100752

First Edition: September 2020

Printed in the United States of America
1  3  5  7  9  10  8  6  4  2

Cover art by Dennis Lyall
Cover design by Steve Meditz
Book design by George Towne

# THE IMMORTAL COWBOY

This is respectfully dedicated to the "American Cowboy." His was the saga sparked by the turmoil that followed the Civil War, and the passing of more than a century has by no means diminished the flame.

———◆———

True, the old days and the old ways are but treasured memories, and the old trails have grown dim with the ravages of time, but the spirit of the cowboy lives on.

———◆———

In my travels—to Texas, Oklahoma, Kansas, Nebraska, Colorado, Wyoming, New Mexico, and Arizona—I always find something that reminds me of the Old West. While I am walking these plains and mountains for the first time, there is this feeling that a part of me is eternal, that I have known these old trails before. I believe it is the undying spirit of the frontier calling me, through the mind's eye, to step back into time. What is the appeal of the Old West of the American frontier?

———◆———

It has been epitomized by some as the dark and bloody period in American history. Its heroes—Crockett, Bowie, Hickok, Earp—have been reviled and criticized. Yet the Old West lives on, larger than life.

———◆———

It has become a symbol of freedom, when there was always another mountain to climb and another river to cross; when a dispute between two men was settled not with expensive lawyers, but with fists, knives, or guns. Barbaric? Maybe. But some things never change. When the cowboy rode into the pages of American history, he left behind a legacy that lives within the hearts of us all.

—*Ralph Compton*

No plan of operations extends with any certainty
beyond the first contact with the main hostile force.

*Helmuth von Moltke the Elder*

# PROLOGUE

THE NIGHT WAS warm, and the desert wilderness was dark as the two men galloped from the camp. Shouts trailed them like the smoke from the campfire, clinging yet growing fainter by the moment.

It was not their camp, and the box tied to the saddle of one man did not belong to them. They had acquired it in a breeze-soft but lightning-fast attack that left their victims stunned—and momentarily horseless, the thieves having cut the reins of their mounts.

But the four uniformed people at the camp—one of them possibly a woman; it was difficult to be certain in the firelight—were not helpless, and they had a desperate reason to mount a pursuit. That was why the robbers had fled quickly. They had pressed their horses hard, the animals' footing uncertain in the deep sand and entangling scrub. The mounts were starting to show resistance, especially the palomino with the blond mane.

The other horse, black as the sky and spotted here and there with white, paid more attention to its resolute rider—the man with the box.

Though they raced swiftly north, the man on the blond stallion regretted their flight. He was angrily chewing down on the tall strand of prairie grass he had picked during their approach, using it to keep his mouth moist as the hot night air rushed in. There hadn't been time to drink from the deerskin, first for fear of making noise and then for being a distraction as they fled. They had to *get away*, he had been told. *Now.*

Frustrated by his uncooperative horse and by the retreat, the tall man had kept pace with his partner before stopping and simultaneously executing a quarter turn to the left so he was facing the other man. The second man galloped past several paces. He stopped abruptly to rein partly around.

This man's face was a long, featureless shape in the dark. The reins were wrapped around the wrist of his left hand. In his right, he was still holding the revolver he had drawn back at the camp. It rested protectively on the small lockbox, the leather handle atop the metal container slung around the pommel. There had not been time to open the box and remove its contents; until then he wanted it where he could see it, feel it knocking as he rode. He also could not destroy what was inside. The items might be needed by his own people. Aggie, if it came to that.

"What the hell is wrong with you?" demanded the man who had stopped second.

"We have to go back!"

The long face grew rigid. "Mister, you're taking orders, not giving them—"

"And you're being reckless. Those men back there—they're veterans. You know as well as I do, soon as they rally they're coming back hard! Best to take the four of them now when we can set an ambush!"

"Veterans enough not to ride stupidly into a trap. They may be making torches right now. They think *we're* hiding, they'll burn brush. We outrun them. That's the plan!"

"Your plan is a puzzle, my friend!"

"You're wasting time!"

"And *you're* being reckless! Those boys are Rebs still fighting a war! You saw how they ran us from Mexico to here—they're not going to stop. Which says to me we fight them now when we have a jump, or we fight them later when we don't."

"They're not the only ones still fighting a war."

"What does that mean?"

"I can't say more."

"Who the hell am I gonna tell anything to out here?"

The other man raised the gun and glared at his companion. "Damn it—ride. Now."

The other peered into the dark, still—and disappointed. "Or what? You gonna shoot me?"

"If I have to."

"For this or for something else?"

"What are you talking about?"

"I saw you and Aggie before we set out." He let that register, then added, "I was coming to say my good-byes to her."

The other man hesitated. "I'm sorry. Truly. But I wouldn't draw on you for that."

"You sure?"

"I'm sure of this. I'd rather have you dead here than

go back and get caught. They will cut you up for what they need to know."

"Even if they did, I couldn't tell them much, thanks to you. 'Some kind of war's being fought, only I don't know what that means.'"

The other man said nothing, but his stance was defiant. The rebellious rider's mind was churning things fast. Something was not right. His behavior back at the camp, their urgent departure—he would say fearful, if he did not know his companion better.

"You could have killed them back in Ensenada, too," the stubborn rider went on. "But that rider showed up— who was he?"

"God*damn* it, there's no time. You coming . . . or staying? Last chance."

The man on the spot did not move. His hand was a few inches from the sheath strapped to his hip. It held his second Bowie knife; he had left the other one in a tree about a half inch from a man's cheek. Close enough to make him talk without inhibiting his ability to do so. He would not be able to reach the remaining knife in time—not if the other man meant what he said.

And the idea of drawing on his old comrade in arms tasted bad inside his cheeks.

Both horses complained simultaneously. The hot night air was picking up, and there were unfamiliar sounds in the night, on the ground and in the skies.

"You haven't even told me why we're here!" protested the man with the Bowie knife.

"Look, keeping secrets wasn't my choice. Those were orders."

The other man considered that, then shook his head.

"Then this is my choice. Kill me if you want, but I run *to* fights. I don't run from them."

And that was the last thing he said before the second man's arm moved, and the gun swung, and the man who was struck swore as he fell—

# CHAPTER ONE

*D*AMN YOU. . . . *DAMN* . . .
Those were the last words he remembered. They were the only words he remembered. The man came to lying on his chest, knowing nothing more except that he was alive.

That much was plain anyway. It was not memory.

As he became dimly aware of his surroundings, and the thick black night in his head became too bright day, he realized he did not actually remember anything more than those words. He did try to answer the involuntary first question, *Where am I?* He knit his forehead. As his mind struggled to get its footing, he found himself wondering: *What am I doing here?*

The question was brusquely shoved aside by a hard, angry pulsing throughout the entirety of his skull. He asked himself, *Have I been drinking?*

He did not know. Like the sweat that permeated his

skin, some insistent and rational piece of him pushed to the fore.

*One puzzle at a time.*

The man opened his eyes to slits and fought through the pain in his head to have a think about what he did know. It was day. He saw blurry yellow-white ahead of him, felt the sun on his back and left cheek, on the backs of his bare arms. He was aware of grit along the outsides of his gums. And his head hurt worse for the effort of just letting in the light. He knew that, too.

The man's face was lying on its right cheek. When he found the strength to inhale deeply, he also found that there was sand in his nose. His nostrils were partly lying in it. He made a valiant attempt to snort out the grit, mostly succeeding after three tries; then he tried to raise his face. The sand clung like pepper on a fish. That was no concern. What was: The instant he moved, the right side of his head kicked as though there was a bronc in his skull trying hard and regular to get out. The man dropped back into the hot, dry sand. As consciousness returned more fully, he realized that his back burned. His chest did, too, because the hot sand clung there, too, stuck in every pore from his exposed waist to his neck. There was something crawling inside his ear, too small to be a scorpion—probably a fly. He shook his head a little, and it buzzed away with noisy protest.

*You remember bugs,* he thought, able to visualize them.

The man's fingers were lying beside his thighs. They were swollen from the heat. He felt along his legs. They were not bare, though he had no idea why he was wearing just long, sweat-soaked underwear bottoms. Worse than that, even as his head cleared and he could picture garments and feel textures, he still had no idea where he was or how he had gotten here. And as the man started to think, he realized one thing more.

He had no idea who he was.

He thought hard. What little he remembered—from when, he also had no idea—came when he used his tongue to try to spit out more sand.

*A picnic lunch. A sunny beach. Sand in the food. But—was that recently?*

He knew what he felt, and also what he smelled and heard—both, nothing. Not a horse, which surprised him. It was time to see. When he finally opened his eyes, they instantly smarted from the sun, which was white and washed-out. But at least he could see the daylight, the sand, and a bit of scrub. When he closed them, all he could see were shadows of a horizon and the foliage against ruddy eyelids. Nothing else appeared to him, not even what he looked like. There was just a deep black well without a bottom or a reflection.

As time passed—perhaps minutes, maybe only seconds; pain had its own way of measuring things—he gave some attention to the sweat that greased his body. It was thick and heating his outsides to near broiling, sucking all the moisture from inside. Moving his mouth, he realized it was not only sandy, but he could not clear it because his tongue was too dry to try to spit. And then, as he slowly raised a hand to where his head hurt—the plumped hand seemed to weigh as much as an iron mallet—he became aware that not all the moisture on his scalp was perspiration.

There was a sticky patch of blood clinging to his hair like morning dew in hell. His fat, shaking fingers spider-walked along the thin trail that ran from the top of his head to deep behind his right ear.

The man's fingertips crept back in the other direction along his scalp, and he let out a raspy yelp of pain as he found the open wound toward the front of his crown. At first he wondered if he had somehow survived a scalping—how did he remember what *that* was, but not his name?—until his crablike exploration found just a gash in the hair wide and damned painful but not very deep.

He had been struck. He remembered a lightning flash behind both eyes. And right before that, before he swore—

A figure indistinct in the dark. Very near with a six-shooter in his hand.

The figure was not shooting. But he was coming toward the man. He remembered, suddenly, his own horse, dark brown with a blond mane. He must have been riding swiftly, since the animal was breathing heavily. Everything else about the animal—saddle, gear, what weapon he might have been carrying—he could not picture or recall. Or what he had been doing right before that. Or why. Or where. It must have been something in this desert, though he could not picture anything.

*Well, a companion and a horse—that's something,* he thought. Was the horse nearby? He would have to open his eyes and get off the damned ground to find out.

Mustering his energy was almost as difficult as trying to remember things. Rising came in jagged spurts, like a marionette being lifted by its strings. It happened with great effort and initially generated little progress. The man dragged his arms from his sides, all stiff and unhelpful joints below the shoulders. He finally planted his palms on the ground, inhaled, and pushed up. Sand clung to half his face as it was lifted from the scalding, sweat-dampened ground. There was a blade of grass stuck to his lower lip, held there as if it were peeling skin. His arms shook, but he locked the elbows. His head screamed, but his mouth was too parched to give the pain more than raw, airy voice. A weak hiss escaped his throat, and then he settled into the rhythm of the pain. He closed his dirty, blistered lips and breathed through his nose, painfully sneezing out the dirt. He lost strength for a moment and fell down, plunking his chin on the sand to support the weight of his aching head. He feared that if he gave up now, he would never get up. He pushed up again.

The grass and some of the sand had come free, his exposed skin baking under the sun. His elbows locked again, and he remained upright. It took a moment for his dry eyes to focus, longer to adjust to the brilliant daylight.

The man did not like what those hurting eyes settled on.

There was an ugly rusty shape about two feet in front of him. It was a scorpion. He knew that it was a danger. But even a horse would know that much. Fortunately, the devilish-looking thing seemed as unmotivated as he was in the white sunlight. Nonetheless, it was best to get away. Pressing his palms to the hot ground and having more reason to get up than he had a moment before, the man rose slowly.

He grunted, his head hammering angrily, but at least his arm and back muscles did not complain much. Breath came without pain. He could not have been here long enough for them to have stiffened, he decided. With effort, he got onto his knees, hovered there until he was steady, then looked around.

There was nothing to hold on to. No tree—and no horse. That was concerning.

"You . . . better . . . get . . . *up*," he muttered dryly.

His tortured voice and pronunciation were not familiar to him.

The man got his bare feet under him one at a time. Sand shook from his chest and arms. He locked his knees and stood. His head argued against rising and then being upright, but he remained like a newborn foal, shifting balance from side to side and accepting that here he was. The pain made him feel nauseous, but there did not seem to be anything in his belly to regurgitate.

*You didn't have time or vittles to eat,* he thought. *Or both.*

Only when the man was sure of his footing did he back away from the scorpion—which seemed, by its stillness, utterly uninterested in him. For all he knew, it was dead. Now that he could see more of his surroundings, he noticed a tarantula nearby. The brown-haired thing was on its back, its legs curled inward. It appeared dead. Maybe the two predators had struggled, the scorpion winning the fight but losing the war. It could be they had never even met, had been scuttling just out of range. Perhaps the spider had failed to find shade or water or whatever it was that a spider required.

Thinking of water reminded him of his own intense thirst. He stepped onto a patch of brown grass to protect the burning soles of his feet. Sweat trickled here and there, mostly old perspiration relocated by his rising.

The man saw nothing but sand and spotty scrub ahead. He did not detect the faint but discernible smell or feel of open water anywhere nearby. That, too, he suspected, was as much an animal sense as a remembered one. He turned his head slowly, looking around. He was on a desert, a dusty plain that was flat in all directions but one. That exception was to his right—the north or thereabout, according to the position of the rising sun. There were hills about a quarter mile in that direction, with bent-over grass and little more. There were cacti, too, but they would be of no help. He recalled that the pulpy interior provided unpleasant water and the unpleasant aftereffect of diarrhea.

That was not instinct. That was something he remembered. He could even taste the damp, sour mush in his mouth.

Blood globbed into his ear, running hot and thick from his scalp. He raised an arm, unsteady with weakness, and scooped the moisture out with a dust-covered finger. He absently wiped it on his underwear.

No horse. No shoes or boots.

*How the hell did I get here?*

He struggled to recall, grew frustrated by running into a wall of nothing. He snorted the last of the sand from his nostrils. He flexed his bloated fingers.

Getting angry was not going to help him. Getting his bearings might. He squinted up into a featureless blue sky without even a passing cloud to offer respite. From the position of the sun, he made it not just morning but early morning. He could not have been lying here very long. With all the nocturnal predators that came out at sundown, he did not think he would have survived the night with a bleeding wound. Besides, if he had been lying there all night injured, he probably would have bled more. Possibly to death.

Whoever had done this, whomever he was talking with or cursing at, had not meant to kill him but might have been content to let death come. Otherwise, they would have finished him. A gun—*too noisy? Were there others around?* Just a second blow might have done it, might have left him here to bake to death.

The blood had not gone hard close by the wound—that was another clue to it being recent. He guessed that it was the heat of the sun that had roused him. Perhaps by design of the attacker? A good thing it had, too. Staying unconscious in the heat was a certain way to perspire to death or suffer— What did they call it? *Sunstroke.*

Even with all those legs, the tarantula and the scorpion could not outrun the scalding lash of the sun.

So it was not intended to be a fatal wound. Then *why* was he here? And at night in the dark.

The man decided to look more closely at the ground for tracks. If he'd had a horse, there would be something.

He looked around on the ground . . . and swore. There was a very slight breeze, hot so that it had seemed like the sun, but it wasn't. It was enough to have blown sand over any footprints or hoofprints that might have been left behind.

There was no time to search around. Detective work was a luxury he could not afford. If he did not find water, he would die. Whoever had hit him had not left any behind. That argued against charity—

*Or else there is water somewhere around.*

The man exhaled and took a moment, his eyes

scrunched against the unyielding sun, searching his mule-stubborn memory for any missing pieces. Like where he was headed. Should he go forward . . . or back, into the desert? Perhaps there was a campsite.

He closed his mouth, set in his determination to recall something, anything. His inclination was to head toward the hills in the south but he had to be sure. If he picked wrong—

Shutting his dry mouth, inhaling, exhaling, he noticed a distinctive smell in his nose—

*A campfire.*

He turned around haltingly, his first steps, and faced in the direction opposite from the way he had been lying. There was nothing. Not the remnants of a fire, nor a stick or a rock covered with blood. He had not fallen.

*A gun butt, then,* he decided.

Hit from behind, from the location of the wound. Lying toward the north, which meant they had been coming from the south.

"The hills," he said, his lips parting to permit the raw rasp of a voice. That was the way he had to go.

The soles of his feet were hot but not unbearably so. That was another indication that the hour was probably closer to sunrise than noon. The sands were not yet furnace hot. Not *yet.* It also meant he had to have been wearing footwear. He looked down. His leggings were worn out well above the ankles, the result of hard leather pressing on trousers pressing on underwear. Caused by boots. He checked the rest of his underwear. The fabric along the insides of his legs was slightly discolored—the pressure of trousers that had been straddling a horse.

Why would someone take his boots and the rest of

his clothes *and* his horse? Again, he did not understand. *Why not just kill me?*

The soles of his feet were not soft, but what about his hands? If he were a laborer . . . or maybe he had been jailed, hammering a rock pile—

No. The skin was not extraordinary, and his fingernails were clean. He must have been wearing gloves. He raised his hands to his nose. They did not smell of horse. They smelled of leather or deerskin—he could not be certain.

What did he do in his life day after day?

He could not walk and think at the same time, and he knew which of those was more important. He took a few awkward, shuffling steps, going wide around the scorpion. Occasionally there were rocks under the sand, some sharp, and he jumped whenever he stepped on one.

Despite himself, he thought as he walked. He wondered if he might have been riding—galloping, perhaps from pursuers—and had been sacrificed by whomever he was with. An offering. Maybe those galoots were still back there, to the south, in pursuit. Maybe they had waited till sunrise.

If only he had a *clue.*

Maybe that was why his clothes had been taken, anything that might help him to remember might identify him to someone else. Perhaps his clothes had been a uniform?

The war. He vaguely remembered a war some time ago.

But whoever had hit him could not have known he would suffer memory loss. Was he, perhaps, supposed to pretend that was what had happened? Was there a plan that he had forgotten with all else? Everything was a jumble.

"God," he said in exasperation.

Did he believe in God? He seemed to feel he had. He remembered praying before a cross . . . Jesus. Thinking of Jesus, he thought of the beard—

He touched his face as he walked. It was clean-shaven and recently. He had to have looked in a mirror or a pan of water—*something* in order to do that. But try as he might, he could not see his reflection.

*What about my age?*

He had no idea. None. He was a grown man; he had lived a life—he had to remember *something.* He tried to look around that chasm in his memory. Along the sides were images of a nondescript town somewhere, some *when.* He might not even have been there. He could be remembering pictures in a book, in frames, on postcards. There were no faces, friends, a wife, or parents—

Walking made his head feel better, but it also rendered the wound active. Blood trickled back into his ear. That had to be addressed before he bled to death, so he stopped, carefully knelt, and ripped off the bottoms of his underwear leggings. He folded one length of cloth into a bandage and used the other to tie it in place, like a bandanna.

His fingers seemed to know how to do that. He had done that before. He must not have lived near a doctor. Not permanently anyway.

Finishing, and touching the outside of the fabric to make sure it covered the wound entirely, the man trudged toward the hills, which, as the minutes passed, did not seem to be getting any closer. Heat was beginning to rise uncomfortably from the sands, not only broiling his sweaty soles but distorting his view of the terrain beyond him. At least, he *thought* it was that. The blow on the head could have been affecting his vision, causing some of that wavering. Or maybe there was something else affecting his eyes, which were not just dry but stinging. They might not be reporting the world accurately.

The past was gone, and the real world was misleading. What a state of things.

*It will come back,* he assured himself as he lifted one foot after another. *You're still just dazed from whatever happened.*

But he could not stop trying to make his brain work, starting with the known or the obvious. Place? United States. West . . . yes, somewhere. He seemed to know that was where the deserts were. Year? It was eighteen something. Month? Out here, it was tough to say. Even winter deserts might be hot. At the moment it seemed as if he had always been hot.

He walked, his legs not hurting but increasingly leaden, his back burning with nothing to shield it, save oily sweat. At least his head throbbed less than it had before. Maybe the sun was doing it some good, like a plant bending toward the light. The thought of shade and, he hoped, water kept him mushing one foot after another despite the heat on and between his toes. As much as his head hurt and as raw as his throat and mouth were, he was not tired. Maybe his memory lied. He could have been hurt when he was asleep, his bedding stolen with his clothes. Everything packed and carted away on the horse he had been riding.

As he walked, he continually directed his attention to the distant, more verdant landscape—searching, smelling, listening for any sign of human endeavor. A warm, soft breeze occasionally picked up dust devils, spinning them in chest-high whirlwinds. There were buzzing insects, and occasionally he had to wave them from his covered wound. Twice he heard rattlers—far enough away to walk wide around them. He remembered, from somewhere in the past, that was the reason he wore boots so high. Snakes could rise up.

The sun had moved a considerable distance and was nearly overhead before he reached the hills—two hours of walking, he guessed. Two hours of perspiring what little moisture was left in him, wrung from him as if he was a cloth in a wringer, his sweat burning off and his skin shrinking around him. Despite the ominous shadow of a turkey vulture that fell upon him, he found his strength waning. Flies swarmed and lit on his bloody ear, only now he was too weak to swat them. Besides, they would only return. If he did not find water soon, the bird and its little black minions would have their lunch.

The bushes he occasionally saw around him must have had access to an underwater stream. It was sad, he thought, that people were not equipped with roots.

The man had almost nothing left to give this pursuit. His knees bent one after the other under his weight. He dropped and fell onto his hands. His palms dislodged a family of pocket mice under a half-buried rock. They surfaced briefly before digging back underground. Whether they were anxious to be out of the sun, away from him, or to avoid a circling hawk, he did not know. What he did know, what somehow penetrated his hazy thoughts, actually gave him hope. In the brief glimpse he had had, he noticed that the mice had not looked emaciated. That meant there was food . . . and whether it was plant, insect, or animal, that also meant there was water.

He turned his face forward. Had the first man on earth felt like this—what was his name?—thrown into a new world with needs but no solutions? And then, suddenly, hope?

He saw fresh ripples ahead, low to the ground and slightly to the east. They were not just rising but moving from side to side. It was not a mirage. It was the air. It was something physical close to the ground.

Half running, half stumbling toward it, the man saw that it was water stirred by the light wind. A moment later he came upon a pond about ten feet across and half as wide. It was surrounded by high, swaying reeds and was composed of groundwater that rolled and was lifted in gentle waves from the northern edge.

The man's approach scared a pair of dark rabbits that moved deeper into the reeds that grew on the eastern and northern side; they were nurtured by the morning light and shaded in the afternoon by a high hill beyond. The reeds on the western and southern side were browned and stunted.

He thrashed through that waist-high foliage and fell on all fours on the other side of them. Like an animal, he pushed his face to the water, recoiling at the surprising heat on his cheeks and sunburned nose, on his cracked lips and swollen tongue. Shaking off the burning sensation, he bent back down and touched his mouth to the surface. He sucked the water up, quickly getting used to the heat. Almost at once, life began returning to his body. His vigorous movements were enough to send the buzzard away in search of less hopeful prey.

As his body recovered some of its vigor, his mind, too, became more alert.

*Maybe now things will come back to me,* he thought. It was more like a prayer than a real hope.

When the man was finished, he cupped water below his eyes, tilted his head back, and rinsed them. He removed the bandage, scrubbed it clean in the pond, then wrung the rest out on the wound. He did not want to dab the gash and risk reopening it. He just wanted it clean enough so insects would stop pestering him.

As he squeezed out the water, he noticed the big eyes of the rabbits locked on him across the way.

"You're safe," he assured them. "I'm hungry, damned hungry, but I've got nothing to trap you with or start a fire."

As if encouraged by the man's gentle tone and undoubted thirst, the rabbits cautiously came forward. Its ears turned back, the larger and darker of the two animals was about to drink when a wooden shaft pierced his hide behind the neck, thrusting him forward and causing him to drop to one side, kicking. The other fled, concerned only with self-preservation. A brief rustle of the reeds and there was no longer any sign of the surviving rabbit.

The man remained frozen for a moment, his refreshed eyes turned ahead; then he slowly lowered himself to his belly. He did not want any part of him visible near the top of the grasses. He looked across the velvety waters as the reeds on the other side began to part from back to front. The shot rabbit was dead, a breeze rustling its fur, thick, dark blood running from the wound. The man noticed that the arrow seemed especially crude. The fletching did not seem to be eagle or turkey. It looked like duck. Somehow, he knew that. And the shaft was a hide-tied bundle of reeds, like those that grew around the pond.

Again, the man did not know how he knew that, but he did.

A figure strode into the reeds at the side of the pond. It was not what the man had been expecting, not an Indian or a settler but a boy. The new arrival was about ten years old and dressed in overalls that looked like they were made from a potato sack. He was shirtless and wore moccasins, though he was white beneath a deep sunburn. His blond hair was short but scruffy—knife cut, it seemed.

The boy's eyes were lively, and he was smiling down at his kill. He slipped the large bow over his shoulder, beside a quiver, as he picked up the rabbit by the arrow. He turned it round and round at arm's length, watching its lifeless head and limbs flop.

"I think I will call you . . . Stew!" the boy chuckled.

Watching him, crouched where he was, the man had a sudden recollection that made his heart rush. He was hiding in brush, a sharpened stick in his hand. Not sharp like that arrow but sharp enough to use in the hard earth. He could feel himself pushing through the dirt with it—

Then, quick as it came, the image left. The beating in his chest slowed. He no longer felt afraid.

*And not of this boy.*

As soon as the youngster had disarmed himself, the man began to rise very slowly. He emerged from hiding arms first, his hands lifted high above his head.

The rabbit was jerked to a stop, and the boy's pale

blue eyes speared past it at the newcomer. With the sun on them, they looked like little diamonds in his bronzed face.

"Please don't shoot me," the man said softly. "I'd make pretty poor stew."

"I don't shoot people, only supper," the boy assured him.

"Very sensible," the man replied.

There had been the briefest hesitation in the boy's young voice, but he had pushed through it. This was a tough frontier kid, the man thought.

The boy lowered his kill and looked behind him as though contemplating an escape. Instead, he turned back and took a moment to consider the stranger. "Were you swimming, mister?"

It took a moment before the man understood what the newcomer was asking. "No. I was robbed of my clothes—of everything, in fact." He bowed his head slightly to show the boy the wound. It hurt when he bent forward like that. "I was knocked out."

The youngster looked for a moment, then shrugged. "Seen worse. Saw a man who was scalped. You?"

The man shrugged the same as the boy had. "Possibly. If I did, I don't remember."

"Really?"

"Really."

"Maybe my ma can fix that."

"Your ma. Is she nearby?"

"Near enough. You better come along. My name's Douglas. Douglas Smith."

"Hello, Douglas Smith. I wish I could tell you my name, but honestly I don't know it."

The boy seemed doubtful. "Someone took that, too, along with your trousers?"

"I reckon they did, in a manner of speaking." The man started to walk around the pond. "Your ma—she lets you wander out here in the desert alone?"

"Nah," the boy said. He jerked his head back. "She's behind that rock. With a rifle."

# CHAPTER TWO

JANE SMITH WOULD never leave the shack, even to hang the laundry, without her .50 caliber Springfield loaded and by her side. She kept at least a half dozen extra cartridges in her apron or, as now, in the pocket of her dress. And she was a practiced shot. Even as a girl, growing up in Austin, Texas, she had preferred rifles to revolvers. She liked having that power against her shoulder rather than in her hand. It was balanced and made a good club if it came to that.

And in this part of Southern California, it was wise to have that protection at the northern end of the desert. People coming over from Mexico were usually affable enough, looking for work; there was nothing here for anyone to steal. Travelers heading south across the border were typically traders or former soldiers, not bandits. But she and Douglas were alone here, and that was reason enough to keep the firearm near.

This morning, when she first heard the voice of someone who was not her son, the woman immediately took to the nearest shelter and covered the boy. He had seen her there when he turned, and known he was safe if the man splashed through the pond to reach him. Douglas knew that it was his job to find out whether the two of them were in danger.

He thought they were. Alone, unarmed, injured, and nearly naked, the man did not seem like much of a threat.

Jane had confirmed this as she listened from concealment, her right eye behind the Springfield, which lay on a rock. Now she watched with an eagle-sharp left eye as her son came forward with the stranger. The man was tall, well over six feet, around thirty-five years of age, with brown hair nearly to his shoulders. He had a lithe build, a narrow face, and deep-set eyes that reminded her of the Texas Rangers she had grown up around—very still but very alert, like a wild horse.

Which made her wonder: How had a man like that come to lose most of his clothing and most likely his horse? Surprise attacked, most likely. He turned sideways as he crossed round the pond; it was then she saw the gash on the side of his head. Either he had trusted the wrong person, or he had been careless in the lower country, the south side of the desert, which was crisscrossed by bandits and revolutionaries.

Her boy kept a careful distance to one side. When Jane was certain that the man did not represent a threat, she stood—still with the stock hugged to her shoulder, ready and willing to fire in a moment.

The man was still about a dozen feet away and watching her. He stopped and raised his hands shoulder high.

"Good morning," he said with a crooked smile.

"Morning." The woman spoke to her son without taking her eyes from the man. "That was a fine kill, Douglas."

"Thank you, Ma. I did okay with this." He jerked a shoulder to indicate the crude bow. He looked back at the man. "I want to get a real one. And a Bowie knife for skinning."

The man's smile remained as it was. But that name Bowie, he knew.

The boy turned back to his mother. "Ma, this man says he don't know his name."

"I heard, son. And the word is 'doesn't.'"

"Sorry."

"I'd like to have a few words with the gentleman. Why don't you go home and skin your catch?"

"Can't I listen?"

"If I'd wanted that, I would have said so," the boy's mother said sternly.

Douglas turned his face down and ran off to the northeast, into the low hills, the rabbit held upright so it did not become dislodged. Jane did not lower her rifle until he was gone. She snuggled it under her arm and regarded the man with a careful gaze, the two of them standing like pillars of salt at the edge of the desert.

"Did you tell the boy the truth?" she asked. "About your memory?"

"Every word is true. I woke a few hours ago in the desert, like you see—for which, madam, I apologize."

"I have seen men and their underwear," she said without embarrassment. "But thank you. Whoever you were, you must have had manners."

As he lowered his arms, he took the opportunity to

frankly admire the woman. She was a head shorter than he, dressed in a faded blue skirt and a blue blouse with the sleeves rolled high. She had sandy blond hair tucked beneath a scarf and strong cheekbones. Like her son, she was red from the eternal sunlight.

The man started forward.

"About manners," he said. "I don't know. I keep trying and hoping that something new will spring up in my mind and I'll remember more things. But right now, everything's like that sky behind you—big and empty but without the sun."

"Maybe you were a painter," she said with an encouraging smile.

He shrugged, then looked at his hands, flexed his fingers. "I don't feel anything that seems to fit. But my fingers want to—not a paintbrush, but they want to hold *something*."

"Did you look around for clues where you woke up?"

"Second thing I did, the first being to get off the ground. There were no tracks. No bloody rock or stick. Nothing."

"Well, there is a fire in the sky," she said.

"I beg your pardon?"

"You said your recollections have no sunshine. But it's there, maybe behind a mountain or cloud. Your memory may return."

He liked that notion, and the woman's optimism. He wondered if he had a woman in his life.

"You may put your hands down," she said.

"Thank you. You and your boy, you live out here?"

"We have a cabin nearby. We should probably start for it before we both melt."

The two set out, over ground that was harder but

slightly cooler against the man's bare soles than the scorching sands he had left.

"The cabin," he asked, "it was built by you, your husband?"

"If you can call it 'built.' We used what materials we could find out here. It's more patchwork than original stones and wood. We planned it as an emergency station for the stage. It was a rough, long stretch between Carrizo in the south and Oak Ridge. We saw a need. And there was until the railroad came through last year. Now we live off the land and our small pension."

"Your husband's? From the military?"

"No, the Butterfield Overland Stage. Nehemiah drove for them."

"Is that a well-known name?"

"Very," she said. "Nothing?"

The man shook his head.

"Nehemiah died on his last run—an accident. Maybe . . ."

"Ma'am?"

"Maybe it was an accident. The wagon tipped over on a shortcut Nehemiah had always warned the driver not to take. He went with them to show them the way. You see, I don't know if my husband could have lived without the stage. I don't know if the boy and I could have lived without the death pension."

"To leave the two of you for that—?"

"I know, which is why I say 'maybe' it was an accident."

"You don't have to say any more—"

"I want to. I think it so very much, it's good to hear it out loud. You see, the wagon fell on him, was righted, and they carried him back. It was such a blow to the boy. Douglas looked up to him, a scout and hunter, then meeting and riding in with the big team of horses. Nehemiah was nearly fifty. I don't think he had an idea how to fill that. Not by adding to the cabin or"—she looked after Douglas—"shooting hares."

"My condolences, ma'am," he said. "I understand the pain of not knowing."

"You may call me by name—Jane. Jane Smith. And thank you." She regarded him, squinting into the sun. "What should we call you for now?"

"I do not have a mortal, foggy notion. What would you prefer?"

"Well, our favorite coach driver was Henry Carey, so how about Hank?"

"That suits me fine."

"Good." She glanced up at his head. "When we reach the cabin, I'll take care of that gash in your scalp and see what we have of Nehemiah's that might fit you. And, Hank? I'm a trusting woman and a good Christian. God organizes things His own way, and I go along with them. I hope you will do nothing to make me sorry for showing you hospitality."

"Ma'am—Jane—I don't know who I was, but I believe I must have been something like what you just described."

"Oh? How do you figure that?"

"I trusted someone, too, and that apparently got me left for dead."

Jane gave him a long, serious look. "That's likely a fact, though it's strange."

"What is?"

"I'm the only one crazy enough to live out here, raising a boy. How do you know it wasn't me who attacked you?"

Hank shrugged. "See what I mean? I must be trusting."

The woman smiled and the two continued along side by side. The walk was mercifully brief, as the invigorating effects of the water wore off and Hank found his stamina wavering.

The cabin was no less than what she had described: a confusion of materials that had the shape if not the certainty of a home. It was made of rocks of different sizes, a thatched roof—which bulged here and there with newly harvested tumbleweed—window frames with traces of bark still present, and a patchwork of repairs consisting of parts of a stagecoach, the colors faded but still red. Like the carcass of a long-dead bison, the remains of the conveyance itself lay a dozen or so yards to the east.

To the east was a small, fenced-in plot surrounding a grave with a cross. The marker had the initials NS branded where the beams crossed. It was propped upright in a mound of rocks, a few leaves spread around it, but the surrounding slats were slanting this way and that, windblown and sunblasted of all color. Ten or so paces nearer to the cabin was a modest garden, fenced a little sturdier, the slats lashed with hemp. A few paces nearer to the cabin was a well. The walls had been constructed from whatever odd stones had been excavated from around the cabin, most likely roped and dragged over by horse.

"You must have had a time lifting those," Hank observed.

"That driver, Henry, was a bear of a man. We couldn't have done it without him."

"That's the same underground water that feeds the pond?"

"That's right. Came near enough to the surface to make mud here. My husband originally thought to build by the pond, but it was hotter out there, of course, and there were also varmints coming and going to the water, day and night."

"Pipes," he muttered.

"I don't understand?"

"Neither do I, but I somehow know that you use them to separate the water from the surrounding earth, to keep from drinking dirt."

"That's a strange memory to have back."

"I wasn't a laborer. I must have watched—"

"It will come," she said encouragingly. "But you're right. Nehemiah listened to all the folks who came through, and he loved all kinds of inventions. This was different from when I was a little girl, and you had to strain drinking water through a cloth."

Hank continued to flex his hands, trying to remember what he held. He noticed then that Jane still wore a wedding band. He looked at his own finger where a ring would have been. It had not been stolen along with everything else. There was no discoloration; he had not worn one.

The man's curiosity remained frustrated as they entered the cabin. Relief from the blazing sun was undermined by the greater heat inside. There were two doors north and south and two windows east and west. Both were open. The small, hot breeze they admitted did little to relieve the stove-hot air. Through the back door, Hank could see a wood block table out back. Douglas was using a small knife to carefully cut the pelt from his catch. A large bucket sat beside the table. Insects of all sizes flitted around the rim and in great number. That was where the innards would go.

"We put the table outside because the smell inside—Well, it would have been awful," Jane said. "Along with the flies and ants. We still have to wash it down thoroughly after each using so the blood doesn't draw scavengers."

Hank was looking around the flat expanse. "Not even any flat rocks you could've used as a cutting board."

"This was not a place created by a generous God for human habitation. I think He put water here to teach us to appreciate the essential comforts of creation."

"Your garden seems healthy."

"There you have it—water, sun. Plus, Nehemiah still provides. When we get too hot at night, we sleep in the coach. As long as there are still walls, it protects us from predators."

Hank was frustrated that the mention of a father and a son brought nothing from his own rattled memory. He took a moment to smell the powdery dryness of the desert home, the pelts that hung on the eastern-facing windows, drawn to block the morning light.

Nothing triggered a memory. No smell, no sight, no action. He wondered if that meant, by elimination, that he had never lived in or near the desert where he had found himself.

Jane pulled back the pelt shades to admit light at both sides. Then she led the man to a chest stuck against the rear wall, to the left of the door. It, a two-person bed, and a small wooden table and chairs, with unlit lanterns, were the only furnishings. A tall stack of pelts sat in the corner, and there was a peg with bundles of snake skins

hanging from it. On the opposite side of the room, near
a large washbasin, were two shelves with kitchen supplies and sundries, and a third with utensils. A few tools
leaned against the wall below—a saw, an ax, and a hammer. Beside the shelves, a row of pegs supported leather
bags. Probably dried vegetables and meat, the man
guessed—though why he should, he did not know. Beside the northern window was a fireplace with a large
kettle suspended above it by two strong chains.

"I've seen one of those before," Hank said, pointing
toward the big pot. "Does it have a name?"

"The Dutch oven?"

"Dutch . . . oven," he repeated as though he were just
learning the language. He considered the words for a
moment before shaking his head. "Dutch are people. I
know that much. But I also know I've seen a fireplace
with a pot like that."

"Let all that rest," the woman advised. "I always find
that when I stop thinking of a thing, I remember it."

"But it's maddening," he said. "I know words. I can
*picture* things—but not specific things that have to do
with me."

She looked down at the chest. "Be grateful for your
life, Hank, even with its challenges. Be that."

The wistful quality in her voice did not go unno-
ticed. He felt suddenly ungrateful for his incessant
complaining.

Jane set her rifle against the wall and raised the lid.
There was a pair of Colts in an old, worn holster on top
of carefully folded clothes. She moved the guns aside
and fingered through garments. They belonged to a
succession of boyhood ages. When Jane reached a sec-

ond set of clothes, she grabbed an armful of the guns
and small garments and set them on the floor.

She rose. "Take your pick of whatever suits you. After
we see to your injury, I can fix them to fit. I don't think
they'll need much. You and Nehemiah are mostly the
same size."

"This is very generous of you," Hank said.

"God does not make mistakes. As I said, I trust in
His works."

Hank was not sure whether he did or did not do the
same. It seemed to him that a woman who had lost
what she had needed an explanation. God was as good
a one as any.

While the woman retrieved bandages, a bottle of
whiskey, and a washcloth from the shelf of sundries,
Hank bent his tired knees and knelt before the chest. He
moved a little so his shadow cast by the lantern would
not fall on the inside. There were denim trousers, a pair
of white shirts, and a buckskin jacket with gray bare
patches. A pair of old boots lay on their sides. There was
a white Stetson, partly flattened, beside them, with a
leather band that bore the owner's name, N. Smith. Below were other clothes, mostly, it looked, having to do
with life and work on the range.

"We buried Nehemiah in his Sunday clothes," Jane
explained when she returned. "It was only the third time
he wore them, the first being our wedding, the second
when he met Mr. John Butterfield in Sacramento. Nehemiah was devoted to that man and his coach line."

Hank removed the trousers, shirt, and boots. He
left the hat, figuring Jane would want that keepsake; he
would not need a jacket out here. Like everything else,

the feel of the clothes triggered nothing. Nor did the pleasant odor.

"What is that?" Hank asked, sniffing.

Jane smiled like a girl caught staring at a soldier. "I used to launder my husband's clothes in mint. Shotgun rider used to tease him, but it reminded him I was always a part of him. I still grow it in the garden."

"The leaves on the grave," he said.

She nodded.

Moved, Hank set the clothes on the table. Then he replaced the other items, carefully shut the lid, which was loose on its hinges, and stood.

"Come outside for doctoring so I can see what I'm doing," Jane said, her arms full of healing.

The two went through the back door, where Douglas was just finishing with the rabbit's feet. A final tug and the pelt was free, in one piece.

"This can go on the pile for Sheriff Russell!" he enthused.

"Mighty fine," Jane said as her son proudly held up the carcass. "You want to do the innards?"

"You mean it?"

"You've seen me do it enough."

The boy nodded enthusiastically.

"Fine. I'm going to take care of Hank—"

"You remembered your name?" the boy asked.

"Not exactly," the man replied. "Your mother picked it for me."

"Hank," he said. "I like it."

"If you two are finished, Douglas—after I dress Hank's injury, I'll pick the vegetables. You hang the pelt and get the fire going."

"I can start the fire? Alone?"

She nodded. "You *may* start the fire. The gutting won't take long."

"Yes, ma'am!" the boy said. He smiled at the man. "Hank. I like it!"

Douglas hung the pelt on a peg on a table leg. Whatever the pests ate from it were remains that had to come off anyway. Then he strode to a patch of dirt that looked well churned. He dug it up with his hands and put the meal inside. That would keep it from attracting varmints until he was ready for it. Then he ran off, spindly arms chugging, to the broken-down stagecoach. He pulled branches and sticks from inside and bundled them to his chest.

"We usually gather them when we go to the pond," Jane said. "The wind always brings along something we can burn. If we hadn't come upon you, we would've gone out and collected them. Further north some, there's plenty of trees, and we have a good hatchet."

"God provides."

"That's right," Jane said. "Sit yourself on the edge of the table."

The man went to a corner away from where the boy had been laboring. Her slender fingertips moved gingerly through the hair matted around the wound.

"You don't mind living with the stagecoach?" Hank asked.

As she reached for the whiskey bottle, Jane's eyes had a distant look. "It's painful sometimes. But Nehemiah loved it, and that spot is special. He always rode out to meet the stage, see if they needed anything. If they did—liquor, water, food, nursing—he'd ride back and get it ready. Whenever he left, Douglas would sit out there, right where the coach is, and look north for signs of dust. A lot of it meant the coach coming in. A little less, it was just the paint that Nehemiah rode. When he came in hard, to beat the devil, it meant there were hostiles on the road. He'd come roaring in like a tornado, quickly gather up extra ammunition and supplies, and then travel to Oak Ridge with them."

"He had courage."

"He did. That and hope." She laughed. "He hoped I was right that God was always looking out for us. Turned out different, though, like I tell Douglas—God has His way."

The mention of hope did not find purchase in Hank's brain. He had none. As Jane dribbled alcohol on his scalp, he tried to place the smell. Not even that was familiar.

"I wonder if there's some boy waiting for me," Hank said as he watched the boy walk to the cabin with his arms full of tree parts.

The woman set the bottle on the table and gently poked through her patient's hair. "Gun butt," she said with a kind of detachment. "Probably a revolver."

"How can you tell?"

"You said you didn't see any rocks or such, and a rifle or shotgun leaves a big mark. Whip handle, knife hilt would have left a smaller one. Grazed by a bullet would have left a trail."

"You know your wounds."

She used the cloth to dab away the loose clots of blood. "Nine years of Butterfield brought me all kinds of injuries. Not just to people but to horses and dogs. Nehemiah broke fingers and toes, especially on those rocks. Douglas likes climbing trees when we go north, breaks off the good firewood. Leaves a lot of skin and blood on those high branches."

"Nine years," Hank said. "I was thinking before—I don't even know what year this is."

"It's eighteen seventy," she replied.

"The Civil War . . ."

"Ended five years ago."

"Yes. I remember that. I don't know why."

"Do you remember fighting?"

"No."

"Your age, you were likely a soldier. Probably for the North, given that you don't sound like you're from the South."

"In those nine years of nursing, you ever see anything like the condition I have?"

"Not out here, but my brother, Wyatt, had his skull cracked by a shot during the War. The shell hit a rock and then hit him. He had trouble recalling things for a while. He wrote to me from Texas every day. He said it helped him remember things by setting them down."

"Maybe I should try that. You mentioned animals—you don't have any out here."

"Not anymore. We had a dog, Dusty, but he died. Of boredom, I think. He was a big shepherd, made friends with the coyotes, so there wasn't much for him to howl about here. We had a horse, too, but he got snake bit about six, seven months ago."

"How do you get supplies? I saw sugar, salt—"

"There is a gentleman, Alan Russell, a retired lawman who rides up from Apple Town every two weeks or so. I'm expecting him today or tomorrow, in fact. Do you know that name? Apple Town?"

Hank thought a moment then shook his head.

"The Central Pacific Railroad? The station at Truckee?"

"Nothing, ma'am."

"No matter. Apple Town has had a general store for about a year. Sheriff Russell brings mail. We give him our pension when it comes—I don't otherwise need money out here—and we give him skins to sell or trade for what little we need."

"Sounds like a kindly arrangement on his part," Hank said.

Jane turned away suddenly to ladle water from the bucket to wash the cloth. Hank realized he had implied something else without intending to: that the man came out to see the widow. She changed the subject.

"The cavalry used to come through every month, when Nehemiah was alive," she went on. "Captain Williams and his company out of Fort Yuma. They'd ask ranchers and homesteaders about the Indians, both the locals and those passing through. Since his death, they haven't been around as much. Maybe once a month . . . less."

"This Apple Town, you've been there?"

"Many times."

"Can you describe it?"

"It's got a general store, bank, saloon, hotel, blacksmith, sheriff."

Nothing in any of that sounded familiar, and Hank grew increasingly disheartened. Even if he was not from this area, he would have encountered or at least heard of one of those ranches or the town. They would have been on maps. One did not simply materialize in the desert.

The woman finished tying the clean bandage around the man's head, then sent him back inside to dress.

"You're patched but don't forget you're still injured!" she said after him. "You push, it'll remind you."

He waved his acknowledgment.

As Hank stepped back inside, the dark settled on him, fitting and appropriate. To the right, Douglas had finished placing wood in the hearth and was leaning forward, poking at the ashes beneath to start a fire.

"I wouldn't duck so far in," Hank suggested.

"I used to watch my dad—"

"He would've been a little higher up, maybe a head taller?"

"Oh, right," Douglas said.

As they spoke, the fire took, and the wood began to burn. Excited, Douglas ran outside to tell his mother and cut into the rabbit.

Hank began to dress. And to think again. Jane Smith had counseled patience. Frustrating as that was, he knew it would be wise to follow her advice. Hopefully, some fragment would show up that would unblock all the rest.

Hank was just pulling on his boots when he heard a sound that was all too familiar.

The sound of a shotgun being pumped.

# CHAPTER THREE

JANE GRABBED HER boy from where he had gone to tend to the rabbit. She threw him through the open door. He stumbled forward, landing on his knees as she followed him in. She reached for her own rifle, but it was gone.

Hank had it. He was walking toward the eastern window.

"Give me the rifle!" Jane yelled, following him.

Hank looked back at her with a hard expression that stopped her cold. "You ever have visitors come around, making as if to shoot at you?"

"No—"

"They could've shot you in the open, both of you, out there," Hank said. "It's me that someone wants. See to Douglas. I'll take care of whatever this is."

Jane did not like being told what to do in her own home, but she did not argue with a man holding a gun, especially when it was her own. She hurried to where Douglas was picking himself up and put her arms around him. They walked to the far side of the clothes chest and crouched there.

Hank got on one knee beside the window. He stayed to the side and moved the pelt curtain a little with the barrel of the rifle. He edged forward to look outside.

A ferocious blast tore the hanging shade from its wooden rod and put holes in the wall near the shelves. The boy gasped, and his mother bundled him closer, her back to the eastern window. Losing the shade threw the center of the room into sharp sunlight, the sides going deeper into shadow.

Hank hugged the wall. "Who's out there?" he yelled.

"Like you don't know, scum!"

The man's voice was gravelly, and the accent sounded familiar. Another piece he could remember that did him no good.

"Scum," Douglas mumbled into his mother's shoulder. "Is that Hank's real name?"

She hushed the boy and hunkered lower. Her blue eyes were lost in the darkness, and the darkness was filled with fear. Neither bandits nor red men had ever menaced her here. Even the winged and pawed predators passed their meager dwelling without bothering them. Maybe they smelled the long-dead skins and were warned off. Now an act of charity had brought hostility to their door. She relaxed her hold on her son, lest her fright brand him for the rest of his life.

Hank had settled back from the window to consider his next move. He looked over at the chest, where Jane and her son were hiding. Whatever he had done to anger this man, Hank could not endanger them further. He leaned toward the window.

"What do you want?" Hank asked.

"What you took!"

"I don't know what you're talking about. Look, let's discuss this. What's going to happen if I come out?"

"That depends on what's in your hand."

"What *should* be in my hand?"

The man outside snorted. "Jesus, what kind of a game are you playing?"

"I'm not playing any game. I swear it. Look, let me come out and talk to you."

"Sure. First, throw out what you stole, followed by that rifle. Then come out with your hands high."

"I can only do two of those," Hank replied. "Whatever you think I have—I *don't* have it."

"You give it to your partner? Where's he?"

*"I don't know!"*

A second shot blasted through the window, sending Hank ducking backward and chipping large gashes in the frame and clanging off a metal pot and pan on the shelf.

"Damn it, man. *Stop!*" Hank shouted when the echo died. "I don't know what you want! I swear to you, I don't even know my *name*!"

"What the hell are you *talking* about?"

"Someone hit me on the skull and left me lying near naked in the desert. I don't know who I am or what I'm supposed to have done. Please. There's a woman and her son here with me—"

"I saw 'em. They can leave if they want."

"This is their home," Hank said. "They were kind

enough to take me in. You stop shooting, and I'll come out, unarmed. I swear it."

There was a short silence. As Hank waited, the wind carried the tart smell of gunpowder into the cabin. He knew that odor very, very well. He tried hard to place it. The War, as Jane had said? Or something more recent? Nothing came to him.

"You sure there isn't anybody else in there with you?" the man yelled.

"You can come in and check," Hank said.

"Yeah, you'd like that. Bushwhack me like you did before. I don't see your horse. Where is it?"

"Same person hit me took it."

"Maybe your partner?"

"Maybe. You seem to know more about all of this than I do."

There was another silence, a little longer.

"Is there a man of the house? Is anyone else expected?"

"You see that grave? It's his," Hank said.

"Awright, mister. I'm not sure I believe a word you spoke, but toss the rifle out the window, stock first. Your knife?"

"What knife?"

"Christ . . . just come out the door to your left." He raised his voice. "The woman and child inside—you two stay where you are. If there's shooting, I don't want you in the way."

"They will stay here," Hank assured him after checking with Jane, who nodded. "I'm gonna push the rifle out now. Don't shoot my hand off!"

"Don't give me cause!"

It seemed strange—stupid, actually—that during the exchange, when his life had been at risk, Hank had not been afraid. Without his memory he felt blameless, innocent of even the most heinous crime conceivable.

*Maybe you* shouldn't *be looking for anything more,* he warned himself—knowing that no man was wise enough to stop where he was now: clean.

"I'm coming out now!" Hank yelled.

"Back door."

"Back door," Hank confirmed.

He looked once more at Jane and her boy. They were a featureless shape beyond the shaft of light. He smiled, hoping they saw. Then, hands raised, he started toward the door in boots that were a little too tight and clomped a little too loud on the plank floor. His heart was beating in his ears as well—again not from fear but from what he felt was a kind of natural animal readiness.

Hank squinted as he returned to the dazzling sunlight. It was hotter now, not just because it was later but because he was clothed. His underwear was already soaked, and the fabric dampened quickly. Hank turned his head and peered through narrowed eyes at the spot where the shot had originated. He saw a hat sticking up just behind the well, the brow below it in shade. Whoever was there had probably came from the south—behind Hank, either tracking him or following him. There were two horses tied to a bush about forty feet south of the well. The man must have used the house as cover when he approached.

"You came with two mounts?" Hank said. "For me?"

"Manner of speaking," the other man said. "Packhorse is for the dead bodies."

"Is there a bounty on me?"

"Not that I'm aware."

The man's replies added confusion rather than clarity.

"What do you want me to do?" Hank asked.

"Come toward the well. Slowly, hands still raised. I know what you can do with a knife."

There was a flash in Hank's brain—just a fleeting vision of a silver blade with a bone handle. Then the vision was gone.

"I wish *I* knew what I could do," Hank replied. "For starters, you mind telling me my name?"

"If I knew it, I would."

"Are you in your right mind? You come here to toss me over the back of a horse, and you don't even know my name?"

"All I know about you is that you're a varmint who took what didn't belong to you, and the weapon you used, and where you headed with that other bandit."

"Okay, let's start with that," Hank said. "What did I take?"

"You can stop walking right there," the man said when Hank was about six feet away. "But keep your hands raised. Also, you can stop talking. I'm sick of hearing you talk bunkum with your mouth."

Hank did as he was told, his feet burning and uncomfortable in the boots. Flies began buzzing around his wound. He blew them away with little puffs of breath.

The other man rose slowly behind his shotgun. His eyes shifted between the cabin and Hank. The man was stocky, dressed in a dusty, perspiration-stained Rebel uniform, and wearing a scruffy beard and soldier's cap that had seen better days. Like Jane, he had a sun-bronzed face. Unlike Jane, he was scowling.

"What did you take?" the man said with open disbelief. "You and your partner took a lockbox that we had carried with us from Ensenada. There were gold coins and documents inside. Stir the pot any?"

"No," Hank said. "I've never heard of that place, as far as I can recollect."

"You've never *heard* of Ensenada," the man said. "What kind of game are you playing, mister? Or are you trying to buy time for some purpose?"

"I'm telling you—"

"You're not telling me anything. You're just *talking*!" The man jabbed the gun forward as if it were an index finger. "If what you're saying is true, I'm guessing your partner took it and your horse and left you for dead." The man studied Hank for a moment. He pointed at the man's head with the shotgun. "That where you got clubbed?"

"Yes. When I woke in the desert, I had my underwear on and nothing else. I got up and just started walking."

"West."

"Yes."

"Why?"

"I needed water, and it was the only place that wasn't desert."

"He's telling the truth!" Jane shouted from the house.

The Rebel stood with his shoulders back, measuring things up.

"What did you mean about me being capable with a knife?" Hank asked. "I've been feeling this—urge with my fingers. What did I do?"

The man turned his head so his left cheek was facing Hank. A red gash ran along the bone, front to back. "You did that from about the distance you are now, into a tree and on horseback. Then you filled your hand with a second one while I was still standing there."

"Then I didn't mean to kill you."

"That seems to be the case."

"That should count for something."

"Maybe you got a soft spot other than on your head."

Hank ignored the gibe. "What else happened?"

"I was bent over the fire, working on something, when you showed up."

"I don't recall that."

"The man you were with—he took the box at gun-point and told you to hurry along. He could have shot us but didn't. We figure he wanted what we carried but didn't want an incident. Sound familiar yet?"

"No." There was not, in fact, a glimmer of *anything* recognizable about this man or his story. But Hank was glad to hear that, at least in this instance, he was not a murderer.

"Might I sit?" Hank asked. "These boots are unkind."

"Go ahead. On the corner of that table behind you."

"Thank you."

Hank hobbled to the table. The man followed him with the raised shotgun. The Rebel snickered at some-thing that seemed to amuse him. Hank was fully con-fused. Perching on the edge where Jane had done her nursing, he gratefully removed the boots.

"I recognize your uniform," Hank admitted as he set the boots on the ground. "Confederate."

"That's right. Lots of proud veterans wear them out here. They got Mexicans and Injuns to worry about. No one bothers us much. Unless they want a fight."

"I don't know about any of that," Hank said, wriggling his bare toes. "Did we meet each other at night or during the day?"

"Late twilight yesterday. There were four of us around a campfire. Your friend stayed just out of the light. But I saw you."

"How far from here did that happen?"

"Twenty miles on the map. When it was over, you scooted into the desert, bound for where I do not know. We left one man behind to— Well, to stay behind. The rest of us three spread out after you in case you cut north or south."

Just then Jane appeared in the doorway. Douglas was behind her, deep in shadow.

"May we come out? It's stifling in there."

The man in the uniform studied them quickly but with a trained eye. "Yes, you may. Let me see your hands first."

She held them out, her palms upturned; then she encouraged her son to come around her and do the same. Hank had felt a brief surge of concern when he first saw them; he was relieved to see that Jane had left the Colts in the chest.

"Why don't you go ahead and stand with your friend where I can watch you all. If you don't mind."

"I don't mind, Mr. . . . ?"

"It's Lieutenant Goodman Martins." He regarded Hank. "Heard of me?"

Hank shook his head, the wound punched back, and he stopped.

"Lieutenant, I am Jane Smith, and this is Douglas."

The boy said, "Pleased to make your acquaintance, sir."

The lieutenant did not acknowledge them. He seemed to regard every move as a threat, every word as a potential lie.

Jane went directly to the table and pointed to the boots. "Mr. Martins, I'd like to fix these."

"What do you mean?"

"They were my husband's. I'm going to fill these with stones. The heat will expand them, stretch the leather."

"Okay."

"Thank you," Hank said gratefully.

"So you really did arrive without much on."

"As I've been saying."

"The word of a thief."

Hank's eyes drifted to Douglas. Maybe the man was right. Maybe he was an outlaw and deserved his contempt. He hoped not. There was a brief look of something just short of awe in the boy's eyes when he gazed up at the man. He had obviously heard the story about the knife.

The woman fixed her attention on the boots as the boy gathered up small stones as she indicated. Hank and the lieutenant locked eyes.

"All of this is for real, not just 'cause you've been caught?" the man with the shotgun asked.

"It's real, Lieutenant Martins," Hank said. He considered the other for a moment. "You retain your rank in peacetime."

"It's not peacetime everywhere."

"Where, then?"

"South. Mexico and the French."

None of that sounded familiar to Hank. "I guess I was involved somehow."

"Somehow," Martins agreed. "If you weren't, you are now."

The man came from around the well, brushing away flies drawn to the sweat running from his hatband. He had a noticeable limp. That was probably why the lieutenant had smirked at Hank's hobbled walk.

"War injury?" Hank asked.

"That's right. You sound like you could be a border country Southerner, maybe Virginia. You remember where you're from?"

Hank shook his head once slowly. Martins lowered the shotgun but kept it tucked under his arm.

"You present me with a dilemma," the lieutenant said, still approaching slowly. "I'm supposed to meet the others further north, at the Butterfield way station. Maybe they caught your partner. Maybe they didn't. I'm thinking you should come with me."

"To do what?"

"Assuming all you've said is true, you still got a partner out there. He betrayed you. Didn't kill you, maybe didn't have the heart. Maybe you two were kinda close, and he didn't want your blood on his hands, exactly." Martins stopped a yard distant. "Or maybe he left you where we'd find you, slowing us down. Or maybe you're supposed to kill us—though I sorta doubt that."

"Why?"

"I saw how fast you were back at the camp. My finger's off the trigger. Where I'm standing, you could've snatched the barrel before I could fire."

Martins backed away a few paces as Hank processed how he had been tested.

"Whatever the case," Martins went on, "when we

find him, and he sees you, you might be able to help us get back what you took."

"Or he might shoot me. He won't know that I can't remember dirt."

"What you say is certainly a chance, save that he didn't kill you back there. Or stab you, though he took your other knife." Martins reached around back with his free hand, drew something from his belt. "I pulled this one from the tree. I intended to use it on you, if I got the chance."

Hank looked at the knife, the bone-carved handle. It was definitely familiar. But only the knife, nothing that might have surrounded it.

"You going to tell me anything else?" Hank asked. "Who you work for, for instance."

"Now, how hen stupid would that be? You might suddenly remember things and pretend you didn't. Like why you should leave me behind and meet your partner somewhere."

"That could happen anyway."

"True, but such a possibility don't mean I have to help."

Hank did not like the man or his deal. He had a swagger in his voice, in his walk, that did not sound like a man accustomed to taking orders in any kind of army.

Jane held her son to her. They had finished with the boots, had placed them on the table—in the sun where the stones would expand and stretch the leather—and were standing at the far end. Hank smiled at them, then regarded Martins.

"What if I don't go?"

"Stay here, you mean? With them?" Martins shrugged.

"I'm pretty certain I do not want you at my back. If you insisted, I'm afraid I would be forced to shoot you now and be done with it."

"Well, put that way—"

"I thought you'd understand. Tell you what, though. I won't bind your hands."

"Why so tenderhearted?"

"It's not that," Martins said. "You gotta drink. I have to give it to you. I'm gonna keep my distance. Besides, we'll catch your partner regardless. If you ain't there, you may not ever find out who you are."

That was true, Hank thought. But whoever he was, there was a strong in-the-present reality: Something about being here, with Jane and Douglas, was appealing. Not only because it was the only thing familiar to him, but because even without his memory, he had felt peace since he arrived. It was not the knife-throwing life Martins had hinted at. But given that natural fit he felt, Hank wondered again if he had a wife and a son somewhere else. What if they were waiting for his return?

"Hey, you busy remembering something, Mr. No Name?"

"No," he replied.

Hank's natural dislike for the man did not take to this new mockery. Perhaps, at one time, he would have answered with a knife through the man's Adam's apple. Now he made no comment.

Lieutenant Martins returned the knife to his belt. "I want to make sure you hear this, mister, because if you *do* remember who you are and what your business was, and you decide to finish what you started, you will wish you died back there in the desert. You hear?"

"It's my memory that's dull, not my hearing."

"Good. Because here's this. If, on the other hand, you decide to throw in with me and mine, that will weigh strong in your favor."

Hank stared at the man and his greasy brow, at dark brown eyes that shined like marbles against his dark skin. "I don't know what kind of man I was, Lieutenant Martins. But your manner makes me wonder who was the good guy and who was the bad guy when we met."

"That kind of wondering is a road to nowhere." He glanced up at the sun. "I have a rendezvous to keep in Oak Ridge, and I've taken enough time here. For all I know, your friend is already captured, and this whole conversation was for nothing. I'll get the horses. Say your goodbyes outside where I can see you."

Martins paused to pick up the Smiths' rifle on his way to collect his horses.

"We need that!" Jane called after him. "To hunt."

"You should've thought of that before you pointed it at me."

"I did that, remember?" Hank said. "She has two Colts in the house, never drew them."

The lieutenant stopped, turned, and then placed the rifle against the well before continuing on. Hank collected his boots, tied the laces together, and heaved them over his shoulders; they needed more time to stretch, and he would not be doing much walking.

He stood there a moment feeling their weight. Swung round his head and released, something like this could kill a mountain lion. Or a man.

It was a thought.

Then he went to where the Smiths were standing.

"Thank you for the rifle," she said.

"Thank you for all you did," Hank replied, looking

down at the woman's face. It had lost some of its initial reserve and seemed . . . pretty, now that he looked.

"You're most welcome, Hank. I'm going to go inside, get you some food to take with you."

When she left, Hank's eyes went to the boy, who remained where he was. "Thanks to you, too, son. You're quite a young man."

The boy seemed a few inches taller and lit by a second sun at that moment.

"You'll come back, won't you, Hank?"

"If it's humanly possible, I most certainly will."

"Even if you don't find your knife, I hope you find out who you are."

"Son, that's the nicest thing I can ever remember hearing."

It took a moment, but the boy smiled like a poked baby. "Aw, you don't remember anything *except* today."

Jane returned with a canvas sack full of jerky and something she held behind her back. Hank accepted the food with gratitude.

"To be honest, ma'am, there's a big part of me wishes I could start over here and now as Hank."

"It's not good to have ghosts. One day your memory will return. I live with memories—you have to make peace with them."

The man smiled tightly as his eyes were drawn to the smoke rising from the crooked chimney.

"You better tend to your own victuals."

"I will." She revealed what she had been hiding: her husband's Stetson. "You'll need this, too."

Hank's smile was big and earnest as he looked from Jane and then over to Douglas. "Son? When this is done, and if I do get my knife back, it's yours."

"Really, sir?"

"Really. Until then, you can practice."

"How?"

"Rub a large stick on a rock till it's got a point. Flip it at the ground like this." The man pinched his thumb and index finger and made a snapping motion with his hand. "And that's not all you can do with a stick."

The boy thought hard. "Like you seen me do with the rabbit and the arrow?"

"Saw," Jane said.

"Sure, that," Hank told him, "if you first stab the critter. No, I recollected something when I was watching you at the pond."

"Really?"

"Yup. I had a stick, and I used it to dig or cut a trench or write in the dirt—"

"Maps?"

"Possibly," Hank thought—truthfully, he could not recall.

"My pa did that sometimes to show where he'd been."

"See? And you can use it to point, too, like a big finger. Or leave sticks on the ground to point a trail you've taken. Thing is, out here, you have to be clever, like I've seen you be. Use the things around you while you're waiting for your knife."

The boy smiled so broadly that his mother laughed. Hank wondered how often she got to do that, and Douglas averted his face quickly. Hank felt another strong tug that bid him to stay. But knew he had no place here. Not now, at least.

Fixing the hat gently on his head—he wore it dipped forward, to keep the band resting just above his wound—

he walked away, tall and suddenly proud in a splash of brilliant day.

"Is Hank going to be okay, Ma?"

"I pray he will be."

"Maybe—maybe we should go with him."

"They'll be on horseback. We wouldn't be able to keep up." She smiled comfortingly. "Do you remember that? When you used to run after your daddy's horse, calling after?"

"I sure do. I fell a lot."

"But you always got up."

"What if we follow and only catch up instead of keep up?"

Jane laid her hand on his sandy blond hair. "You heard—Hank has some things he has to settle. And we've got a smoked rabbit to attend to."

Douglas watched as Hank and Martins met. The new rider took a moment to stroke the horse.

"He's making friends," the boy remarked.

"He is indeed," Jane said wistfully as she put her arm around her son and walked over to the sack where the rabbit waited patiently.

# CHAPTER FOUR

IT WAS A very natural thing for Hank to sit a horse.
Having done it enough, he guessed that was something you did not have to remember. The ability was
just there.

*With a knife, too,* he thought. He wondered what he
would do if he had the one Martins had shoved in his
belt. He suspected he would feel better just possessing
it. And it might help him to remember.

The men rode single file onto the plains, with Hank
in front. He had shifted his boots so they were wrapped
around the saddle horn, where they thudded dramati-
cally and rhythmically against the sides. Sweat had
quickly saturated the band inside the Stetson and droplets ran along his scalp. They stung the wound but not
enough to distract him. The bandage sagged so quickly
that it was not long before he tore it away. The slight

breeze, warm though it was, felt soothing on the hot wound.

Hank did not try to talk to the other man. If Goodman Martins had wanted to say anything, he would have. If Goodman Martins were any kind of human being, he would have helped him just a little. Both were indicators of the kind of challenge Hank faced in the hours to come.

The farther north the men rode, the more verdant and rolling the countryside became. They were still on a mostly scrubby plain, but there were trees here and the first water he had seen since the pond: a creek where they stopped to water the horses. Hank had seen no sign of any other animals having gone this way, other than those with small padded paws. He figured that Martins was looking, too.

Hank ate a strip of the jerky and offered some to his companion.

"Got my own," Martins said, but he did not offer to share.

They rode on with nothing but the terrain and the occasional shadow or cry of a hawk to distract them. Hank felt nothing as smaller birds and mice fell victim to their diving attacks. Was that the uncaring coldness of the old Hank or the new?

He half turned.

"There's something I'm trying to understand," Hank said, "and I'm wondering if you can help me."

"Depends."

"You said I was on horseback? I seem to recall one—had a blond mane."

"I didn't see it. I said you boys stayed outside the fire."

"I thought maybe you caught a glimpse of markings, of what I was wearing—"

"I did not. First thing I knew was when you threw the knife and your friend collected what you came for. Then we heard you ride off."

"How did we get such a big lead?"

"You cut our horses loose first. Took us a while to gather them in the dark, shouting out plans and scaring them more, holding burning brands for light with one hand, grabbing reins with the other. I wanted you dead, the two of you, but I had to admit you were good. Damn quiet."

Hank shook his head. "It just happened a few hours ago. How can I not remember any of the—" He fell silent.

"What is it?" Martins asked.

"I can't remember any of the plan," Hank said—not just repeating the words but thinking about them. "A plan. A *bad* plan . . ."

The lieutenant kicked his horse forward until he was beside Hank. "You had a plan. What was it?"

"I don't know. I said those words to him."

"Said them to who?"

"Bill. Bill . . . *Beaudine.*"

The other man's harsh features showed interest. "Your partner?"

"I don't know," Hank replied. His own brow was creased in the middle as he tried to fill in that dark hole in his memory. "Do you know the name?"

"Don't ask. Damn it, think. Bill Beaudine. What *about* him?"

Hank tried to put a face on the name, a form, a horse, a place . . . anything. He saw only that empty hole and shook his head slowly. He silently repeated the words over and over. *It's a bad plan. It's a bad plan.*

Martins swore and came to a stop. Hank's grip on the reins was loose, and his horse walked on several paces before stopping on its own. The rider was not quite present. He was hunting through his emptied mind.

It remained empty, and Hank turned sharply in the saddle. "Lieutenant—*help* me! Give me something. Have you *heard* that name?"

"I've heard it," Martins said.

"Tell me where! I'm not holding anything back—"

Hank looked at him imploringly, but Martins was done.

The lieutenant looked ahead. "C'mon. We have to reach the way station by nightfall."

Martins spurred his horse to move. Hank did not bother asking what the urgency was about, did not press him more about the name. The man was either a self-made bastard or a great soldier, possibly both.

Hank followed, mentally repeating the name Bill Beaudine.

*William Beaudine. WB. Bill. BB. Sergeant Beaudine. Captain Beaudine. Colonel Beaudine.*

No version of it, no rank, seemed to be quite right. None brought up a face.

A gust of wind lifted a tumbleweed, blew it against him. Strands stuck to his sweat, and he brushed them away, spit a few to the side—

*A blade of grass.*

He had been chewing one on the back of that horse. The grass had been stuck there when he regained consciousness. He did not bother to tell Martins about that. But it was *something*, something new.

He reminded himself of something Jane had said, to let things sit. Don't look straight *at* them. Hank turned his struggling mind to Lieutenant Martins. Hank and, presumably, Bill Beaudine had been seeking the soldier and his companions. Why?

Martins had been fighting in Mexico, part of an army. The lieutenant had not said whether he was siding with the natives or was fighting for the United States.

"Are we at war with Mexico?" Hank asked suddenly. Jane had not spoken of it, but then it was not necessarily the topic a busy frontier woman might think to mention.

"Not since forty-eight. My pa served. Cost him an eye and an ear, fighting those dust rats."

"Was your father a soldier, too?"

"Stop talking," Martins said.

Direct questions had not worked, and the back door was shut, too. But it did not sound as if Martins would have fought for the locals. Another nation? Any political information Hank might have possessed was gone. If Martins was against the Mexicans, did that mean Hank had been for them? He did not seem to recall any language other than English. If he worked down there, he would have to know *some* Mexican.

*Unless you were down there for just this one thing: attacking Americans and not locals.*

The sun was just past overhead when dust rose on the northern horizon. That was the direction Martins was headed, toward the next way station. Lieutenant Martins "whoaed" to a stop. Hank did likewise.

Martins dismounted. Hank did not. He had been considering for the last few minutes, separating himself from the other man. This vague hope that scraps of knowledge would return or be triggered did not seem to be bearing fruit. Not with this man and his unwillingness to help anyone but himself and his mission—whatever that was. Hank was getting restless to try something else, almost anything else. The only thing that prevented him from galloping off was the very real fear of being shot in the back if he tried to get away. Or having the horse shot from under him and having to trot after the lieutenant, noosed to the saddle.

But this distraction might be the opportunity he needed. It depended on who was riding hard to get here. Martins obviously considered the newcomers potentially more of a threat than his unarmed companion. He had walked his horse ahead and not looked back once.

"You think they're your friends?" Hank asked.

"I said, don't talk."

Martins still did not look back. He was peering at that sudden activity, shotgun in hand. Then he did something curious: He took the horse's reins in his left hand and just stood there.

*That's not to escape,* Hank realized, whether remembering it or figuring it. Martins' intent was to pull the animal around for cover, if need be. That was why he had dismounted . . . and didn't mind if the other man stayed in the saddle. Hank would be the first to draw fire.

Hank looked at the terrain east and west. There was no cover in the low hills that he could reach in time, and there was no way he could outrace a shotgun blast. Especially on a horse, which made a considerable target. Yet if flight was impossible, there was still an option.

Hank dismounted, slowly and quietly. He kept his head steady so he wasn't shocked by a jolt of pain. Without the slight breeze he had felt on horseback, the sun and the heat quickly became oppressive. That meant Martins had to be feeling it, too. Despite his care the injury throbbed again, though not as bad as before. The parched grasses protected Hank's bare feet somewhat, enough so that when he started to move, he did not feel the burning . . . or make any sound.

*I've done something like this before,* he was certain. His legs knew to bend for flexibility, and his right hand felt empty . . . as if it needed a knife.

Hank did not bother trying to remember where, when, how, or why he had done this. He only knew that he must do it again. He let his body move, slightly crouched. His eyes were on the shotgun, in case Martins turned—

Hank was about five feet from the lieutenant when a sudden chittering sound, some flying instinct—or perhaps an Indian—caused the man to spin around. Had the officer turned and raised the shotgun simultaneously, Hank would have died there. But that was not what Martins did. Hank was able to take two more steps, then spring at the man before the weapon could be fully lifted.

The leap caused Hank's wound to ache, and he screamed from deep in his belly to release the pain. Fortunately, the cry livened his senses, his eyes, his movements. Hank's hat flew away, and the shotgun discharged, injuring only the dry earth in front of the soldier and scaring Hank's horse away; Martins had been forced to release his own reins, causing the paint to buck and back away as the men fell. Hank landed with his left arm around Martins' neck, pulling the man down as he himself hit the ground. Hank landed on his right side, braced by his right arm, but the drop had knocked the breath from the Confederate soldier.

Time mattered now. Whoever was approaching would have heard the shot.

Hank did not waste time fighting for the gun. As they scrapped for position, Hank had two goals: to get on top of the other man and to get his right arm around the man's waist . . . behind it. Hours of frustration fueled by desperation helped Hank achieve both. Straddling the lieutenant, Hank put his left hand on the man's throat, putting his weight into the grip and pressing the back of the man's head to the ground. Martins had to use both hands to try to wrest the attacker away so he could breathe.

While that fight played out, Hank slipped his right hand round and felt for the hilt in the back of the gray jacket. He grabbed the bone handle through the fabric and tugged the knife to pull it free. Martins suddenly realized he had two battles to fight but Hank had the advantage—and then he had the knife.

The men were both inarticulate, grunting savages as they fought. Hank poured his desperate situation into the assault, lifting his full weight briefly from the straddled officer and coming down hard, knocking the breath from his adversary. Martins' fight dissipated as he wheezed, as Hank freed the knife from under the coat, flipped it over in his right hand, and laid the blade against the throat of the man trapped beneath him. Hank stopped choking the man as the blade drew blood and the officer ceased struggling. Hank used his free hand to pull the shotgun from the man's fingers. His eyes blazed down at the lieutenant.

*"Who am I?"* he screamed.

"I—I don't know!"

Hank dragged the sharp blade like a pendulum, cutting side to side in the man's leathery neck and drawing more blood.

"I swear, *I don't know*!"

"Who is Bill Beaudine?"

"A Pinkerton man."

"What?"

"A detective!"

The explanation meant nothing.

"Who are you working for?" Hank demanded. "What did we steal?"

Martins wriggled, clamped his lips shut, snarled in his mouth as blood trickled down both sides of his neck.

Hank grabbed a fistful of his hair, yanked his head back to expose more throat, and pressed down. The lieutenant winced, but his lips did not open.

Lieutenant Martins was more of a soldier, of a man, than his attacker had guessed. Hank stole a look up, saw the dust cloud nearing, two riders visible. He glared back down at his captive and pushed the knife hard enough to draw more blood. He felt the resistance of the man's voice box and stopped.

"Give me *something*, damn your eyes!"

Martins looked up. And spat.

There was no more time. Hank raised the knife, hilt down, and brought it hard against the man's forehead, audibly cracking Martins' skull. Rising unsteadily, blood once again running behind his own ear, Hank took the shotgun, recovered his hat, and carefully approached the lieutenant's spooked horse a few feet away. His own had run off too far to catch.

Hank climbed into the saddle. He did not know if the men approaching were friends or enemies. Obviously, neither had Martins, and this was not the time to find out. Without making any stops, his companions would likely have beaten him to the meeting place, been watching for his dust.

Pulling the reins to turn the mount around, Hank made his way past the other horse, slow enough not to scare him and close enough so he could reach over to grab his boots without stopping.

He and Martins had been heading northeast, by the sun, and Hank continued east—the direction the horse was facing. He kicked him to a gallop, as unsure of where he was going as he was unsure of everything else in his life at the moment. All he knew was that he could not go back to the Smith cabin. However bad Martins was hurt, he might return there when he woke. It was not fair to put the family in further danger. Hank's fast-made plan, the entirety of it, was to circle wide around the newcomers and, at least for now, make his way to the stagecoach stop. If they were headed there, chances were the hard-riding Beaudine might have done so as well.

Besides, at the moment, the stop was one of only two places he knew of on God's entire earth.

T HE TWO RIDERS, both in dirty Confederate uniforms, rode in with urgent speed. They stopped just a few feet from the fallen man. One of the men slid from his saddle and looked off to the east. He saw a galloping horse and rider small against the sky and another horse grazing much nearer.

The mounted man was also looking east. "Should I go after him, Frank?"

Colonel Franklin Voight looked around and shook his head. "Seems like he took the lieutenant's shotgun. No point running headlong into that. Bring water, a cloth, something to patch his throat. We gotta bring the lieutenant around, see who that was."

As the other man dismounted, Voight glanced at a compass hanging from his belt and marked the fleeing man's exact direction. There was nothing out there, so the rider was likely to turn back at some point. The other horse out in the field—that was the one Martins had brought to carry a dead man. It wasn't.

The second man came over with his canteen and removed his kerchief. Private Paul Stevens was a strong six footer, his head covered in prematurely white hair. The man bent over the unconscious Martins was the shortest of the trio.

Stevens knelt and dribbled water sparingly on the injury inflicted by the knife hilt, then used his sweaty kerchief to dab it away. Lieutenant Martins did not move. Voight listened to the man's breathing, touched lightly on both sides and around the small of his back. Nothing was broken. Voight put the damp cloth on the man's neck wound, then sat back on his heels.

"You see the head wound, Private?"

"Yeah?"

"Bruising already. Hard, sharp, pointed hit."

"A rock?"

Voight shook his head. "I'm guessing it's the same knife that was held to his throat. Probably that Bowie knife the lieutenant pulled from the tree. Unless he stashed it elsewhere, it's missing."

"Seems careless of the lieutenant to have had this happen."

"Man tied up can slip off the horse, slow you down. You gotta do everything for him. Go collect the other horse. We'll get the lieutenant on it, go to the meeting point, figure out what to do."

"He'll want to ride on, cuts and bumps or not," Stevens said.

"Likely as not, but he'll need 'em patched all the same."

The private looked to the east. The horse and rider were no longer visible. Perhaps they were in the small clump of velvet mesquite about a quarter mile away; it was difficult to see into the shade.

"I still think I should ride after the one who did this."

Voight shook his head. "He could be hunkered down out there, waiting for us to do just that. No, you've got to cover our move north so we can regroup, fast. Get Martins' horse. And, Paul—watch that whoever is out there ain't waiting for you to do just that."

"Right."

While Voight patched Martins' throat as best as he could—using mud he made from canteen water—Stevens remounted and went off after the other horse. It had stopped about a quarter mile away and was grazing. He rode toward it and then halted abruptly.

"I see him!" Stevens shouted.

Voight spun but remained low to the ground. "Where?"

"Off to the east—"

Voight shielded his eyes with both hands and looked where the private was pointing. He saw a small shape just north of the trees. It could have been a horse or a rock or a stunted tree; it was too far to be sure.

"Let him be!" Voight ordered.

But Stevens didn't hear, as he had simultaneously driven heels into his horse and taken off in that direction.

Voight stood and bellowed, *"Private!"*

Either pride and a desire for vengeance or distance rendered the private deaf. As Stevens rode, he pulled his carbine from its scabbard and held it at the ready. The figure beside the tree had not yet moved. Maybe the man had been thrown, the crazy way he was riding. Or it could have been that Martins hadn't taken punishment without giving some, and the man was injured.

The private charged ahead, sucking the hot air through his teeth, ready to stop in an instant. He was riding low, hugging the neck of the horse, using a tight rein to pull the horse into unexpected zigs and zags. As the point man of their Tennessee regiment during the war, he was accustomed to short pursuits and antelope-fast attacks.

The ground spit dirt and grass ahead of him. and a moment later the air erupted with a deep, rolling crack. Private Stevens made one of those sudden halts, nearly upending the horse with the forceful ninety-degree turn. Stevens was off the horse in the same move and tugged the reins sideways, leaving the animal between him and the shooter. He held firm on the reins with his left hand while with his right he brought the rifle up and over the saddle, pointing north.

He peered ahead. The horse was still in the trees. Stevens squinted at it.

"Eh?"

A horse. Just a horse was standing there. The rider had doubled back on foot, probably belly crawling, taken concealment in the rolling terrain, and fired off a shotgun—likely Lieutenant Martins' Crescent double-barreled, from the familiar boom of it.

That was more cannon than Stevens wanted to deal with. Especially because that first shot might have been an intentional miss.

None of the old unit had ever surrendered, but they had retreated. Still behind the horse, he raised the carbine so it was pointed up, above the saddle.

"I'm leaving!" he shouted.

The private looked down at the scraggly earth. He always found he could listen better if he wasn't looking. There was no response, but there was also no additional gunfire. Stevens stood a moment more, then cautiously stuck his head up over the back of the horse. He looked ahead.

The horse was gone, leaving behind an empty settling cloud of dust.

"Goddamn, you've done this before, too," he said.

He returned his brain to the other missions: tending to Martins and the big one, recovering the box. Though he could not help but wonder if a big clue was departing fast to the east.

Without further hesitation, Stevens climbed back on his mount and kicked it in the opposite direction, scooping up the stray horse as he rode back.

When the private returned, Voight was kneeling beside Martins. The officer's jacket was off, and Voight was checking the muddy poultice on the lieutenant's throat.

"Had your ration of full-steam stupid for today?" Voight asked, glancing up.

"Colonel, there's a reason the lieutenant was traveling with that fella."

"You mean the lieutenant who's lying on the ground

here?" Voight reminded him. "You're saying he had a reason that he could tell us if he were awake?"

Stevens dismounted, still holding the reins of the second horse. His hard landing, his kick at the ground, showed he wasn't ashamed of going, just of failing.

"How is he?"

Voight turned back to the man lying on the ground. "Despite having his bruised sides painfully poked, he has not made a sound."

*Like too many of our boys in too many of those bloody campaigns in the last American war,* Voight thought. And now here they were, on what was supposed to be a milk run, hoping they could get their leader healthy again.

"You want to sit him up or—"

"No," Voight said. "We'll take off his jacket to pad the saddle and just drape him over carefully."

"That's what the lieutenant planned to do," Stevens observed. "Throw two dead men across it."

"I was there, Private. I heard."

"Just remembering," Stevens protested.

"Would've been better if you'd did some thinking, too. And waiting."

Stevens scowled. "You're being a little harsh, don't you think, Colonel?"

Voight shook his head. "The shotgun was gone—and so was the Bowie knife. Remember that?"

Stevens seemed surprised. He had not forgotten the incident, which had taken place just hours before, but he had forgotten that Martins was carrying the knife.

"So he was the guy," the private said.

"Yeah. A professional. I want to know how the lieutenant got him before we go after him."

Stevens nodded; it was short and conciliatory. Voight handed Stevens the jacket. The private draped it over the back of the spare horse. Then he took the lieutenant's head, and Voight grabbed the legs, and they hoisted Martins facedown across the saddle.

"I still don't like the idea of letting the one who did this get away," Stevens muttered.

Voight was losing his patience. "We came late and lost that battle—that's a fact." He gave the prostrate Lieutenant Martins a little push on the small of his back to make sure he would not slide off. "Let's think about winning the war."

With that, and after delaying to stomp-clean himself off so he was not blinded with his own dust particles, Stevens looped the reins of Martins' horse over his own cantle and mounted. It would be slower going than both men would have liked, but it was either that or separating. With at least two adversaries, that was not going to happen. Not after fighting shoulder to shoulder through four ugly years on American soil, under Colonel Nathaniel Jackson Ahrens and the 1st Regiment Tennessee Volunteer Cavalry, and then five years of working against the Juáristas south of the border. Stevens had little interest in their cause one way or the other. With the overthrow and execution of the tyrannical Emperor Maximilian I, President Juárez had canceled all foreign debts. The governments of France, Spain, and Great Britain didn't like that and sent their armies over in 1861—while the United and Confederate states were in no position to intervene, distracted by their own problems. After the Civil War was over, many soldiers came south to work for the high-paying Europeans.

Most of those had been defeated; only the French

maintained a small, harassing presence. This mission was designed to make them more than that.

When Voight and Stevens had put together in something resembling a train, with Martins in the middle, the men rode out at a trot, toward the way station in Oak Ridge.

# CHAPTER FIVE

A LIVING MAN. A *free* man.

Even if he did not know who he was, and despite the dull pain that beat on his skull with impressive resilience, Hank savored the moment of liberation. He had not only escaped captivity; he had turned back an attempt to retake him. Martins' shotgun had not felt as natural to wield as the knife. Fortunately, Hank only had to put buckshot near the target, not in him. His concern was that he might actually hit the man without meaning to.

Martins had forced him to behave aggressively. So had this man, and Hank was glad he had kept checking behind him—common sense? An instinct? Whatever it was, it had saved his life. He had not wanted to shoot this man, not because he found it abhorrent but quite the opposite. It had felt too, too natural. Whoever he was, lawman or outlaw, perhaps a soldier like these men, there was nothing random about whom he hurt or killed. When he had thrown the knife at Martins, before all this, he had only sought to warn him. The lieutenant had said so himself.

Fortunately, this encounter was done—for now. He also had his liberty—for now. He held the Bowie knife in his hand, hoping it would reacquaint him with his past. Other than feeling as if it belonged, nothing came to him.

The caress of the air, the sun, the horse did more to soothe his injury than anything. Freedom won filled him like nothing he had experienced since his recent rebirth.

Riding at a slow gallop, he selected another strip of snake meat. Chewing it seemed familiar, just like the grass, though the salty taste was unfamiliar. Hank still occasionally turned back in the saddle to make sure the men were not in pursuit. Since the man who had chased him had turned back, they had not moved from where he had left Lieutenant Martins. Then, suddenly, after a few minutes, Hank turned, and they were gone from view.

*They probably have to get somewhere to doctor the lieutenant,* Hank thought. It would have been a two-man job if they intended to take him anywhere—and they must have realized, by now, that it would be a two-man job if they had attempted to take the man who had done that to Martins.

The brim of his hat dipped low, Hank kept up his pace until he felt it was safe to stop. He did not know by what instinct, what animal sense, he judged that; it was something he simply felt.

Hank slipped the Bowie knife in his belt. *That* did

not feel right. It belonged to a particular sheath. Above all, he was eager to have that back where it belonged, on his left side.

Stopping on the near side of a low rise, Hank slipped from the saddle and retrieved the boots. He untied them from one another, shook out the stones, and—bless Jane Smith—put on his now roomier boots. With a final glance at the western horizon, he began to take stock of what was in Lieutenant Martins' saddlebag. There was the additional food the lieutenant had mentioned, including sun-dried bananas, a tinderbox, and shotgun shells. There was also a pouch of tobacco. Hank had not seen the man smoking or chewing, so he must have used it for trade. That suggested to him that he was not operating with the U.S. Army as such. Otherwise, he would not have needed to swap a smoke for anything.

There was a large map that, when unfolded, covered the terrain from just below the California line to Sacramento in the north and the Arizona Territory and Nevada to the east, with trails indicated but nothing other than the stage trail and its stops marked on them. There were a pencil and a notepad with nothing written in it, but there were pages torn out.

"For leaving messages under rocks?" he wondered, though Hank had not seen the lieutenant write or leave any. Perhaps the men left notes for one another when they separated. Maybe they had finished down south and were headed home. Could the lockbox have held their wages?

*That would make me just a common outlaw,* he thought unhappily.

There were a half-full canteen and a sheath with the man's own smaller cutting knife. Hank slipped it out.

The four-inch blade smelled of fish. It seemed dainty, ineffective, used for scaling and filleting. He replaced it and took out his own. Once again he felt the heft of it, flipped it, and caught it, and looked around. There was a black snake in the grasses about six feet ahead. He did not know the kind; he only remembered rattlers. He took the knife by the point and hurled it, planting the blade deep and confidently in the ground, just behind the tail—close enough to cause the serpent to rapidly wriggle off.

"I guess some things can't be knocked out of you."

He wondered what else his body knew, what secrets his muscles retained.

Shooting a shotgun had not been one of them. That had seemed heavy, firing it overkill.

Hank recovered the blade. He noticed the stain of Martins' blood on the bottom of the hilt. He looked, saw the man's neck blood on his pants. Hank rubbed the stain in the dirt and went back to his horse.

He stood there a moment, looking in every direction. "You're living and you're free, but where are you going?"

He considered heading back to the desert where the present adventure had begun. Now that he knew Lieutenant Martins and his party had been situated farther south, there might be clues as to what he himself was doing there. But the way the man had described the attack—in the dark, sneaking—made it sound like it might be hostile territory. Especially if someone down there recognized him.

Indians or Mexicans? he wondered. It didn't matter. If he encountered anyone who knew him, it would not be with much liking. They would more likely kill Hank than tell him who he was.

Besides, going south he would be tempted by the Smith cabin. That would not be fair to the easily busted hopes of a young boy—especially when Hank could not yet afford to be without the knife.

It was better to go north, to the way station. If nothing else, someone there might know or have seen Beaudine. Or him. Maybe they had come through it at some point. That plan had its risks as well. But it seemed to him he had to locate William Beaudine, or at least learn more about him, to find out anything about himself. One unsuspecting man could be tracked and approached with caution.

Climbing back into the saddle, Hank decided this much: He must have been riding long days before the incident that brought him down. His thigh muscles ached, and his seat was uncomfortable. He adjusted his posture as best he could, mindful not to agitate his wound, and he kept the pace slow to save both himself and the horse.

The countryside quickly took on more color, mostly reds in the form of grasses and berries, though it added no human population. The shotgun was in its cutoff scabbard, ready for quick-draw use, since Hank had no idea what kinds of wildlife or Indians might live hereabout. Circling buzzards, at a distance of maybe a half mile, told him that either two- or four-legged killers were out there. It also told him which direction to go for water: away from where animals were dead or dying.

As Hank rode, his mind returned, unbidden, to trying to remember. He had no mental memory of the sheath, only a physical sensation. His thigh recalled the weight of it. He put his hand above the spot where it would have been. He let his fingers hover just above the spot—

He could *almost* feel it against his fingertips—the scruffy touch of the deerskin sheath the knife had been in. There was a worn-out roughness to it. It had been through river water, sun, gritty winds. He let his fingers remember more of the texture. There were beads . . . and along the sides big piggin strings, the rawhide laces that held the sides of the sheath together. The deerskin was so worn, it was like soft leather in spots, but he kept it—

*Because it was special.*

"Why did someone *take* it after leaving me?" he wondered aloud. It was just one more thing to carry. Was it distinctive enough so that, seeing it, someone would know who Hank really was?

There were laces. He had flashes of himself bending and tying them. Why would he do that? They were long laces, long enough to go around his—

"Thigh. I tied it there so it wouldn't shift when I drew it."

Hank was sure of that. He couldn't quite visualize it, but he knew. You had to be able to trust your weapon no less than you trusted your horse.

He wondered if he trusted William Beaudine.

"If not, it was surely with good reason," he said.

*Trust.* Right now there was only one person he trusted; at least, that he remembered. Jane. Once again, Hank looked at his fingers. He raised his left hand and looked at the ring finger, rubbed it clean against his trousers— against Nehemiah Smith's trousers. He suddenly felt covetous *and* a usurper.

As he had done with the knife, he imagined the

fourth finger. He flexed it, believing that he would recall the presence of a ring. It didn't seem like there had
been anything there. There was no empty longing, except for the woman he had left behind.

*Seems that a family would have to be one of the first
things I'd remember,* he thought. Holding a wife, a child.
Their smell.

Spurring the horse, Hank made his way north with
greater urgency, leaning forward in a manner that also
suddenly seemed comfortable and familiar—

And something else.

He could feel himself having stopped, suddenly. Turning the horse to the left. Looking at the shape of a man
who stopped his own horse a few paces ahead. There
was something knocking on that horse. *Whap . . .
whap . . . whap . . .*

It was dark, and it was laden with *something* . . . and
then it was gone.

But Hank felt encouraged by it. The vision, if truth-
ful, was another piece, and he rode on hard in search
of the rest. . . .


JANE SMITH WAS working out back, trying not to think
about Hank, about the thought of perhaps never
seeing him again, when fate helped take her mind off
the man and his plight. She did not know what had happened to make her cabin so popular this hot summer
day. She loved her God and her Bible, and the wisdom
they imparted, and the great and stalwart liberators
like Moses and Joshua, the leaders and poets like David
and Solomon. Flawed men all, but *men* all. Reading
and rereading their sagas reminded her of her man.

But this day left her wondering what the heavenly plan was for her.

As she and her boy were busy composing the remains of the rabbit that was now, finally, in a stew, there was a faint vibration underfoot, like when the underground stream that fed the pond and their well was flushed and full and running.

Only it was not the stream. That mostly happened months before, in the spring.

Douglas was busy using the fireplace poker to alternately churn the mound and pretend he was a pirate in one of the picture books his father had brought from Apple Town. Without showing alarm, Jane left the rifle behind and wordlessly went to the eastern side of the cabin. Shielding her eyes from the early-afternoon sun, she peered southwest and saw a column of riders approaching.

Wiping her hands on her apron, she turned to go back to the compost heap and started when she saw Douglas beside her. "You gave me a fright!"

"I'm good at stalking, right?"

"You're good, you are," she agreed. "Now I want you to stalk right inside."

"Why, Ma? Who are those men?"

"I'm sure I don't know, Douglas James Smith, but horses are unpredictable, and men are more so. Go!"

If he heard, he made no sign of it. He was staring over the poker, held straight out in his right hand, as he ticked off numbers.

"There's thirteen of them," he concluded. "Hey, you didn't bring the rifle. Want I should get it and my bow?"

"You should do as you're told!" his mother said. She

started toward the back of the house, gently shoving her boy before her. "Now!"

"I'm going. I'm going," Douglas said, swinging his head from side to side with defiant disapproval. But he did as he was told and retreated to the hot cabin.

The column riding toward them was visible beyond the well. The men were dressed in a uniform of sorts: not military but white peasant garb, black sombreros, and bandoliers. The wardrobe was common enough in these parts, though not in such numbers. She saw the ammunition from far off, which was why she had not gone to get her own rifle, which sat within reach against the table. She did not want to provoke violence by someone misunderstanding her nature.

Only one of the riders was quite unlike the rest. It was a woman wearing a white top with big sleeves and a low neckline. It was embroidered with red curls on top and shoulders. She also had on a tricolor lace skirt and a white shawl to protect her from the sun and wind. She was not a peasant, and Jane's first impression was that the men were an escort for the lady.

*Those soldiers Hank encountered must have been waiting for these other men or scouting ahead,* she thought.

If their uniform was not military, their carriage was. Jane had seen enough horsemen in her thirty-three years to recognize trained riders, probably cavalry and not bandits. Except for the bandoliers, they had none of the hallmarks of brigands who haunted the local ranges. Each man was rigidly upright, riding an equal distance from the man beside, before, or behind him, and was silent. No one sang; no one spoke; no one smoked. And the man in front—of medium height and build with a thin chin and a thin mustache—held his head emphatically upright and straight. He was at least a captain, she suspected.

*And they are pasty faced,* she thought. Desert outlaws were sunburned, mountain men wind burnished. Except for the man in front, no one wore facial hair, which suggested they did not spend many nights out-of-doors in the cold. As they rode past the well onto her property, she could see under the circular brims of their hats they were not just fair skinned but several were blue eyed or green eyed.

Jane moved from the compost heap to where her rifle stood against the table. She did not pick it up but put the shovel down so her hands would be free.

The column came to a practiced halt when the leader raised his right arm. Jane was not surprised when that hand descended and swept off the man's hat. She had guessed them to be Americans—Southerners, from their grooming, former soldiers working in Mexico, training Juáristas from the ragtag guerrillas they had been to the disciplined military force they needed to be.

She was surprised, then, when the leader spoke to her with a heavy French accent framed by a big, insincere smile.

"Forgive our intrusion, madam." His eyes shifted briefly from the woman to the rifle, then back. His smile widened without adding conviction. "You and your family need have no fear."

"We don't. Caution isn't fear."

The man's expression took on a moment of sincerity. "I respect the distinction, madam. I am Raoul Dupré."

"I'm Jane Smith."

"My pleasure." He cocked his head toward the cabin. "The boy I saw. Your son?"

She nodded.

"And is Mr. Smith nearby?"

"He is."

"May I ask where?"

Without taking her eyes from this verbal peacock, Jane nodded to his grave.

The leader had been in the process of replacing his hat. He looked over, halted, and bowed his bare head slightly toward her.

"My condolences, Mrs. Smith. The War?"

She nodded again. "The coach."

"I see."

The captain turned toward the well. "Might we impose on your hospitality for a canteen of water?"

"Help yourself."

He bowed courteously once more. That was not, however, all he wanted. The pond was just a half a mile distant the way they had come. This was a stall. She could tell by the way he was looking around, but only at the ground.

"Madam, we are searching for comrades who have gone missing. They would have been wearing gray uniforms, late of your Confederate Army. Like this gentleman." He pointed to his left.

"Not my army, Captain."

"My pardon," the Frenchman said.

"There was one such, Captain Dupré. He called himself Lieutenant Goodman Martins."

The name got a reaction from the man in gray. His eyes openly wandered the property, then the ground beneath their feet. From his expression, the man apparently just realized their careless approach had obscured any tracks.

"That is one of the men, yes," the Frenchman said after doing his own visual check of just the cabin. "Was he alone?"

"He arrived without any companions."

"But he is no longer here."

"As you see," she said.

The man in the uniform said something to the captain.

"How many horses did he bring?" Dupré inquired.

"Two," she said.

"Can you tell us in which direction he headed?"

"North," she answered.

The leader peered toward the distant horizon. "Did he mention why he was going that way?"

"We did not speak much," she said. "He had a shotgun turned on my boy and myself."

"Why?"

"You'll have to ask that when you catch up with him," she said. "He has, I'd say, a three-hour jump on you."

The man continued to study her. "May we talk to your boy?"

"About what? He's ten."

"Ten-year-olds have eyes . . . and ears. Perhaps he noticed something you did not? For instance, where Martins may have been headed? Did he say anything about his destination?"

"He mentioned the way station, I think."

"Oak Ridge?"

"Yes."

"Why did you not tell me that before?"

"You asked me what direction, not what destination," Jane said.

The captain was not pleased. He looked like he wanted to charge her with a saber.

"I do not know what you are playing at, madam, but now I will speak with your son."

Jane hesitated but only for a moment. The captain and his right-hand man were like bobcats on a ledge. It was not really a request.

"Douglas!"

"Yes, Ma?" came a muted voice from the dark interior.

"Come on out. There is a gentleman who wishes to ask you about the lieutenant."

Her comment drew a lingering, knowing look from Dupré. She had been very specific, as though giving her son instructions. The captain smiled crookedly at her and then, more broadly, at the boy as he approached. The youngster was holding his bow and arrow. The shaft was loaded but pointed down. He was openmouthed as he walked toward the array of men. He had not seen so many horses or riders in one place in his life. He stopped when he reached his mother's side. She slid her arm around his spindly shoulders. Jane could feel his heart drumming hard. He seemed so young and small to her just then.

And fearful.

"Hello, Douglas," said the leader. "I am Captain Raoul Dupré of the French marines."

"Oh!" the boy said, his mouth falling open.

The man had hoped, correctly, that the military rank and reference would impress the boy.

"Did someone make that for you?" the officer asked, indicating the bow and arrow.

"I made it myself, sir."

"Very commendable. I would like to see you shoot it sometime. But first, Douglas, what can you tell me about the man who came to visit?"

"Hank."

The word was like a small detonation, and it was as though the sudden gray smoke of cannon fire had settled on the captain, Jane, and Douglas, binding them in unpleasant union. Perhaps that had been the captain's intention. Perhaps it was an accident. It did not matter; the damage was grave.

The boy recognized the sudden change in his mother, in the officer, but he did not understand it. He pulled at her blouse. "Ma?"

"It's all right, son." Jane pulled her son closer.

The captain considered the two now without expression. "Which of you is going to tell me about Hank?"

Jane said, "I'll tell you what we know of the man, which isn't much. We found him near to being naked and dead on the edge of the desert, at the pond. He had no memory of who he was. We took him in, fixed a considerable head wound he had suffered, and gave him clothes, and that was it. He left with Lieutenant Martins."

"Why?"

"Lieutenant Martins forced him at gunpoint. That's why," Jane replied. "The lieutenant believed that Hank had taken something from him. But Hank had nothing on him."

"Including his memory," the captain said dubiously.

"That's right. He struggled and couldn't even recall his name. We gave him the one he used."

"When did the lieutenant and this Hank leave?"

"Early morning—maybe three hours ago."

"Headed?"

"Already told you," she said, pointing to the north.

"I assume the lieutenant had a destination."

"Your man did not confide in Hank, and he did not share any information with us."

"I see. And did Hank leave on a horse taken from you?"

"We don't own a horse. I already told you, the lieutenant brought a spare. I don't know why."

The captain looked at the boy. "Do you know why?"

The young man shook his head instantly and vigorously.

"Douglas," said the captain, "are you telling me the truth?"

"I'm trying to, sir."

"Do you know *anything* else about Hank or the lieutenant? Anything at all?"

Douglas looked at his mother, and she said, "Go on, son. You may tell him anything you recollect."

The boy's eyes returned to the officer. "A knife," he said. "Lieutenant Martins—he said Hank was handy with a throwing knife."

"Did he throw one at the lieutenant?"

"I—I think so. Not when he was here. The lieutenant, he said there were four of them sitting at a campfire when he threw it."

"The lieutenant and three others?"

"Yes, sir."

"Does either of you know where these others are?"

"They spread out," Douglas said. "I think that's what Lieutenant Martins said."

The captain looked at Jane. She nodded.

The boy looked up at his mother for reassurance. She looked down at him with a benign, reassuring smile that said he was doing fine.

The captain kicked his horse forward several paces, stopping just a few feet from the Smiths.

"You were listening very closely, weren't you, Douglas?"

The boy nodded.

"You liked Hank?"

"Yes, sir."

"Do you think he liked you?"

"He said he was going to give me a knife, once he found his and remembered who he was."

After a moment, the officer's eyes slid back to Jane.

"It seems your son remembers a good deal. Perhaps you have something to add?"

"I do not, except that a boy's hopes do not always align with the facts. Whatever is going on with Hank, Lieutenant Martins, and you has no purchase here."

"Sadly, madam, as in any war civilians are called upon to serve. It is possible that you know nothing more. It is also possible that Hank has some affection for you both. That might discourage hostile action, if such he has in mind."

"He was here less than an hour," Jane said.

"Long enough, it seems," the officer said, looking at the boy. "You will come with us."

"Where?"

"To find Lieutenant Martins and this 'Hank.' Room

will be made for you on horseback. Bring clothing for nighttime."

"You intend to—*abduct* us?"

"Say, rather, that I insist you both join us. At least until we know more about this gentleman."

"I tell you, we barely know him, or he us."

"Then you will have nothing more unpleasant than an outing, perhaps broaden the boy's experience with the world." The captain gestured ahead grandly.

"You have no authority here," she protested.

"Our numbers say otherwise." He glared down at the woman. "Get your things, please."

Jane stood as stiff as the rifle leaning against the carving table, unsure whether to cooperate or to run. If it were just herself—

*But it isn't.*

Douglas was looking from his mother to the captain, waiting for guidance. She touched his head and once more looked smilingly down.

"Would you like to take a trip?" she asked him.

"Sure, Ma. It could be exciting," he confessed. "You could still learn me writing and reading when we stop. I could practice shooting rabbits."

"A wonderful and very practical attitude," the captain cheered.

"Then let's get some things we'll need," she said, coaxing the boy along. There were no tears, no wavering in her voice. She faced this as she did unexpected danger every day.

"Only clothes," the officer said to her back. "We have food . . . and weapons."

"This?" the boy asked, holding up the bow and arrow.

The captain did not want to appear afraid of something that was little more than a toy, not before his men.

"Of course."

"And his reading book," the woman said.

"All right."

"We also have to douse the hearth."

"One of my men will do that," he said, looking at the man behind him and snapping his eyes toward the house. One of the French marines dismounted, looked around, and headed for the water bucket.

Even before the captain had ordered a man inside, Jane had already considered and dismissed the idea of taking a firearm from the chest and concealing it in her wrap. They would be killed or taken anyway, and most likely treated harshly. One thing she had learned living in this unforgiving land was that nature was inexorable—you moved with it; you sought refuge; you did not fight it. With men, the only difference was that you picked your time to fight. Here and now was not it.

She entered, followed by the soldier and Douglas. The boy watched while the man began to extinguish the blaze as though it were a campfire—pouring water on it.

"Sir, not like that," Douglas said.

The man froze.

"He may not understand you," his mother said.

"Like this," Douglas persisted, flicking his fingers as if they had water on them.

The man snorted and finished what he was doing, exactly as he had been doing it.

"That's not very nice," Douglas mumbled.

"Come here, son," Jane insisted. "Now."

The woman was kneeling beside the bed; she had

stiffened during the encounter but relaxed when Douglas stalked over, the exchange ended.

"We have to be careful around these men," she said quietly.

"I know. But this is our house. That's my fire."

"True enough. Let's see if we can get them away from it without further incident."

The boy nodded and stood beside her as she pulled a small, flat wooden drawer from under the mattress stand. It had belonged to a dresser that had been used for firewood during a long rainy spell.

Jane removed a heavy shawl for herself and an Indian blanket for Douglas. It was a gift from a small band of Pechanga Indians who had been traveling from the west and to whom she had given water. It was disheartening, as she thought back over the years: Most of the men she had known over the years, those who had leaned toward savagery, were white skinned.

Jane took a pair of kerchiefs from the box, returned it to its place, then waited until the soldier had left. She stood and paused to take a look around the dark cabin. She had rarely been away from here herself, this home in which her son had been born and her husband had died. A place where, just a few hours before, she had met a man who had brought a moment of real fellowship to her life for the first time in years.

"God would not have done that without a reason," she said in a prayerlike manner.

"Done what, Ma?" her son asked.

"Just thinking out loud," she said, hugging the garments to her as they walked back into the sunlight. A rigid and seemingly impatient Dupré gestured sharply, directing them to a pair of horses at the rear of the line. There was a rider midway up the line pulling a sledge behind him. He dismounted and handed both Jane and Douglas their own canteens. The two riders in back had also dismounted to help them up. Despite the woman's very real concerns about this adventure, Douglas smiled when they approached the horses, and he was beaming as he was raised to his horse's back.

"I haven't been on a horse since Fury died," he said. "This one feels different."

"That's because he's a military horse, not a nag," Jane said, raising her voice and looking ahead at the captain.

There was accusation in her tone, bite in the word "military." It held more contempt than when she talked about wildfires and dust storms. Nature was mighty and at times destructive, but it was not malicious. It did not want to do harm to anyone.

Jane handed her son one of the kerchiefs and told him to tie it behind his head, over his mouth. Then she climbed onto her own horse, helped up with a hoist from the soldier, and covered her own mouth. As soon as the two men had mounted behind them, the column moved out. Their departure stirred dust as well as memories old and recent—of stagecoaches and Nehemiah, of lost pilgrims and wanderers like Hank. The memories hovered in her memory, shifting and colliding, until they had reached a stretch where the cabin was no longer visible. Only the mountains on the distant horizon looked familiar to her.

Jane watched ahead and to both sides, carefully marking their passage across the plain just as she did each time she ventured into the desert. The terrain, even landmarks changed with the light. A traveler who failed to notice that could well become lost and perish. However far they went, and by a means she had not yet conceived, Jane vowed that she and Douglas would make their way back.

# CHAPTER SIX

"T HEY WILL BE sorry they shut it down."

Tall and rangy, the speaker was looking at a barren plain, an expanse that had once teemed with anticipation, promise—and people.

The man shook his head, sending bugs flying from his long graying hair and from his woolly white mustache. He absently brushed it back with a big leathery hand.

"They'll be damned, *damned* sorry when the plains out here ain't nothing but those iron herds and the daytime is like a thousand war party Indians sending smoke signals, nothing but black with teeny spots of blue. And the population—dear, sweet Lord, what will that be? Not the finest and hardiest folks who ever crossed mountains but *all* of them. People will come from everywhere, funneling through the high rock and snow in a metal contraption. They won't be tough. They'll just be here. And not coming for a visit with Grandpa but to stay. To *stay*, y'hear?"

The speaker turned to the only other man in the room. That other man continued to eat his meal without looking up. Having stared so long into the daylight, the speaker could barely make out anything inside the log cabin. He turned back outside.

"Some of them will come to take a job that wasn't needed before the train: working in stores that wasn't here before the rails, raising horses and fixing wagons and selling new fashions that don't belong out here. And cattle! Train, I hear, will need ten times what gets cattle-drove now. Kansas will be chin deep in cattle patties and will stink for the next hundred years. Then these folks'll be sending for their kinfolk, causing clutter, angering more Indians—like a human plague of locusts that will, dear God, eat what grains we have and meat we raise down to the root and bone. Then we're all in trouble."

Zebulon Moore paused but remained standing by the back door, breathing air that did not come from inside the dark, musty room, which was once the dining hall of this formerly illustrious and crucial Butterfield way station. He was in his sixties, fancied himself in his forties, and looked like he was in his eighties. Like his bent frame and stiff fingers that he now and then flexed or wriggled or rolled, his social skills had seen happier times.

The other occupant of the room imagined that this was the same speech Zebulon had made to himself many times over the course of many days, spoken aloud to whoever stopped by, just as he was doing now. The man continued to eat, still only half listening when the first man resumed. There was a job to finish but a delay was also necessary not just for food but for safety.

"Oak Ridge," the grizzled man went on in a voice that frequently broke like snapping bark, and his crooked smile showed mostly gums. "I can say it in three languages, Spanish, Chinese, and Chumash. I learned all of them from living and working here. You happen to notice, friend, that on my out-front sign, the chains are rusted? I used to have a hand who worked for me, Pedro, who put a shine on them every day. *Every* day. You could see each link bounce the sun a good half mile off, like the chains that bound— Who was that old fella? The one brought fire to men and was tied to rock?"

"Prometheus!" said the man's wife, who was doing laundry outside, just within earshot because the shade happened to be nearest the house just now.

"That's the one. Thank you, Lizzie!" he shouted. "Well, got no cause to buff them now or replace them. Just let the windblown dirt have them. Down with the old iron, up with the new. Is that why we all fought a war, to pitch everything that was?" He nodded thoughtfully. "I bet Mr. Lincoln would've done things different. Old Andrew Johnson—the bankers controlled that Southern boy."

The man turned back and walked over, shaking his head like a starving elk that had just found a watering hole filled with mud.

"Friend, the name of this place once meant comfort and adventure to all who heard it. One of the drivers, now departed Nehemiah Smith—he used to tell folks they was in the *best* hands in the West when he would escort them here if the Injuns were warring, and then leave to hurry back to his wife and child. And he meant it. Now? Now it's just me and my wife and our dog. And old Windy ain't much of a hound at that."

The man at the table had not even realized there was a dog until Zebulon broke a corner of bread from the loaf on the table and underhand-threw it at him. The golden dog belly-walked near, then stretched his neck and jaw as if the whole thing was nearly too much effort. After chewing down the treat, the dog apparently had the energy to go outside. Or else he, too, was tired of his master's voice.

Zebulon stood beside his guest, who sat on the side of the table facing outside. The narration ended, the proprietor would now and then look out at the backyard, wince into the bright light, and watch his wife work over the oak bucket and washboard. Not once, however, from the time his guest had arrived through the serving of food and drink—for which his wife had briefly stopped her labors out back—had he stopped reciting the history of this station, his own essential function as a stableman for every teamster who drove a coach, and his dissatisfaction with the state of things.

Like so many old wounds, his bitterness kept the cause current.

As if silence signaled defeat, the man went on.

"The *rail road*," he said, pronouncing it as two accursed words. "I seen it up close. With my own eyes, I watched it cough all over Apple Town on its way to Truckee. It was late by ten hours getting in, like a steer that had no fight left reaching the stocks in Abilene. I rode like the Express riders used to, and by God, I beat the dang thing to Truckee! And when it finally came coughing in, it was all ugly hot iron and choking engine smoke and mobs of riders who had been crushed by noise and unwanted fellowship. Too many for the train crew to give personal care, you know? Not like it was here. And that station?" he said, throwing up a hand. "Nothing more than a sooty room with birds and flies inside, plus chairs and a stove that didn't work. I told my wife, 'Elizabeth, you would not last a minute working there without grabbing that new turkey-feather duster you bought by post.' It was not clean like here. Well, we don't scrub every day like we used to, but this is still better. People used to appreciate that after a short hop on the stage lasting no more than the daylight hours, as you can see, as you can attest, sir, we provided whatever a traveler requires."

Without passengers and fresh linen on the table and goods to vend, the man's voice was a hollow echo of a structure. And Zebulon Moore, dressed in buckskins that had seen better times, was like the caretaker of a forgotten tomb, a tributarian without an audience of mourners—save himself.

Fortunately, William Beaudine required nothing more—unless it was silence, which it would have been ironic to ask for. And pointless. He knew men, knew them well, and nothing but a bullet, probably two, would silence this man.

It really did not matter. In his years as a detective, he had grown accustomed to shutting out nearby sounds, even in a busy saloon, to hear who might be riding into town and when. You learned a lot from the speed made by hooves on hard-packed dirt streets or wooden sidewalks.

But Beaudine also was not in a mind or mood to "attest" to anything, if a compliment was what Zebulon Moore sought. Upon arriving, he had shot the lock off the box he had stolen and examined the contents, and now he was considering them carefully. There had been three items, not the one he had been expecting. Three things that made a bad situation uglier.

The diner's dark eyes were turned down with long black hair falling over them. His strong jaw chewing, he ate the stew of beans and chicken quickly, not because he was tired of hearing the owner of the way station but because he had to be on his way. He had made the decision to travel a little out of his way north to refresh himself. Lives—nations—were at risk.

Contemplating what he had done was pointless. He had bought himself time, perhaps only a little, off Quinn's stubbornness. It was a decision forced on him, and done. What remained to do was the reason Beaudine ate in silence, letting the other man prattle on. He also ignored the sound of the utensils scraping or stabbing the metal bowl, the chewing in his own ears, and most especially any sounds from outside. At least Zebulon Moore was utterly lacking in curiosity. He did not ask anything about his guest.

Even if Beaudine had been interested, he also did not have time to waste on talk or something he needed more—rest. The horses needed it, too, and the only reason he was here was to let them feed, drink water, get some shade, and—one of them, at least—be free of someone bending his back.

Beaudine also wanted to make a delivery, and he would get to that soon enough.

Fortunately, the man was used to hardship, not just as a career but as a way of life. He was accustomed to enduring it but also managing it. Where in the Snowy

Saw Range—the Sierra Nevadas—the temperature was cooler and the sun met its match when it climbed the towering, impenetrable peaks, breaks like these were necessary, he had learned long ago. Push yourself, and eventually, you lost more time than a rest stop would have saved. He loved it up there, and he had left because he had been summoned.

A telegram sent to him, general delivery, at the new and struggling town of Jefferson Cue in the foothills. Take the train to San Francisco. Meet Mr. JP—never a full name. Not where other eyes could see the message or the man himself.

The work was challenging, as always, though this particular job had not given Beaudine the time to prepare as carefully as he would have liked. The aggressive Pinkerton detective, whose motto was "Stop or Die," knew that haste increased the chance of failure, though in this case he understood the need for it. Back in Washington, Congress was busy taking the first steps to putting together something that by all rights should have been turned on that body itself: an apprehension unit for the new Department of Justice. There was loud talk that the twenty-year-old group founded by Allan Pinkerton would land that contract.

"But only if," the fifty-year-old Pinkerton had told him in their meeting in San Francisco, "only *if* we can convince President Grant that we are not just capable, not just exemplars, but superior to anyone else they might possibly or creatively consider."

After all, President Grant was a former military man. He would be inclined to trust them; a military detachment perhaps with men culled from regional police forces was among the other ideas. Such men were trained to serve and would not drag departmental corruption with them.

But the president feared that such men would be subject to the same bias as he himself was: They would be more sympathetic to anyone who had fought in the war—certainly for the North, maybe for the South. The integrity of the enterprise would always be in doubt.

In that respect, and in terms of devotion to duty and reputation, Pinkerton was the only choice, which also meant that Beaudine could not afford to foul this up. He had to succeed, at any cost.

*At* any *cost,* he thought, feeling the kind of regret he could ill afford.

Pinkerton had emphasized those last three words in a way that left no mistaking the risks and leeway. Even if Beaudine or anyone else died in the attempt, he must not fail. Any possible injury, even to innocents, had to be considered dispassionately and within the larger framework. The men they were dealing with had to be stopped, and they were ruthless.

*You got that information from Aggie and me, Mr. Pinkerton,* Beaudine thought as he pushed his plate across the table and rose.

Zebulon had resumed talking about the Butterfield Overland Stage, littering his reminiscences with praise for the vision of John Butterfield. Beaudine had no opinion of the man other than, like Pinkerton, he was a visionary who had commanded and deserved respect.

Beaudine picked up his dirty white hat from the table and left a quarter-dollar coin in its place. The proprietor's watery brown eyes went wide.

It was worth the extra cost to shut the man up, if only briefly.

"Thank you, sir!" the owner said, smoothing his mustache with his left hand while reaching for the coin with his right. He inspected the braid-haired lady on the front as if mistrusting her authenticity.

The payment was more than double the actual price. Beaudine had long ago learned that money bought discretion, a commodity whose value far exceeded its price.

Beaudine finished his glass of warm but wet pale ale and turned to the door. The nattering of the owner of the station resumed as the man followed him out. Beaudine saw the proprietor's wide, strong-shouldered wife still washing laundry out back and waved. She was cleaning the cloth that he had seen on top of the vegetable garden when he arrived; it had been covered with bird droppings. Crows sat unmolested on the remains of crosses atop three graves well behind her. They scattered when the woman raised one sudsy hand and flicked soap at them; it was a dance they had apparently shared before when the birds trespassed. Casting a look back at the still retreating birds, the woman went back to her work. The big mutt of a dog lay flopped between her feet and the big basin, seemingly glad for every cooling splash that landed on him.

There was something world-weary but clear-eyed about the woman. And she was handsome in both her face and energy. In his forty-three years, Beaudine had known many saloon girls, a number of Mexican and Indian ladies, and a few bored Washington socialites who wondered about frontiersmen. But he had never known a frontier woman, and he wondered about them, too. Was she the aggressor when the door was closed? Did a woman like this attack everything like it was a vegetable-patch cover?

The proprietor continued to chatter. The Pinkerton man did not really hear what his companion was saying just now about the patio and a fiddle player. Beaudine was searching the southern horizon as he made his way to the hitching rail. It was clear. Not so the air out here. The yellow grass underfoot smelled foul—like death. Death of a place, death of an enterprise. He had to get away from here. Beaudine had stopped not just for food and respite, not just to clear the dust from his face and hands and to eat, but also to see—from a defensible shelter, should that be necessary—if there was anyone in pursuit. That applied not just to the men whose camp had been invaded, and the troops who Beaudine believed were riding hard to join up with them. It also applied to the man the detective had left behind, Jason Quinn.

Beaudine walked slowly to his horse, thinking about his old friend and colleague. Now, there was a man to set against a foeman. That was the reason Beaudine had hired him in the first place. Brave, with courage and knife skills, and also somewhat mad, Quinn could never have been a Pinkerton. He had no use for a standard code of conduct. But that was another reason any corporation, government, or individual hired the agency. It was something that had to be on the mind of President Grant. Pinkerton *knew* firebrands like Quinn and employed them as needed.

The road in the direction he'd come looked clear. There were no clouds in the sky, which meant no local rain to muddy the ground and keep dust from rising.

The clearness meant that if anyone was headed this way, they were at least two hours off. That was how far the dust showed against a generally flat plain under a clear sky.

Beaudine stood beside the trough and looked at the stuffed leather satchel he had lashed to the second horse. The horse was a striking animal, dark brown with a blond mane. It was as majestic as the bundle was fat and ungainly, and everything he had taken from Quinn was in the leather-bound heap, including the sheath. That was in Beaudine's saddlebag. Quinn loved that nearly as much as he did the horse, a gift from the widow of Jim Bowie himself. He would want that back more than he would want to take any kind of vengeance.

Beaudine turned to where the proprietor stood complaining now about the dry heat that reached all the way to the west from the desert. Beaudine pulled a dollar coin from his pocket. He held it so the sun shined in the eyes of the chattering man.

Zebulon raised a hand. "Say, watch that there—"

"Be quiet and listen," Beaudine said. "This silver dollar is yours, and here's what you're going to do for it. You paying attention?"

The coin and the hand both came down. Zebulon was a changed, attentive man. "I'm listening."

"Okay. Put this horse in your stable. Feed him, care for him, and keep him there. This satchel? Put it with the horse, out of sight, and leave them until one of two men comes for him. The first one would be me. If I don't come back in a week, and the other man hasn't come, the horse is yours—and burn the satchel."

"Burn it?"

"The second is a man by the name of Quinn. But you only tell Quinn about the horse if he shows up alone. Do you understand all of that?"

Zebulon held out his bony hand and flashed his gums. "My friend, I do!"

"Fine. Repeat what I said."

The man cast his eyes up, remembering. "Coulda used one of those pints," Zebulon said, clearing his throat.

"Come on, you're used to talking," Beaudine replied, looking back at the southern horizon.

"All right now: You said that no one gets near the horse or satchel but you or Mr. Quinn, and Mr. Quinn only if he isn't in the company of someone else."

"That's right. Now, don't forget any of that. Also, tell no one other than Quinn I was here."

"Is that for the same price?"

"You do everything as I instructed, and I'll give you another dollar when I pass back this way."

"And if you don't come? You said— Well, you said you might or mightn't."

"I will get it to you somehow. My word."

Zebulon grinned. "You seem trustworthy. You have a deal. Might I ask where you're going? In case this Mr. Quinn wants to know."

"He knows."

"What if he forgot? And come to think of it, why do you have his horse instead of him?"

Beaudine was already impatient, and now he was growing irritated. "Our business is done, Mr. Moore."

"If you say so, Mr. Beaudine. Sorry. I'm just naturally curious."

"Oh, and one more thing. Don't be shocked by Mr. Quinn's appearance. He's had a rough day."

Zebulon snorted dismissively. "I've seen lots of folks with plenty of rough days under their belts. He won't surprise me."

"He may not have a belt," Beaudine said as he passed the dollar to Zebulon.

"I won't ask no questions. Oh, except what do you want me to do with the box you left?"

"Bury it."

"It's a perfectly good—"

"Worth dying for?"

"Huh?"

"Use it, someone finds it, they may think you took what was inside. They will want it back."

"But I don't have it."

"Exactly. Keep it hidden, except for the man I told you about."

Beaudine untied the reins and jumped into the saddle, refreshed and eager to get away from here. He looked back at the proprietor before he rode off.

"That better be more than a lick and a promise."

"Mister, at the risk of sounding something other than modest, St. Peter's got nothing on me. I'm a gatekeeper who also keeps my word." He jerked his head toward the north. "Where you're going, where the train is, where lost souls gather—that's hell. Even got the fire in the maw of the big locomotive to prove it. The day that men like me don't honor my word is the day it all falls apart."

Beaudine looked south, and content, he looked down after settling himself for the long ride ahead. "I believe you, Zebulon. Thank the missus for me."

"Sure thing. I've greatly enjoyed the jawing."

Beaudine gave him a look as he reined the horse toward the southeast.

"Hey—you know you're doubling back, heading inland, yeah?" Zebulon shouted after him.

"Thank you."

"Most people here, they're San Francisco bound!"

"To hell, you mean?" Beaudine said over his shoulder as he rode off, mercifully out of earshot.

"Yeah," Zebulon said under his breath. "And who ever thought it would smell like oranges."

As Beaudine headed into the plains, part of him—a large part—wished he were going the other way. He would rather get into this business now. But the contents of the box had given him an idea that required assistance. And there was only one place he could get it.

That being the case, things would get mighty sticky if and when Quinn caught up. But the mission came first, and that was all Beaudine could think about as he hurried toward Apple Town.

# CHAPTER SEVEN

*D*ON'T FORGET YOU'RE *still injured!"*
Jane Smith's kindly, gentle words returned like
a forgotten faith as Hank's skull exploded with fire. No
sooner had the man leaned into the bobbing head of
his galloping horse than the world around him swam
red and his grip on the reins lessened. He dropped them
and instinctively wrapped his shaking arms around the
animal's powerful neck to keep from falling. He succeeded but just barely.

The swirling ruddy black opened briefly to reveal a
woman. A handsome woman wearing a red floral-
pattern day dress with detachable white cuffs and a frill
collar. She was in a sunny room with a wooden desk and
writing implements, an unlit lantern upon the desk. Her
black hair was parted in the middle and pulled into
braids.

She had a reason for doing that, he knew. It kept

them out of the way when she rode, prevented damage from the wind and grit.

Framed by the hair was a big open face and a look of concern.

"You're sure about this?" she was asking, her voice a hollow echo in his brain.

"Yeah. Yeah, I've gone over it every which way I can think of. It's not a great way out, but it's the best way."

"I'm worried about you," the woman had told him. "I've *met* these people. They are venomous."

"Bill told me all about them—"

"Did he?"

"Yes, but if he's going, I'm going." He looked into the woman's concerned eyes. "He won't do anything. In case I don't come back, I wanted you to know I believe that."

"Thank you. You're both leaving now?"

"Soon as I pack my grip. He'll be waiting with the horses."

She smiled at him, crinkling the skin around her green eyes. He remembered her having looked away quickly.

*Why did she do that? I didn't.*

He remembered hesitating there, then abruptly leaving, but he did not know from where. He went outside, was on a town street, the sands golden beneath his feet, the smell of horse piss and patties pungent and familiar. There were people walking about, but they were washed out in the sunlight. He could not read any of the signs behind those folks, but there were a handful of vaguely familiar storefronts.

Did he live here?

*"Quinn!"*

He could feel himself stopping but not turning as Aggie walked toward him, making her way toward a couple of horses hitched in front of the place he had just departed. He felt a deep, deep sorrow in his heart—he felt it now still.

"However this works out, I'm sorry for the rest," she had told him.

"Yeah."

"No, truly."

Till that point, he had pointedly showed her his back. He had turned then. There were no tears in the woman's eyes. He had not been surprised.

"You were playing by rules we didn't make," Quinn had said.

"I know. And I'm sorry about how it ended."

"Just tell me," he had said. "Was it all a script? Everything?"

"I think you know better," she had said, looking away.

Hank remembered the words and her look. The young woman's smile was weak but earnest. He remembered trying to smile back but failing. He did not know if he hated or loved the woman just then. They both seemed tired. She had started to reach for his hands, but he had withdrawn.

"That was only in case I don't see you again—," she began.

"I hold nothing against you," he said. "Not against the folks who will try to kill me, not Bill, not you. I swear it, Aggie. This is the life I chose."

"Why don't you go see Father Garcia?"

"For another homily?"

Suddenly, she vanished from his mind—along with the street and the buildings, the horses and the people, the empty feeling and the memory. Hank was once again holding on to the neck of the horse as it ran across the plain as though it, too, was acting by its own natural rules.

With the colors fading behind his closed eyes and the pain in his head once again growing manageable, Hank felt for the reins, found them, and gradually slowed the animal. It stopped and stood, wagging its head from side to side as Hank tried to raise his own to an upright position. It came slowly, painfully, but it did come. Somewhere during the run his hat had flown away. He turned his head slowly, spotted it about fifty yards behind him, gleaming in the sun, and rode back to fetch it.

*What was that?* he asked himself. *Where? Who is she?*

Aggie and Quinn. He *knew* those names, one of them apparently his own.

"Quinn . . . ," he said. "Quinn." He was trying to figure out what came before it. Or after? Was that his Christian name?

Hank dimly recollected the woman—but he did not know why or who she might be. He could almost hear her voice, low and purposeful. He seemed to recall she was never in a hurry. As for the location, that was a total blank.

Reaching his hat—Nehemiah's hat, he reminded himself—Hank stared down at it.

Another man's hat. Given to him by another man's woman. Why did that suddenly make him uncomfortable?

The hat had landed near a scorpion. "You again," Hank said. He remembered something then. "'I will beat you with scorpions.'" It was from the Bible. Maybe he had gone to see Father Garcia before departing wherever it was he left.

Hank—or was his name Quinn?—looked around at the desolation and combined it with his own isolation. Christ, how the hell had he gotten here? Alone in the middle of a plain, hazy visions, a lazy brain, a skull that pawed like a cougar and seemed always ready to pounce. Was God or fate or stupid luck responsible for this mischief?

*I'm Quinn,* he decided, and dismounted slowly, bent carefully, and retrieved the hat. He swatted it against his hip, then fanned away the dust that spun in the air. As he stood there, Quinn saw riders to the west. He put the hat on to shade his eyes. He saw three horses, moving north.

They were the men he had left behind. He had obviously gone more east than north in his flight. The trio was just spots on the plain, like ants crossing a pie on a windowsill. He pictured the map, saw that he and they were probably intending to converge on the same spot, the way station at Oak Ridge.

"If I can see them, then they can see me," he reminded himself.

But he suspected that, chastened earlier, they would likely not charge across the plain. And as he watched, the three horses made no move to change course. Quinn did not, however, presume that he was free of them. They had Lieutenant Martins with them, and he needed mending. That was likely the big reason for their steady, direct ride.

*And why should they chase me if they figure I might be going to the same place?* he thought. After all, that was the direction Martins had been headed. And these men likely did not know—or, if they knew, they did not believe—that Quinn had lost his memory. "What do you want to do?" the man asked himself. He could withdraw and forget this entire affair; he could shadow them, moving north at a safe distance; or he could wait until nightfall and then race north, to the way station, however precipitous that maneuver would be in the dark. He was not fully clear about whether he should try to finish something his "other" self had begun. Other than the possibility of learning who he was—and perhaps not liking that fellow much—he did not see the sense of continuing.

"Because you're not Hank any longer. You're Quinn," he reminded himself. "Already, something's changed." He had to find out the rest. Maybe he could still make new choices then.

He wondered if he had ever liked *having* choices or whether he preferred fate or someone like Beaudine to do the deciding.

Gently replacing the hat on his head, Quinn mounted and rode north, as he had been doing. It occurred to him that if he could get to the way station first, he might be able to learn something about William Beaudine or himself before the other men arrived.

With a little less exuberance than previously, Hank kicked the horse to a trot and spent the next few minutes timing his rise and fall in the saddle to the punch and calm in his head.

IT MADE JANE angry, as she had time to think, that she had gone along with the bullying Frenchman.

There had been the practical reasons, all of them concerns for the safety of her and her boy. But now resentment had set in. These men from another continent had come to the shores of Mexico, crossed the border into the United States of America, then presumed to dictate instructions to her. Nehemiah would probably have resisted them for that attack on the sovereignty of a man, his home, and his nation.

*And he probably would have died for it,* she thought. *Willingly, but no less buried.*

At least Douglas seemed to be enjoying his adventure. He was mounted to her right, his owl eyes missing nothing. After some initial mistrust of the men around him, he tested his mettle by sitting tall, slightly away from the man behind him, as though he were alone on the horse.

Jane had access to the canteen, but she used it sparingly. The scarf protected her from the direct rays of the sun, but it was still hot, and the horse radiated even more heat. So did the ground where nothing green grew, which was often. As one hour became two, Jane also found herself drowsing. Slipping into a physical and emotional limbo, she was instantly awake when the line of soldiers suddenly halted.

Jane and her boy were at the end of the line, too far back to see why the captain had stopped the unit or to hear what he was saying to the man at his right. The second-in-command handed Dupré a pair of binoculars. The leader studied the horizon.

Douglas was trying to see around the near dozen men in front of them. "What's happening, you think? A rider?"

"I don't know," she said. Though he was mostly in shadow from the rider in front, Douglas was clearly sweating, his clothes soaked; Jane noticed that the boy's canteen was dusted with sand. It had not been used. "You should drink, son."

"I will when you do," he answered. "I think that's what Pa would have done."

Jane was not surprised to hear that. She smiled inside and did not instruct him otherwise.

Neither of the men with them spoke, not even to each other. She wondered if the other riders even understood English. In Mexico, that would not have been a requirement.

Because they were standing still, blockaded from the breeze, the heat quickly became oppressive. She felt faint, took more water. The man behind her said something harsh in French. She finished her short swallow and returned the canteen to the pommel. Suddenly, two men—those directly behind the captain and his second—peeled off from the line and rode forward.

"I wonder if it's Hank," Douglas said.

"Hush."

The boy pressed his lips together tightly. Back at their home, even though he was telling the truth as his mother had always instructed, he might have said more than he should have. The woman's caution back there made him determined not to do that again.

The two Smiths looked ahead, waiting. Jane found herself torn. She did not know whether she wanted the captain to find Hank or not. It might mean her release and his finding out who he was. But those good reasons did not lift the sense of omen that pressed on her chest.

And there was something else, too, something that surprised her. A yearning deep in her belly, a strong part of her that wanted it to be Hank . . . just to see him again.

Motionless, the entire band of soldiers, their guests, and their horses was becoming restlessly hot. Eyes were constantly turning back toward her, with occasional low chatter among the men. Jane moved forward from the man behind her, whose shirt and face had begun dripping. He put an arm around her waist and drew her back. He left it there. It had nothing to do with her safety. Jane turned to get the canteen hanging from the saddle, using the action to wrest free. She drank, and her son followed suit, thirstily, looking sideways so he could stop when she did. Canteens were also active and clanging up and down the line. Aware of the situation—and perhaps having an idea that the new arrival was not an immediate threat— the captain ordered the men forward.

It was then that Jane saw who was approaching and realized who it was. It was not, alas, Hank. The new arrival was Alan Russell with his wagon full of Apple Town goods bound for the Smith home.

# CHAPTER EIGHT

WHEN HE HAD been the law in Apple Town after the War, Sheriff Alan Russell could not wait for the town to grow. And it was not only because he was growing—belly out with inactivity. There was talk, never more than rumors, that a train was coming through. He was a mustered-out cavalry sharpshooter, age fifty-and-some, when he took the job, mostly to keep the cattlemen and the sheepmen from killing one another over water, grazing, and general hotheaded bad humor. He liked the word Mrs. Lewein of the Triple L cattle ranch north of town had used to describe all the men: "They each got too much *wax*," she said. Like the moon growing too full each month.

No one blamed the men, not entirely. The territory contributed to that state of being. It was so empty of comfort, entirely overbaked with hardship, that even pastors had trouble staying for very long without becoming hostile. Father Garcia had stayed mostly because he had seen the Mother of Jesus seated and all aglow, he said, on the back of a horse ridden by the outlaw Joaquin Murrieta when Garcia was nine years old. That kind of belief died hard.

Mrs. Lewein preferred more substantial "religion" and took to carrying a rolling pin the way her rancher folk carried firearms. She used it more often and to greater effect, too.

The only time the men rallied shoulder to shoulder was when the Chemehuevi or Modoc got pushy. It usually started with attacks on miners or prospectors and spilled over to the spreads. Once the threat was neutralized, the citizens went back to spoiling things for one another.

Usually, all Russell had to do was show up to calm things down. Even without his gut, he stood an imposing six feet five. The men were often unreasonable, but they weren't stupid. More often than not, Mrs. Lewein was his ally in making temporary peace, even against her own kin and hired hands.

Then the railroad finally did come. And with the growth came masses of Easterners who were looking for *something* and sometimes got swindled of everything they had by fake cowboys and real gamblers. There was also an influx of guns, men looking to make a reputation. Russell had killed two of them, both in their twenties, within the space of a month.

Realizing that the challenges would not stop, and that most deputies were unreliable, he changed his line of work. Because Russell was near sixty, being a messenger and deliveryman instead of a peace officer let him make his own hours and also enjoy the open plains while they lasted. He saw a time when the restless and bottomless-greedy railroad men from the East would crisscross the land with tracks. And towns. And people. He did not think that becoming a mountain man was in his future, though he had considered the possibility that building a house out in Jane Smith's corner of the desert held appeal—for a variety of reasons, one of which was the widow herself.

Hidden beneath a floppy straw hat that repudiated the harsh sun, and bolstered by his own natural endurance to heat—born of a youth spent in humid Louisiana before his family came west seeking gold, which, like so many others, they failed to find—Alan Russell had been thinking fondly of the woman when he spotted what looked like a column of migrants . . . except they were riding too orderly for that, and more than likely should not have been riding at all. Then he saw a pair of riders peel away and gallop toward him.

Russell had a pair of single-action Smith & Wesson .44s on the buckboard beside him, with an extra six shells tucked into pockets on the outside of each holster. He was not wearing his gun belt because, with him being seated, it rubbed his belly red. The sheriff's four-year-old Winchester rifle—which had fired more attention-getting bullets into the air than into people—rested in a scabbard hitched to the side of the buckboard.

Upon seeing the riders, he had removed the rifle and put it under his right arm. He did not stop. There was no reason to assume hostile intent. That kind of thinking had a way of triggering unintended action.

He was good, and fast, but there were two of them and more behind.

As the men neared, Russell could see that they were indeed dressed like Mexicans, but they did not wear their garments like clothes. They were costumes, sweaty but not creased or worn through. The men sat stiff like they were tucked into uniforms that only they could see and feel. He relaxed a little when he saw that they did not carry sidearms, just carbines tucked in leather. *New* leather. These disguises were not just poor; they were of very recent vintage.

The men had ridden up side by side. They separated when they reached the wagon, one going to each side. Russell was on his guard when he stopped his two-horse team. The bundles and two crates in back rattled a little. They were unsecured; there had never been a reason for Russell to race or tie them down. The men beside the wagon looked to be about thirty and were clean-shaven.

"Our captain sends greetings," one man said in a heavy French accent. "He seeks a word."

"I'm always open to talk," Russell said. "About what?"

The man shook his head. Either he did not know or he did not know any more English than what he had just said.

"Captain," Russell chewed on the word. "Of what army?"

"Police," the man replied.

"I know all the police hereabout. Can you be more specific?"

"Sir, please, will you come?"

"Well, I'm going in that direction anyway. I'll follow you in."

Either the men did not understand that last exchange either, or else—more likely—they had contrary orders. They did not lead the way but remained on either side of the wagon while Russell continued on his way. As he guided the horses forward, Russell pulled the holsters a little closer to his left hip.

The man on the left seemed to have noticed. He slowed a little so he was just behind Russell. Reluctantly, the sheriff relaxed his readiness. He had no reason to suspect bad intentions other than that was his natural way.

The unit was in motion forward by the time he arrived. There was little dust to stir, and he looked from front to back to make certain no one was openly armed.

That was when he saw Jane Smith.

"Whoa!" Russell said, now highly alert.

The wagon crunched to a stop some ten feet from the two men at the head of the column. The riders beside Russell stopped. The captain raised an arm to halt the others. Russell leaned over the side of the buckboard to peer around them.

"Mrs. Smith, what are you doing out here?" he asked, loud enough to reach where she was seated.

"She was invited," one of the men in front answered.

"I wasn't asking you," Russell replied. He craned even more to the side. "You got Douglas with you?"

"Yes," she answered.

Russell straightened, his eyes shifting back to the man who had spoken. "What is this?"

"Sir, I am Captain Raoul Dupré. You are?"

"Alan Russell, former colonel in the United States cavalry and retired Apple Town sheriff. Answer the question."

The captain's eyes lingered a moment on the weapons that were convenient to the man sitting before him. "We are searching for a renegade, a thief who stole something before making the acquaintance of Mrs. Smith. We seek what he took, nothing more."

"Why are Mrs. Smith and her son *with* you?"

"It was my hope, Sheriff Russell, that they could persuade him to cooperate, to avoid violence," the captain answered pleasantly.

Russell leaned out again. "Mrs. Smith—did you come willingly on this hunt?"

She nodded stiffly. Russell did not believe her. The man behind her had his arms close to her waist, holding her. He looked back at the captain.

"Who are you to be pursuing an outlaw? By what authority?" Russell asked.

"You are a former sheriff," the captain said. "By what authority do you ask?"

The Frenchman's gaze continually shifted from the man to the buckboard. A good officer, he was obviously evaluating, moment to moment, the threat represented by a potential enemy.

"From your answers, or rather the avoidance of them, what you're telling me is that these two are hostages," Russell said angrily.

"It's all right, Alan," Jane said quickly.

"There, you hear?" the captain said.

Once again, Russell's instincts were active. There had been an uncommon touch of insistence in Jane Smith's voice. It told Russell that just the opposite was true. She wanted *him* to cooperate—and move on. But that would take some convincing.

"What did you stop me for?" Russell asked the captain.

"We believe that the man we seek came this way. Did you see any riders?"

"Not a one since I left Apple Town. This isn't a thickly populated area. Not yet. But I know these trails. Where are you headed?"

"Just northwest," the man answered.

"The old Butterfield Trail is the place to look, not the plains. There's a road, after a kind. And a way station at the end of it."

"Thank you," the captain said. 'We have maps."

"This target of yours—is he American?"

"We do not know, sir," Dupré said with a sudden show of impatience. "We only know what he stole from our party."

"I am not without connections in law enforcement throughout these parts," Russell said. "If you give me more information—"

"Thank you, no. Good day, sir."

Russell looked out at Jane. The proximity of the man behind her crossed the bounds of decency. If it bothered her, she made no indication. After that brief exchange, she had assumed a reserve that was also unfamiliar to the outgoing woman.

The captain ordered his two men back into the formation. The pair left the side of the wagon, which made Russell feel suddenly less safe, like a bear on a cliff: big and exposed. Because of his specialty in the military, Russell had never been in the heart of battle. He had always been in a tree or on a ridge, picking off enemy observers or commanders. As sheriff, he had rarely felt any personal jeopardy. The worst that happened whenever he failed was someone else got shot and Russell would have to bring in the perpetrator.

This was different. His fingers tingled and his heart began to race. He was alert for any sign from the captain that an order other than "March" was forthcoming. Beyond his own safety, there was the matter of Mrs. Smith and her son. He did not desire to take a stand against a dozen guns, especially when gunfire was fickle enough to strike the innocent.

"Might I ride with Mrs. Smith for a bit?" Russell asked. "She and the boy might be more comfortable in the wagon."

"We are going north. You are going south, are you not?"

"In fact, I was going south to bring Mrs. Smith supplies she requested." He jerked a thumb behind him. "That's what I have here. That's *all* I have. If she's not going to be home, there's no reason for me to finish the journey."

"Perhaps it would be best if you deliver the goods while we continue on our mission," the captain said with finality as he motioned the line ahead.

Russell's eyes moved to Mrs. Smith. As the woman neared, he could see the urgency in her taut expression. She did not want a showdown any more than he did.

*But she does not, by God, seem like a woman who wants to be doing what she is doing,* he told himself.

The former lawman waited a moment longer, then made a *chucking* sound in his cheek and guided his team around the company. As he passed them, he looked past Jane and saw Douglas Smith sitting on the other side of his mother. The boy did not look fearful; but then, he was a trusting boy.

*They'll find their man and let the Smiths go,* Russell told himself. *Best not to excite the situation.*

Yet there was something else. He was snakebit by the idea that foreign agents would cart away any American— even a so-called thief. What would they do to get back whatever he was supposed to have taken? Torture the man? Threaten the mother and child? Perhaps do more than threaten? Accepting that possibility meant that he had spent his life fighting for America and its citizens for nothing.

There was a point that Russell had never crossed in his honest career, when impulse and virtue take control of common sense. He had reached the line between them a few thoughts back; now he was across it. If he were to allow these men to carry a family away in pursuit of a man who would likely get no trial, then he was unworthy of calling himself a man, let alone a lawman.

Russell stopped the wagon. He slid one of the six-shooters from its holster and held it low, beside his right thigh. Then he turned, half rising, and faced the front of the line.

"Captain! I just remembered something!"

The officer lifted his arm, and the riders stopped smartly. Dupré swung his tired charger from the front of the line and faced the retired peace officer.

"What have you remembered, Colonel Russell?"

"I remembered that this is America and you have no lawful business here. And something else."

"I'm listening?"

"I don't believe this lady and her son want to be part of your expedition—"

"Don't!" Jane said, turning in the saddle. "Mr. Russell, it's all right!"

"Mrs. Smith, it is anything *but* right." Russell glared at the captain. "Tell you what, Captain. I'll make a deal with you. To avoid gunfire, you let me take the boy."

"Gunfire? You will die."

"Yeah, I can count. But some of your men will fall, too," Russell said. "Possibly you, sir."

The captain was silent for a long moment. He had no time for this, yet a part of him appreciated the fortitude of this man and relished the challenge of an unexpected command decision. Life in Mexico was rote and dull. This was not. He noticed that the handgun had been removed from the holster. He saw the steady demeanor of the American, the unwavering eye. Against that, he weighed this bold and intolerable challenge to his authority. Most of the men had no idea what these two were saying. But they would know what had happened if the boy suddenly peeled off.

The captain said something in French. Something that had meat, Russell thought, judging by its duration. Several men became stiffly alert as the man with the boy broke from the line and trotted over. He passed in front of Russell so that the former lawman could see his own six-shooter low at his side and pointed up at the boy's back. Neither Douglas nor Mrs. Smith was aware of the danger. The men, of course, would have heard the captain's command.

"Colonel Russell, we are not monsters, nor do we wish to be savages. I commend your courage, but we really must be on our way. You will leave your guns on the plain, beginning with the one at your side. Then you will continue on your journey. When we return the Smiths, we will return your firearms."

Though Jane could not see either of the drawn weapons, she had known from the start that weapons had to be in play. Russell's stand, just that, would not in itself have softened the hard heart of Pharaoh.

"Mr. Russell?" the woman said plaintively, more to herself than to him.

Now Russell was perspiring. He knew he had three courses of action. One was to submit. Another was to fire at the man holding Douglas. Russell knew he could get the shot off fast and clean, throw himself over the back of the buckboard, and bring the rifle into play against the captain. But unless it was trained army stock—and it might not be—the Frenchman's horse would buck at the shot. It was a lead-pipe cinch that Douglas would end up in the dirt—likely injured or worse. The column would probably be thrown into chaos with gunfire flying at them—and at the Smiths—from every direction.

The last option was to appear to cooperate and, when the column was out of sight, turn and follow them, as he had done to so many riders during the War, then wait for an opportunity to liberate the Smiths.

*Without guns, that'll be pretty difficult,* he told himself. *But it'll be more difficult if I'm dead. Awright, Colonel. You created this newest situation. What's your play?*

The Frenchman seemed to be trying to give them all a way out. Reluctantly, Russell took it.

"Okay, Captain. I yield."

"A sensible move." Dupré's voice was not a commendation but something thick and heartless.

Pinching the gun barrel between two fingers, Rus-

sell raised his sidearm slowly and, seeking out a clump
of grass, tossed the gun down. He followed that with
the other .44, still in its holster, and then the Winchester. Except when he bathed or when he slept, he
had never been this far from a firearm since his pa first
taught him to shoot. He felt no less a man, but he did
feel quite naked.

At the captain's command, the rider holding the
boy raised his gun. It was aligned with the boy's ribs.
The French soldier pointed it at Russell and fired. The
bullet caught the retired sheriff in the right shoulder,
spinning him nearly a full turn. The second shot was
immediate, higher, more precise, and it entered the
rear of the man's skull. Bone and brain were ejected
from the front, a red-and-white rainbow that the dead
man followed into the wagon. He landed limp, motionless save for the torrent of blood from his head. The
wound created several streams that dripped through
the floorboards of the wagon, splattering as they hit
the ground like an ugly rain.

Jane screamed. Douglas froze in openmouthed horror. At a command from the officer, the same two men
who had accompanied the wagon rode over to steady
the two cart horses, which were rearing and colliding.

"Collect the weapons and horses and leave the
wagon," Dupré ordered in French. "It will only slow us."

Jane went to dismount, and the man behind her
grabbed her hard around the waist. At a signal from
the officer, the man with the boy returned to the column. Douglas did not struggle with his own captor but
screamed at the man to take his hands off his mother.

"Mrs. Smith, you and your boy will stop! Now!"

"Captain—*Captain*! You cannot just *leave* him!"

"Madam, you will not speak again. Is that quite clear?"

"It is, but I don't care! You must bury—"

"I *must*?" The captain drew his own sidearm and fired into the air in a single fluid move. The horses barely shied. Unlike the cart horses, they had been inured to gunfire.

Dupré made no other sound, and the woman fell silent. Small moving shadows suddenly fell on the plain as buzzards began to move toward the human carrion. Putting her face in her hand, Jane wept until she heard the soft voice of her son beside her.

"Ma, it wasn't our fault. You tried to tell him. We didn't do nothing."

She raised her face and forced a smile and did not bother to correct his English. "No, son. We did nothing. And Mr. Russell—he did what a good man was supposed to do."

"I wish he hadn't," Douglas said.

"So do I."

Jane wept as the line moved on, her face in her hands as if they could expunge the horror of what had been committed. She did not see Douglas glancing back, filling his eyes with the carnage they had left behind.

Filling his young heart with the wish that they would find Hank and that Hank would put a Bowie knife into the captain's foul guts.

Suddenly, the captain stopped the line. He said something to the woman beside him. Nodding, she broke her horse from the column and rode back to where the Smiths were. She fell in beside Jane. This was Jane's first good look at her. She was a swarthy woman with dark hair that was pulled back by a bow from her strong cheekbones. There was something aristocratic about her, despite the peasant dress.

"I do not speak English much," the woman said. "I am Maria. The captain wishes you to ride here." She pointed at her own saddle.

"With you? Why?"

"The men . . . they are looking backward too much."

"Discipline is not my problem."

"He will not like that," Maria said.

"I don't care."

Douglas interrupted the conversation to request permission to dismount briefly.

Jane nodded and looked at Maria. "Tell our riders to stop. My boy needs a moment alone."

"You ride with me, he can do that."

Jane had not considered this to be a negotiation, but now it was. She weighed Douglas' needs against her desire not to cooperate with anything the captain wanted.

"All right," Jane said. "But we ride together, my boy and I. Either you come back here, or he comes up there."

"I will ask."

Maria told the two riders to break from the line and stop. While Douglas ran behind the line for a moment of privacy, Maria relayed Jane's request. When she returned, Douglas was already on his horse.

"I ride here," Maria said.

As Jane dismounted, Maria relayed the changed marching order to the two men. Jane's former companion trotted ahead while Maria caught up to the still moving column and took his place.

"He is not happy," Maria said.

"He does not deserve to be," Jane replied.

"A word. The captain has a job. You make it easy, you have it easy."

"The captain is a savage," Jane said. "I do not believe anything I do henceforth will please him."

"Then, *señora*, I do not think you will like very much what is ahead."

# CHAPTER NINE

THE PEARL WHITE stagecoach crossed the frontier with an urgency that challenged horse, driver, and passengers.

It was a conveyance that had been, literally, built for an emperor but had now become merely presidential. There were chips on the exterior and weather-beaten reds and regal shades inside. It was distinguished now only by the iron-reinforced luggage rack that helped to keep three large trunks from shifting.

The men riding in the rear boot were young and working in shifts. While one slept—uncomfortably, fit-fully but enough—the other watched the surrounding terrain. They were dressed in the costume of their trade: a white shirt buttoned nearly to the top, dusters, and sturdy trousers. They wore wide-brimmed crown hats, pulled low in front to prevent them from blowing off. Up front, the two men were dressed in similar attire. The man riding shotgun was napping now; when he awoke, he would switch places with the driver. He wore a white kerchief across the bottom of his face. He lowered it only to fit a fresh plug of chewing tobacco in his yellow teeth—an indulgence that would never have been permitted were the passenger a noble personage. The driver wore no such covering. He relied on his full beard and mustache, and keeping his mouth closed, to prevent grit and bugs from landing inside.

Both men had swarthy skin. But unlike other drivers and shotgun riders crossing the southwestern plains, these men were not bronzed by the sun. They were from Veracruz, with ancient Indian blood from farther south.

Inside the rocking, jolting carriage were three male passengers, one of whom had an exceptional calm that the other two lacked. All were dressed in military garb with braid and brass buttons. One had a less martial, more ceremonial flair; the other two wore functional, traditional naval uniforms. These two men sat stiffly, restless as fish in a bowl, now and then peering out from behind the drawn shade on either side. Occasionally they took a sip of water from a canteen, offering some to the third man, who sat across from them, facing forward. He declined with a wave of his large hand. Both men had Spencer repeating carbines on their laps and wore Colt six-shot revolvers on their hips.

Each time the man sitting alone saw the weapons, he could not help but think that here was a portrait of progress. Not very many years before, he and his men had carried slingshots.

But the two sitting shoulder to shoulder were used to cannon and sword—weapons that were impractical or useless on the plains. The anxiety they felt was actually higher than when they had risked everything for the cause. Then, had they lost, had the emperor and his foreign supporters won, the men had only faced hanging or a firing squad. Now they faced something worse: failure. Losing victory would be worse than being unable to achieve it.

Yet that was what they faced if they and their American informants had anticipated wrongly.

The three men had said very little since leaving the inn in Ensenada, El Territorio Norte de Baja California. There, they had enjoyed not just a full breakfast, but the vocal acclamation of the owner and her staff. That was some four hours earlier, just before sunrise, after they had ridden through the night. There was nothing to say now. The plan was set and the decision made. The frigate would sail now from San Diego as if they were on it. They would arrive in San Francisco by coach to meet, with full panoply and cannon salutes, the ship where they were going to meet Ulysses Grant. The only stops they would make now over the next two days were at rivers and lakes to water the horses and in San Pedro to eat and freshen up before the final leg to San Francisco.

Of the three routes presented, that was the decision of one of the two men, *Contraalmirante* Esteban Allende, who was in charge of this expedition. It was his marines who had been overexuberant, who had had American intelligence from a pair of agents and taken it upon themselves to try to arrest the would-be killers.

They had failed.

Now the risks were worse: The land route he chose was the hardest path but the least traveled. It avoided towns and most spreads, including the old Butterfield way stations. They felt they could fend off any attack, with seven armed men aboard. There were reports from an outpost in Zamora of a column of French soldiers dressed as peasants, but they were rumors. His own daughter said she knew the man who had started the rumors, a soldier who wanted to be a writer like Cervantes. The only real hazard Allende envisioned was at night, when they planned to stop for two or three hours to rest the horses. He hoped that the absolute quiet in the plains would alert them to anyone approaching.

In his forties, the *contraalmirante* was the older and more experienced of the pair. That also made him frustrated by the limitations he faced on land: impediments to his view and the din the wheels and the thoroughbrace made. There was noise on the ocean—the slap of the surging water against the hull, the creaking of the masts, the shouts of the sailors—but at least one could *see* if anyone were approaching. Out here—

But that had not been an option. Not after the plot had been unearthed by that American woman. The plan had been designed and financed by the French. Since the long-planned meeting could not be changed, the conveyance had to be used. *Capitán* Donato Ortega—the other officer, a veteran of countless artillery engagements—had arranged this stagecoach quickly, and without intermediaries, to minimize the chance of the change being discovered. Allende had sent his daughter, Maria, ahead to inform the captain of their plans; she was the swiftest rider he knew and the only one he could trust. They had personally interviewed and hired the two young cavalry lieutenants in the boot, men who had repeatedly distinguished themselves since the Battle of Camerón seven years before.

What remained was to reach San Francisco. It was a journey that would have gone much quicker had they taken the frigate *Jalapa* from the port of Ensenada, as planned. But the two American agents had uncovered a plot based on information provided by a third member of their team, a woman at the palace. A woman who even the presidential guards did not know had been there, one who also had contacts among French sympathizers—in particular, a man named Raoul Dupré, who was said to live among the peasantry stirring dissent. In itself, her ability to infiltrate the ranks of both sides was alarming and reassuring at the same time.

Now, at the suggestion of those two men, the party traveled by land. The senior man, Beaudine, had the trust of the American president, and more important, he had a plan for dealing with the would-be killers.

*"They are not in this alone,"* Beaudine had told a trusted Juárista at the port, a man who worked as a rider. *"There is an elite French unit in concealment, one that must be exposed and stopped."*

Allende was glad that President Grant was such a good friend of Mexico, or at least a strong enemy of European intervention on the continent. Either way, the officer was glad to have the Americans as allies rather than enemies, as they had been for too many years.

*It will all be well,* Allende assured himself. *God is with us, and perhaps as importantly, so are the Americans.*

Which is why the trip was so vitally important. The alliance forged by President Grant must be reinforced by images, mutually signed decrees, the exchange of let-

ters. The previous American president, Andrew Johnson, had not wanted the French army or any other
European army on the continent, but the American
Congress had not wanted to give the unpopular leader
anything he wished. As a result, and without any official
sanction for his actions, the president had ordered U.S.
general Philip Sheridan to leave rifles and ammunition
near the border, where they could be collected by the
freedom fighters.

The foreign intervention had ended officially, but in
fact it had simply gone underground, where fewer numbers could obtain their destructive designs by more
insidious means. Napoleon III still had designs on an
empire in North America. More than that, he still had
troops in Mexico—well concealed and well financed,
many secreted in Guatemala.

Gold stolen from these ancient shores, then returned
for favors—it was an insane world.

It was Napoleon's view that it was no longer efficient
or wise to attack the body of the state. He had to do
what had been done in France a century before: remove the head.

And that head belonged to the third man in the
stagecoach, President Benito Juárez.

There was a serenity about the sixty-four-year-old
politician and revolutionary that his companions envied.
Even during the height of their struggle, with death
around them or imminent, his vision was uncompro-
mised, his valor absolute. To date, his had been a full,
active, and difficult life that had included political office
and even exile for opposing the corrupt leader Santa
Anna—who had been chased to Cuba fifteen years before by Juárez and his comrade Ignacio Comonfort.

There followed battles with invaders and with the Catholic Church over their unseemly wealth. Neither he nor his closest advisers had known peace. Yet the man himself was at peace with everything he had done.

Juárez did not blame the other men for their agitation. If anything was to happen to him, his life of proud service to his liberal causes would be over, and the republic would continue. However, the loss of the great leader was a stain from which the two officers would never recover. That responsibility would not be over even after the meeting with President Grant, but at least this plot would be ended.

Along with French designs, the assurances from Washington were based on sound action and not the kind of brawny, improvised tactics for which Grant and his associates had been famous on the battlefield.

Juárez liked and respected Grant, as he had liked and respected Abraham Lincoln. Whether it was the American president or his clever secretary of state, Hamilton Fish, who had the vision, Washington also wanted to work out a plan to help forestall any future incursions from Europe. That included the nefarious efforts of Russia, which had made repeated efforts to trigger rebellion and secession in California. In the day after the presidential meeting on the Pacific Fleet steamer USS *Resaca*, Juárez intended to visit with railroad men and banking executives. Independence and cross-border alliances were good. Money was better. It amused the president to think that of all the things Europe had not effectively tried to gain influence over in his nation, it was support for the struggling national economy.

But all of that was for the future. At the moment,

the stocky man with a benevolent face was just enjoying the break from his duties. He had spent the night
reading documents by lantern light and was focused on
big plans for his nation, not personal security. It was
for others to worry about plots against his life. Like his
beloved wife, Margarita, who had done little more in
her adult life than worry about him and their twelve
children. At least she had the vitality to do so, being
younger than he by twenty years. Perhaps, though, it
was exactly such activity that had taxed her overly. She
had been planning to join her husband, to meet the
American president, but the lady was ailing.

He was sorry, for her sake, but the trip was a hard
one. She would have been so disappointed, making the
journey and being in no condition to board a rocking
vessel exposed to the raw sea air.

For his sake, though, this was a journey well worth it.
This was the kind of statesmanship Juárez had fought to
achieve and most enjoyed.

*All I need do is follow the path destiny has decreed,*
*whatever that may be,* he thought as the wheels clattered and threw up pebbles and the horses' hooves
clomped loudly.

And the assassins who had been thwarted by their
absence in Ensenada were forced to scramble to find
Juárez, or his destination, and stop him.

# CHAPTER TEN

T HE CHANGE FROM daylight to twilight was familiar to Quinn.

Pushing his horse to cover as much ground as possible while the sun was still out, the man knew he had experienced sunset before, of course, even though he could not picture where or when. All of the transitions of light and shadow were strangely reassuring along with the slight cooling of the air, the first hint of the full moon staking its claim on the horizon.

Yet that was where the comfort of dusk had ended. Every sound seemed strange—like he was a primitive man hearing something for the first time, and being especially alert because he was uncertain what was out there, only knowing that it probably wasn't good for him.

But those were all surface feelings, something that came naturally. What was deeper and had been troubling him since noontime was that Hank felt as though he did not even belong here, in this place, in this body.

His name had to be Quinn—why else would he have seen and heard it so clearly? He must know a woman named Aggie, for the same reason. And he had, without the full vignette, remembered the name Beaudine, a blond-maned horse.

Yet what if that was not part of his past but rather an elaborate delirium or dream, some kind of fancy brought on by the damage to his skull? The present was reliable because he could see and hear and smell it. The images in his head could be anything.

They certainly had not triggered a cascade of memories or images or a continuation of the little story that had played out. Hopefully, those would come. He did not want to exert himself the way he had earlier, since he did not know what might happen to him physically while his mind was wandering through the past.

"And anyway, you have more immediate concerns."

Such as which way to go. He had checked Martins' map as he rode. It would have been easier, by moonlight, to take the Butterfield route to the way station, but he had to assume Lieutenant Martins' accomplices possessed the same map he did. They would be looking for the most direct trip, and that was it. So he would stay the course, guided by the setting sun and the few landmarks on the map. Hank had already decided not to stop for the night, counting on the full moon to illuminate any gopher holes or gullies along the way.

Quinn's plan was rewarded when, well after dark, he saw moonlit curls of smoke rising from a shadowy chimney. As the rider neared, the moon-tinged outline of the overall structure came out in relief against the dark mountains behind it. The log building was long, low, and set behind a lattice fence that only ran along the front and was covered with dead vines that had probably once held flowers. There was a two-story barn out back that likely doubled as stables. He saw a pen with a coop for chickens—for eggs, he reasoned. What meat they served here no doubt came from game like deer and wild turkey.

*What made me think that?* Quinn wondered. Had he himself hunted in the wild?

As he approached, lantern light peeked through the unshaded windows. It did not appear that anyone was about in the yard. Except to use the necessary or to get well water, there was no reason to be out. He could not tell if there were footprints. The moon was not high enough for that. There were no horses hitched to the post that sat at the east side of the fence. He did not smell tobacco. He did not hear voices. There were no children moving about inside.

That told him what was not going on, not what was. He needed to be careful.

Quinn decided to go wide around the compound and check the barn. The back door of that outbuilding was shut, and he left his own mount there, tied to an oak at the front of a small cluster of trees. The open front door would be visible from the station, but he risked going around the far side to at least have a peek inside.

With his knife tucked into his belt, he crept in a careful, sure-footed manner that made him certain he had done this kind of activity before. The moon did not reach here, and he felt his way along the dark barn wall, which was covered with peeling paint. It turned

out there was no need to go to the front. There was a
window here—on the eastern side, probably for morning sunlight—and Quinn raised it without effort. He
climbed over the sill and saw six horses filling all six
stalls on the opposite side of the barn. The animals
were facing out, where feed buckets hung from metal
hooks on the northern wall of each. Moonlight spilling
high through the front door illuminated the first three
stalls.

*Damnation.*

Sticking to the Butterfield Trail, the men had gotten
here first. He recognized one of the animals as the
horse he had ridden when he was Martins' guest. The
other two belonged to the men who had found Martins.
Two more, he suspected, were owned by the way station. He did not think either of them belonged to William Beaudine; neither of them was equipped for travel.
Then there was the last animal. Quinn could not quite
make it out, and so he moved in closer.

He swore again. In the last stall was a dark brown
stallion with a blond mane. That meant it had all been
real, everything he saw in his mind.

The horse whinnied lightly when Quinn reached
over the low door of the wooden compartment.

"Hi, boy," he said soothingly. The horse responded
with a gentle shake of its head. "Seems like you know
me. I guess I know you, too, though I'll be damned if I
can tell you why."

The man stroked the animal's muzzle for nearly a
minute. There was nothing about the touch or smell
that triggered any memories. The mane, tumbling long
and wild over both sides, was all he really seemed to
remember.

"Listen, horse. I want you to remember me good because I may have to leave you. But if I do, I'll be back. I swear it."

The animal bucked its head playfully, and with another strong pat on its side, Quinn turned back into the barn. Bent low, he crept just beyond the thick cone of moonlight toward the open window, his boots crunching on the thick dirt and hay.

He was facing another decision. Inside the house were more answers from the men, not just who he was but what he was supposed to have stolen. But there was also danger. He had injured one of their own, and that would not earn him any charity.

He decided to leave but to stay near, wait till morning, follow the men—

"Snowcap!" he said suddenly, stopping and turning back. He walked back toward the animal. "That's your name, isn't it? Snowcap."

The horse whinnied, and Quinn leapt over the door to quiet him.

"Hush, boy! We don't want to attract attention."

Standing inside the stable, comforting the horse with the light of the moon inching higher, Quinn noticed something he had not seen earlier: a bulging leather satchel sitting in the back of the stall. He went directly to it, knelt on the hay, and ran his hand across the worn hide, the faded initials in dirty, frayed metal leaf: JQ.

"Quinn," he said, then said it more emphatically. "Quinn. Quinn—Jay . . . Jason. Jason Quinn. I'm *Jason* Quinn."

That felt right. It sounded right. And it fit the bag that he was certain belonged to him. There were two well-worn buckles holding the fat parcel together. Quinn worked them open with anxious fingers. He threw back the flap of the case, which was partly torn away from use. It was too dark here to see, so he felt inside. He slipped a hand in, but it was a jumble to the touch, so he began pulling items out, feeling them and trying to see them in the faintest spill of moonlight. After examining each one, he set it on the ground.

There was a compass, first. Below it, a book, an *Old Farmer's Almanac*, as long and thick as his hand. A pencil. A second Bowie knife and a deerskin sheath. He drew the blade; that, too, felt natural and right. Smiling, he attached that to his belt and put the other on the ground. There were some extra socks, underwear, leather gloves—and his clothes. They were still faintly damp, clammy, from being crammed inside.

"I was wearing those," he muttered as he drew them out, releasing musk as strong as the horse smell. It was not a memory but an observation. Whoever had hit him had put the clothes inside for him to find, along with the rest of these items. "Then it couldn't have been an attack. Was it a *plan*?"

Was he supposed to be found, but with his memory intact?

At the bottom of the case were two other items. One was a thin, slightly scratched tintype of a handsome woman. It was the same gal he had seen in his earlier vision and it was inscribed, *Love, Augustina-Rose*. There was no writing on the reverse side of the metal.

The picture did not trigger more memories. The name, a mix of American and Spanish, evoked nothing. He recalled only what he had seen in his pained memory earlier.

There was something else below that. His sheath—

beads, piggin strings, well-used hide. Eagerly, he took it out, handled it in the dark, reacquainted himself with a belonging that was immediately familiar to the touch. His fingers found something surprising then: paper tucked inside.

A map folded to fit snugly within. He took it out, held it between his teeth as he attached the second sheath to his belt, then carefully returned the tintype to the bottom of the satchel. He replaced everything but the map and the notebook. There might be something written on both; he could not tell in here. When he was finished, the man who was now Jason Quinn closed the satchel, picked the other items up, and rose slowly so as not to aggravate his wound.

He patted Snowcap on the neck. "You're a good guard, my friend. I'll be back—just you be patient."

The horse neighed, and Quinn took the two items to the window. He climbed out and stepped back, toward the edge of the trees where he could read them in the moonlight. He opened the map with eager fingers. He scanned the terrain and the markings.

The document was no help. Physically, it was a little smaller than the one Lieutenant Martins had had in his saddlebag, maybe twice the size of a writing slate. The terrain on both maps was the same, though this one had no printed names anywhere.

*Why was this in my sheath?* he wondered.

He began to fold the map when he noticed something odd about it. The paper had been folded with the map side out. He opened it fully once again, saw that there were smudges on the back side. Examining them more closely, he noticed that the blemishes each concealed a small black dot in the center.

Quinn put the notebook down and raised the map over his head so that the moon shined through it. The white light revealed that the map had been intended to be viewed this way and only this way. One dot seemed to be south of where he had woken in the desert.

*Martins' campsite,* he guessed.

The other was off the coast. Remembering the contours of Martins' map, he put this mark around San Francisco. He looked more closely. The spot was not where the city was marked on the other map but just to the west.

In the water.

Whoever had hit him could not have known he would lose his memory. This had to have been marked and left behind for another reason.

*Of course,* he thought.

"You did not know where we were going, Mr. Quinn," he said.

Beaudine had left it where a knife fighter would surely find it.

It did not seem possible that events could be clearer and muddier at the same time, but that was how Quinn felt. He knew his name, and there was clearly a place he had to go, but he did not yet know why—and what exactly his relationship was with the man who had hit him. Was his partner William Beaudine, or was that someone he was to meet in San Francisco? If the latter, whom had he been traveling with, from where, and why?

And Au . . . Aggiena . . . Aggie. His wife? His gal? His sister? The way they'd been squabbling, it could have been any of those.

He went to the horse he had left tethered to a tree

and put the items in Lieutenant Martins' saddlebag. He could not take Snowcap. The stallion was not saddled, and he did not want to make a commotion. And whoever was here might just notice that such a distinctive horse was absent.

As Quinn stood there, he heard muttering from the direction of the way station. He walked slowly back along the side of the barn and heard someone shifting around inside the outhouse, all elbows from the number of times he bumped the walls. Quinn moved cautiously to the edge of the barn wall and, looking around, drew the knife and moved stealthily through the dark.

He had done this before many times. There was nothing to remember. The reflexes were all there.

Quinn had to cross moonlight to reach the small but sturdy structure. He did not know if the place had a dog, but he stayed upwind of the house, which was also upwind of the outhouse. He breathed through his mouth to avoid the odor—then shifted to breathing through his teeth to avoid the moths that flitted in the heavenly light above.

"You go a week or two, no visitors," a voice from inside was saying. "Then it's a flood. And not from the damn train, don't you know. And not even listening to me. 'Doctoring is extra,' I told them. 'My wife don't work for free. No way, no how.' Do they care?"

Quinn bent—the location of the sounds suggested the man was probably seated now—and moved his face close to the back wall.

"My horse is in your barn," Quinn said softly.

"Jesus' spit! Who *else* is creeping—"

"*Hush*, damn it! My name is Jason Quinn, and I

want to know how my horse came into your possession. These men, your current guests—they didn't bring it."

"No, sir, they did not," the man inside whispered. "Hold on! Dear God, a man can't even visit the privy without a crowd. I'm gonna move up to— What the hell's that new town? Where the Suquamish Indians are?"

"Seattle," Quinn said—remarkably and without hesitation.

"Yeah. I'll take Liz if she cares to go or get me a squaw, or maybe both, and live in timber country where no one will bother me."

There were sounds of movement inside the shack, and then the tall man emerged in the bright night. Bare chested and fixing the suspenders on his red range trousers, he came fully around back and regarded the man crouching in the shadows.

"Only varmints hide in the dark," the owner said. "You a varmint?"

"I don't think so."

"That's a curious reply. Can't you talk straight?"

"Friend, all I know I can do is throw straight," he said, realizing that might have been perceived as a threat and sheathing the knife. "What about my stuff, my horse? Why are they here?"

"I was told you might be showing up."

"Told by who?"

"A Mr. William Beaudine. Said I should hold the horse and some belongings for you. You say you found that, too? The satchel."

"Yes."

"You always feel free to go nosing about a man's—"

"Look, mister—"

"Moore. Zebulon Moore."

"Mr. Moore, I don't have time for this."

"You have money?"

"No." He added menacingly now, "Just the Bowie knife."

Moore took a moment and then nodded, not a show of acquiescence but answering his own unspoken question: *Do I want to survive this encounter?*

"When was Mr. Beaudine here?" Quinn asked.

"This morning. Ate, paid, dropped off your stuff, then left."

"He gave you no instructions?"

"All the gentleman said to me was that the horse was to go to no one but him or you—"

"He's coming back?"

"Said he would, didn't say when, only that he would pay me more—which is why I asked, Mr. Quinn, not to be greedy but it was our agreement—"

"Go on," Quinn said with mounting impatience.

"He said to give what he left to you, but only if you was alone."

"Did he anticipate I would be with someone?"

"Didn't say. I told you every instruction he gave me. There wasn't a word more. Oh, excepting he had me bury a box. It's about two paces behind you, about a foot down. You can feel where the earth was turned over."

"That's it?"

"That's all," Zebulon said.

If there had been more, Quinn was certain this talkative man would say it. "The men inside—one of them has a head wound?"

"That's right. A lieutenant. The other two are a pri-

vate and a colonel. They keep talking about some sergeant, but they say 'she,' so I guess it's kind of an honorary
name. At least, that's what they call each other."

Quinn was still secreted in the darkness behind the
outhouse. Zebulon looked hungrily through the dark,
like a rogue coyote searching for a meal.

"You, uh—you want more information? I can probably get it."

"I don't have any money," Quinn said.

"Oh."

"I'll tell you what, though. I've got a horse tied to a
tree behind the barn. I'll claim mine. You can have
that one."

"Is it stolen? I don't want no trouble with the law.
Retired peacekeeper Sheriff Russell, he comes around
now and then. He'd know if I was hiding something
like a horse."

"It was roaming free when I took him," Quinn answered. He nodded toward the station. "Are any of the
men awake?"

"Not when I left, but if we keep jawin' in a loud
whisper—"

"Just go inside and do something for me. You can
have my horse, Snowcap. That's been mine for a while."

"Mister, that's a fine horse, and you got a deal . . .
depending on what it is you want done."

"What you said. Ask about me, by name. Did you
tell them Beaudine had been here?"

"No, sir. The privacy of my—"

"Tell them."

"Okay."

"Come back and tell me what they said, how they
reacted."

The proprietor nodded and set off. Quinn did not like the bargain at all, but he had nothing else to offer. Rising to his full height, Quinn eased cautiously around the outhouse and into the moonlight.

"Say, Mr. Quinn?" Zebulon said, no longer whispering.

His heart going dull on him, Quinn stepped cautiously to the side of the outhouse, the knife still in its sheath. He used his toe to feel for the box, but before he could dig it up he caught the glint of a moon-kissing shotgun barrel pointing at him and his host from the open back door.

# CHAPTER ELEVEN

WILLIAM BEAUDINE WAS getting set to sleep where he did not sleep enough: under the blanket of heaven, with the million eyes of heaven looking down. It made him feel like a part of something bigger—bigger even than the United States of America, which was a dangerous thing to be reminded of. It challenged his commitment to just how important his mission was.

"I sure hope that when you die, that's where you are," he said, looking at a swath of stars so opaque that it seemed like God's own robes. Now and then the sky was split by a white streak. Beaudine was not a churchgoing man, but he suspected those were local souls that hadn't quite passed muster and were headed the other way.

He lay in his bedroll with his head on the bulging root of a towering pine. He had softened the natural pillow with his shirt; it was a hot night, and he would not need any extra covering.

Beside him, on the right, in easy reach, were his two revolvers and his rifle. He was hopeful about that being the path to heaven above him—what else could it be? The lights were not good for anything else. But he was not overeager to make the trip. Beyond the guns were twigs he had strewn on four sides for a considerable distance. Their crunch would let him know if a man or an animal was approaching. He did not worry about being shot from a distance: He did not have anything worth stealing, other than the horse and the guns. A horse was its own alarm, if anyone came for it. And he could reach his guns and fire from a deep sleep as fast as a hammer could be cocked. In his work, accuracy was not as important as speed. Second to speed was the ability to pencil-roll away before a shot could be fired by someone else. He had survived these five years with Pinkerton—and the War before that— following that policy. He had seen marksmen die because, while they knew they could hit what they fired at, they did not always have the time.

On his left side, close in, was the box that he and Quinn had stolen from the American mercenaries hired by the French. He had carefully opened the box, studied its contents, and then returned the box to its original condition.

He needed all of it intact.

Lying there, his eyes taking longer, slower blinks as the minutes passed, he thought about Quinn. He was a good man, a very good man. But damned headstrong. Beaudine truly hoped that the man had survived. He prayed that Quinn woke before the others found him. But there had not been time to argue, and Quinn was clearly of a mind, a very set mind, to disobey his instructions.

Beaudine's eyes finally closed, tired from too much sun. His mind journeyed back—was it only just a day?

*"You haven't even told me why we're here!"*

*"Look, keeping secrets wasn't my choice. Those were orders."*

*"Then this is my choice. Kill me if you want, but I run to fights. I don't run from them."*

That dispute, which there had been no time to settle, had risked the success of the mission. That was why Beaudine had struck him with his gun butt and left him on the desert sands, unarmed, near undressed, and bleeding more than Beaudine had intended. But according to the map that Beaudine had memorized down to the smallest hill, Quinn was close enough to water that he could fix himself up and move on when he woke. And, after he had refreshed himself, there was an old halfway house still occupied by a family where he could hopefully get some nursing. The only reason Beaudine had not left the other knife was that, coming upon Quinn, the mercenaries would have known that this was one of the men who had attacked him. They would still likely figure that, but not knowing much, Quinn would not have been able to tell them anything other than two names, one of them William Beaudine. They might have heard of him, which could actually work in his favor. The men would be unlikely to rush into anything without due consideration. Anything that slowed them down helped him.

He still heard himself hurriedly, angrily talking to the unconscious man as he took his belongings, hoping that something he said might get through:

*"The order came from our employer, Mr. Pinkerton himself, which is that I can tell you no more than I*

*have. His orders came from the president of the United States. And that, Quinn, is the devil with his horns on."*

As he fell asleep, Beaudine had one other thought. It rose from somewhere deep in his mind, unbidden. He would probably forget it by morning. But reliving the blow he had given Quinn, Beaudine questioned the choice not only because he was one man down in a two-man operation, but because he could not help but wonder if he had turned a very deadly man against himself. . . .

MARIA MIGHT NOT have been fluent in English, but what knowledge she had said was no less accurate for that.

Jane lay on the ground with her hands tied tightly behind her back.

It was a visibly, now consistently strained captain who had put her in that position. It was not in response to something she had done but something she had requested.

Earlier in the ride, as Douglas had begun to weep after finally reacting to what had happened to Sheriff Russell, his mother had leaned toward him. She spoke quietly; her words would be understood by none of the men within earshot, but her tone had to sound conversational.

"What happened back there was inhuman, but it was something that got out of control," she had said. "That's why we have to be reasonable."

"Ma, Sheriff Russell was trying to help us," he had replied. "I'm sad because I couldn't help him. And I'm

angry. That man who was holding me—he didn't have
to shoot twice. Sheriff Russell dropped his gun after
he was hit."

"I know. It was barbaric," his mother had agreed.

"I'm okay now," Douglas said, sniffling up his sorrow and becoming steely eyed. "I'll think about Hank.
He would know what to do."

Jane nodded, smiled inside, and returned to her upright position and, like her son, rode on.

The delays at the Smith cabin and then with Sheriff
Russell were two of the reasons the French column
reached neither their American allies nor the Oak
Ridge way station by nightfall. They were also on a
forced march, which had tired the men. The horses, too,
needed rest. With open reluctance and dismay, Captain
Dupré ordered that camp be established atop a low hill.
There was the Scouse River at the eastern foot of the
hill, and both men and horses were allowed to water
themselves before the sun was completely gone. Torches
were set, more to frighten predators than to provide
light. While that was being done, he conferred with the
woman who was back with Jane and Douglas.

"I've decided that we cannot keep up this pace," he
had told her. "Do you think you can get aboard?"

"It is possible," the woman had replied. "But I am
concerned about the gold in the box along with the
other documents."

"Why be concerned? The *Louis XIV* from Roche-
fort shall be arriving shortly after off the California
coast, south of San Francisco. A rowboat will meet
you. You will be bound for a French port the day we
strike."

"And you? You have not said when you will join me," Maria protested.

"*L'Officier Généraux* Marais will be carrying my orders. We will know then." He had moved closer to her, looked down into eyes that were nearly as gray as the dusty sergeant's uniform that Martins had provided for her. "We have waited this long. A little longer can be endured. What is most important is the present. I am going to abandon the chase of Lieutenant Martins and this mysterious 'Hank.' We must turn west in the morning, before the Juárez frigate sails."

The woman nodded.

"I will plan a route," he said, urging her to rest while she could.

The men gave Jane a blanket, and she gathered what grasses she could to make the ground softer. She would need to be under the blanket, or she would be gnawed to distraction by insects. She did not bother to inform the men of that fact.

Not that she expected to sleep. She was tired, but despite what she had said to her son, she was both angry and afraid. She had to think of a way out of this. The camp was set up without a campfire, the horses in the center and the men circled around them. One sentry was posted on the north, one on the west—the only directions the captain felt an intruder was likely to come from. Jane was between the fringe of the group and the northern sentry, a few yards from both. Douglas was initially situated on the other side of the camp. So far away, it was unlikely he would be tempted to sneak around the perimeter and plot with his mother.

Jane was openly hostile to this arrangement, and

she had gone to the captain to impress on him the need
for her to be near Douglas.

"My son has witnessed a great deal today," she had
told him pointedly. "He may have nightmares."

"All children have nightmares."

"You cannot be so ignorant," she charged.

Dupré had not acceded to the request, stating, "Not
so ignorant to keep mother and son close so they can
plan an escape."

"Merely escape?" she asked, the threat emerging
before she had a chance to crush it down.

There was a thick, tense moment of silence. She
found the officer more menacing than he had seemed
all day.

"Monsieur Reynaud!" he had called out.

A beefy, sweating sergeant had hurried over. The
captain spoke quickly, in French, and Jane soon learned
the gist of his instructions. Dupré had ordered that her
hands be bound behind her back and that her son be
placed on the other side of the horses in the center of
the encampment.

When the sergeant had approached with the strap,
and Jane discerned his intent, she yelled at the captain
and nodded toward Douglas, "At least *wait*!"

Dupré did that much, ordering the sergeant to pro-
ceed when Douglas was led away.

"It will be all right!" she said after her son. "I promise."

"I know, Ma," the boy had replied. It was not a
statement of hope but strong with purpose.

After being roughly bound, Jane was returned to
her crude bedding, rubbed uncomfortably with the
hard edges of the leather strap, and told to lie down. At

least she was not thrown to the earth. Perhaps the sergeant had a particle of decency; or it could be that he was too tired to make the effort.

The captain came over before retiring. "My apologies," he said without sincerity. "Though I have, in Paris, dealt before with women who possessed murder in their hearts, this is the first time I have had to restrain a lady."

"Your conquests never cease," she said mockingly.

The captain showed no remorse for his actions and seemed proud of the remark. He acknowledged her comment with a little bow. She reminded herself it was dark, and maybe he just did not understand English well enough to recognize disdain.

Jane had spent the next hour or so in deep, silent reflection. On the one hand, she was concerned about her son. He had been so young but so present when his father was brought home, gravely injured. He had not seen the worst of the blood and breaks, and Nehemiah was unconscious by the time he arrived. Any cries of anguish—and she knew there would have been many—had been spent inside the limping return of the stagecoach after the accident. His shotgun rider, Gonzalez, had borne the worst of it.

This was very different. Douglas had been stunned to silence by the violent destruction of a man he knew and liked. An adventure had suddenly become a horror about a single violent event. Like a photograph, it would never change or fade or do anything but glare back at him in shocking red.

Jane wanted to believe, to trust, that with her own love and attention, and by his own growing to manhood, her son would get through the shock of it. She had. As a girl, she had witnessed the aftermath of Indian massacres and wolf attacks and a bison stampede. They were grotesque and indelible. But so were many of the images she had seen in church. One, in particular, was as vivid in her mind as it had been the day she had seen it: A figure of the most serene Jesus with his heart outside his body, the organ burning, surrounded by the crown of thorns, had kept her awake many a night. As long as there was an adult to calm her, to explain how the evils were part of Satan's plan to weaken them, she had recovered.

There was, on the other hand, the larger question of whether Jane and her son would survive this journey at all. The French had orchestrated the casual slaughter of a human being, an upstanding member of their own local community. She had no reason to believe that this captain—who had ordered one murder that she was aware of—would hesitate to have his men commit two more. Maybe he had never intended for them to survive. Captain Dupré was not just a murderer; he was the leader of a war party, an invading army in a foreign, hostile land. He could not allow anyone to survive who might provide information about the present operation, the men, their weapons, their strength, their movement, or their eventual retreat. Surely Fort Yuma in the Arizona Territory or some other outpost would mount a counterattack.

She knew those policies well. They were the very things Nehemiah used to talk about with Major Lancaster and his alert cavalry. Their lives and mission depended upon accurate information, and they listened carefully as her husband described the Indians he had seen or been confronted by along the stage trail. A lone, experienced rider saw much more than a coach whose comings and goings adhered to a timetable. That, plus the dust of the stage, gave the native population time to conceal whatever hunting, trading, or war parties were about. They were even known to interrupt skirmishes among one another to hide.

If the visit of the troops did not align with Nehemiah being at home, he would leave behind his report—spoken to his wife since he could not write. In exchange, they would leave her with supplies including ammunition if Jane had spotted any Indians herself.

The woman wondered about their chances of running into the mounted troops out on patrol. The cavalry tended to ride a circuit marked by water sources, since those were the paths the Indians also took. Thanks to the French captain's ignorance, and not his tactics, they were not exactly following one of the trails known to the locals. Major Lancaster would cut the French down and save her and Douglas. But she could not rely on that.

*No,* she thought. The cold reality of the ruthless heart behind Dupré's affable facade made it imperative that at least Douglas get away. And not during the day when they could be hunted down, but at night.

*This* night.

Deciding to do something, Jane carefully considered the situation. Dust storms, wild animals, drought, fire—she had dealt with those kinds of afflictions. This was new for her. Even if she could bury her pride under a rock, she did not think that charm would work on this commander.

*And I'm out of practice,* she thought, amused that she could *be* amused at such a moment. Or maybe it was not so strange. She thought of Sheriff Russell, of Hank, of Nehemiah. She had been self-sufficient for so long, she did not know how to approach men as men.

The night was filled with small sounds both inside the camp and without. One of them in particular caught Jane's ear. The sound came late, when the sky was star-spangled pitch. It sounded like the scratching noise made when their old dog, Dusty, had shamefully belly-walked through grass one morning after being licked by something smaller, his tawny self spotted with little rodent teeth marks.

Her eyes sought details among the dark, low grass and snagged tumbleweeds. When they finally emerged, she was no longer sure she was awake.

It was her son, using his elbows and knees to snake toward her. She suppressed a cry, but her eyes were wide with both surprise and concern. He crept next to her, low as only a young boy could make himself, before lying on his side, face-to-face with her.

"Been crawling for a long time," he whispered.

She moved closer; he immediately noticed the awkward placement of her arms. Following them with his eyes, he raised his head and saw that she was tied up.

"I thought that's what they done," he said softly. Then added, "Did."

"It's all right," she whispered back.

"You're tied like a chicken!"

"Don't fuss about that. Just pull the blanket to my nose, and you get under it."

He did as she instructed. "Like when I was a boy."

"You remember."

"Uh-huh."

When he was hidden in their small, tented way, she asked, "How are you here?"

"It was easy. I came through the horses. Calmed them, just like Dad once told me."

"My clever boy!"

"I also made this." He drew a stick about a foot long from inside the sleeve of his shirt. His chest expanded proudly as he held it in his mother's face. She moved her head back to see.

"I sharpened it like Hank said," he announced proudly, adding, "I pretended to snore so I could rub it on a rock."

Despite the danger lurking just beyond the moment, Jane was smiling. She kissed her son on the forehead and then moved the blanket back with the upraised side of her head. She saw his bright eyes in the bit of moonlight that struck him. An idea had occurred to her—lunatic on one level, but no less uncertain than the fate they presently faced.

"Ma, let me untie you."

"No, love. You gave me a blessing of an idea that needs me to stay bound up. And I want you to pay very careful attention, better than you have on grammar or when I warn you not to lean over the well," she said softly but firmly.

There was movement outside the blanket, and Jane put her hand over her son's mouth so he would not speak. The sentry had come over. He was behind her, Douglas in front. She craned around and looked up.

"Yes?"

*"Rien,"* the man replied, and walked away. He had probably been given instructions to check on the woman.

Jane muttered after the soldier as he left. If he heard her talking to her son, he was likely to return. She turned back around and spoke into the blanket.

"You are going to listen, yes? Nod to show me that you understand."

The boy nodded once.

"I want you to leave the camp—"

"Ma, no—"

"*Shh!*" she said. "You are to listen to me. If I were to leave, they would chase me. I don't think the captain will spare the men to go after you. They're tired enough as is. As long as he has one of us, the captain may not care."

"But he'll be mad—"

"*Son!*"

"No, listen. It's like Pa warned you when we helped that runaway squaw. What did he call it?"

"Pride," she replied. "This isn't the same. The captain will be angry, but he needs to move out at sunup, and he cannot spare the men. He won't chase you, and he won't hurt me."

The boy took her hand under the blanket. "Come," he whispered. "We can *do* it."

Jane found it difficult to keep back tears at her son making his first sounds like a man. She looked back, saw that the sentry had not heard, and stopped telling Douglas to be silent.

"You must trust me," she said. "And I don't want you to come back whatever you hear the captain say. Even if he says he's going to harm me. Even if he *does* hurt me. Promise?"

The boy did not answer.

"*Promise?* It will hurt me more to know you are here, in danger."

Upon consideration, the boy relented. "Yes, Ma."

Jane moved closer. "You keep your pa and Hank in your head. Be brave and steady."

"Like Pa. Like Hank."

"Good boy. Now, here's what you do. Stay under the blanket, and when I get up, you crawl off the way you just did—but to the east. They don't have a guard there. Go to the Scouse River and follow it north. The captain will probably think you're going south to get home. If he sends men after you, it will be in that direction." She put her fingers around the stick. "Anyone sees you and makes a commotion, run. Or get in the river and let it carry you. Use the stick if you have to, if someone grabs you."

"But, Ma, if I'm not going home, where do I go?"

"You *are* going home, just not right away. When you're sure nobody's following double back downriver—"

"What about looking for Hank? He's north."

"With one of those men. You can't swap one jailer for another." She nodded and kissed his brow. "You can do this. If you need to, if someone comes to the house, go to the pond and hide there for a spell."

"Like I do when you're looking for me for schooling."

"Exactly like that. Now, pull the blanket over you while I get up."

The boy threw his arms around his mother and then, without hesitation, did as she had instructed. She prayed that he got the chance to play hooky again very soon.

Rolling from her side to her belly, Jane got her knees under her and rose. She intended to ask to be untied to tend to her private needs.

Even before Jane had her feet under her, one of the men yelled something from the center of the camp, near the corral. She did not understand the alarm, save for one word: *Garçon*.

Boy.

# CHAPTER TWELVE

"WHO IS OUT there with you, Moore?"

The speaker stood tall in the doorway. His inquiring voice punched hard through the still, silent night—raw and unyielding.

Quinn eased back behind the outhouse while his companion pretended to finish hitching his pants, which he had already done.

"That was just me keeping myself company," Zebulon replied.

"On the side of the outhouse?"

"Thought I heard a coyote. We got chickens, y'know."

The man at the door, Colonel Franklin Voight, just stood there.

"Would you lower that firearm?" Zebulon said, walking forward. "It might go off!"

"I asked who was out there, Moore, and 'coyote' ain't

the answer I was looking for," the man said without altering his stance.

"Who d'you think is with me? Who *would* be with me while I'm doing my business, out here on a trail that no one travels anymore save when they miss the train or get lost?"

"All right, you idiot old coot. Move away from the latrine unless you want to die."

"Why? What you gonna do?"

"Air it out," the man said, cocking the shotgun. "Damn foul thing could use it."

"Oh, no. No, you don't. I'm not gonna toddle aside while you destroy my property!"

"Then you can be shot up with it, old man." The man raised and aimed the shotgun. "I said step aside, and I mean now."

"There's no need for shooting," Hank said from behind the structure. "I'll come out."

The man in the doorway grinned. "I thought so. I oughta shoot you for a lying buzzard, Moore."

"Why? For seeing to the survival of one of my guests?"

"A guest."

"That's right. He's here, and he can pay. What would you call him?"

"A man on borrowed time," the man said. "Now, why don't you just shut up and move away, Moore?"

"In my own home," Zebulon muttered as he stepped to one side. "No one has any manners no more!"

While the men chattered, Quinn rose, raised his hands, and stepped very slowly from behind the outhouse. Like frozen lightning, full of portent and danger, the barrel of the shotgun remained pointed ahead in the white light. Below it, he saw a dog slink into the night, its tail low.

Quinn walked along the outhouse wall, well away from Zebulon. In case the man recognized him and decided to shoot him, he did not want the proprietor harmed.

"Stop where you are," the man said when Quinn had cleared the building. "You got any weapons?"

"A knife."

"Moore?"

"What?"

"Take it and toss it on the ground."

The grizzled older man turned to Quinn and saw the blade. He approached. "Sorry to leave you naked."

"It's okay. It won't be the first time today."

The proprietor was puzzled by the remark, but Quinn was actually pleased. It felt good to clearly remember *something* that had happened to him.

The Bowie knife was removed from its sheath and *thunked* on the dirt.

"Awright," the man said. "Resume walking toward me. Slow, hands where they are."

Quinn did as he was told. Another man, roused by the commotion, came to the door. Behind him, the wakened Elizabeth Moore stood in shadow. In a corner, the dog raised his head, then set it back down.

As Quinn moved closer, the second man took a few steps forward, standing shoulder to shoulder with the other. He was holding a Colt.

"Jesus Lord," Private Stevens remarked. "The Almighty is on our side and has delivered a bounty to our doorstep."

"You figure it's him?"

"I figure it can't be no one else, slinking around at this hour," Stevens said. "You come to finish what you started?"

"I came to talk."

"Like you talked to the lieutenant?"

"I was his prisoner."

"Now you're ours," Voight replied.

Quinn considered explaining that he had very few specifics on what they were talking about. But he decided for the moment to say nothing that might provoke them. Whatever his life was before today, Quinn felt it was wise to let the men with the weapons do all the talking.

When Quinn was just a few paces away, the man with the shotgun finally pointed it at the ground.

"You can stop there."

Quinn began to lower his arms. "Thank you, Mr.—?"

"*Colonel* Voight. And raise 'em. No one said you can get comfortable."

Quinn did as he had been instructed. The second man also lowered his gun.

"Where's Beaudine, and where's our box?" Stevens asked.

"I don't know, but I'd like to show you something."

"If it ain't the box—"

"It isn't, but what I have to show you may help us all figure things out. I'd like to remove my hat."

Voight and Private Stevens were silhouetted against the light inside the station. They stood still in shared confusion.

"Your hat?" Voight said.

"That's right."

Stevens lifted his gun again. "Go ahead and show us."

The three men stood silently watching as Quinn raised his hands higher and lifted his hat straight up. He turned slowly so the men could see the wound on the back of his skull. It was no longer bleeding, but the blood had caked there.

"This Beaudine you mentioned," Quinn said. "I believe he hit me on the head and left me for dead in the desert. Gentlemen, I don't know who I am, what I'm supposed to have done, or what I'm supposed to be doing."

"You gonna tell me you don't recall hitting Lieutenant Martins?" Stevens asked.

"Yes, that I do. He held me prisoner. I needed to get away."

"To do what?" Voight asked.

"To try and find the man I was traveling with, to learn who I am."

"Heck," Zebulon said, "it's gonna cost me a silver dollar when he returns, but if one of you makes good, *I* can tell you both of those things."

The three men looked at him.

"You've seen Beaudine?" Voight demanded.

"Why didn't you tell us this before, you old idiot, when we asked if anyone had been through?" Stevens asked.

"This morning, early," he said, then straightened with importance. "The privacy of my guests is sacred to me, like a wedding vow—but these are particular circumstances we have here."

Voight swung the shotgun toward him. "And this isn't church! Start recollecting."

A voice came from behind the group. "Take that gun off my husband and put it down."

The voice, stern and unruffled, came from inside the way station where only Voight and Stevens could see, but everyone could hear. The two Rebels looked back.

Elizabeth Moore stood with a revolver pointed at the head of the unconscious Lieutenant Martins. The man lay on the dining table, surrounded by two pans of water—one dirty, one clean—and the bandages and implements that had been used to dress and redress his injury.

Voight and Stevens stood still.

A hammer cocked. "The graves of two Confederate renegades and one Injun are behind the chicken coop. I'll dig more."

"All I done was dig 'em," Zebulon remarked.

"All right, stay calm," Voight said quietly.

"She's always calm," Zebulon said. "Else she couldn't shoot straight."

Voight showed disgust with the proprietor but lowered the barrel.

"Put it on the ground," Elizabeth added.

Voight bent and placed the shotgun in the dirt.

Elizabeth shifted slightly so the gun was on Stevens. "You with the Colt. Disarm yourself as well. Then both of you come back inside, though by all rights I should send you to the barn to saddle up."

Stevens did as he was told.

"You're guests here," Elizabeth went on. "You don't come to a place and start pointing gun barrels and making demands. Not under the Moore roof you don't."

Zebulon came over and, talking to himself, collected the weapons. Quinn turned and picked up his knife, wiped it against his trousers, and flipped it so the point faced toward him, along his wrist—to conceal it? To throw? He did not know why; he only knew that he had done it before.

To sheath it, he realized as he naturally slid the knife into its beaded sheath. Zebulon waited while the two unarmed men reentered the station. The proprietor followed them in, Quinn coming after.

"Good manners sometimes has to be enforced with bad ones," Zebulon confided to the other man.

Quinn made no comment. His heart was beginning to thump harder as he looked at the two men who were now both covered by Elizabeth's six-shooter. She had moved and was standing behind the table so the men could not jump her. She had gray hair piled on her head and a stern, set expression that seemed to move only by the shifting light of lanterns. One lamp sat on the table, the other hung on the wall on the opposite side of the group near the front door. There were only the faintest pinpoints of ruddy light in the fireplace behind the woman.

"Close the door, Zebulon," she said. "I saw that rogue coyote."

"See? I told you," Zebulon said to Voight. He laid the guns on a rocking chair and shut the door.

Quinn was standing beside the door, and he moved so Zebulon could close it. Elizabeth motioned him closer to the other two and looked at the three men.

"I don't care what any of you has done, and I'll patch anyone who's injured as best I can. But I *won't* have harm committed under my roof." Cocking her head at the door, she added, "That means any of my roofs."

"Ma'am, I understand your sentiment," Voight said.

"But this is the man who left Lieutenant Martins for dead."

"So I heard. I also heard this man was your man's prisoner. I'm no judge, but that seems a good reason to crack someone's skull."

"This fella and his partner stole from us at knife-point," Voight went on. "We only want what's rightfully ours."

"I heard that, too," she said.

"We got quite an education standing there," Zebulon said.

Quinn shook his head slowly. "Mr. and Mrs. Moore, if I did such a thing, I don't remember it. Lieutenant Martins found me being nursed at a station east of here, on the desert."

"The Smith place?" Elizabeth asked.

"That's it, ma'am. Mrs. Smith was most kind, generous, and trusting. The injured man took me from Mrs. Smith's care in the hopes I'd remember something. But a hope is all it was. Until a few minutes ago, when I saw the satchel in the barn, I didn't even remember my name."

"What satchel?" the woman asked her husband.

"Something Mr. Beaudine gave me to hold."

She looked at her husband.

"For a silver dollar and another to come," he added reluctantly.

Elizabeth gave him a look that said the discussion was not over; then she glanced back at the others. "I'm sorry for you, Mr. Quinn. I should send you on your way, too. Mrs. Smith could use a man around—"

Elizabeth Moore froze in midsentence. Her eyes and mouth were both wide, her extended throat wheezing down air. The lieutenant had been awake, his eyes shut, and he had found the scissors Elizabeth had used to cut his bandages. He had turned suddenly on his shoulder and pushed both wide-open blades into her belly. He withdrew the shears for a second thrust, but she had already dropped her gun and staggered back. The woman hit the wall beside the fireplace and slid to the floor. She sat stiff against the logs, and her thin fingers slapped audibly on two patches of blood that merged to one on the fabric just above her waist. The dog rose, slunk toward her, and pressed his nose to her cheek.

A chaos of motion followed. Zebulon cried out and ran to his wife, bumping into the table and upsetting the lantern, the glass chimney shattering, the flame starting a small fire with the upended kerosene. Voight immediately jumped to where Zebulon had been standing, beside the chair with the guns. Shocked by Martins' action, Quinn was a moment late following Voight. But his old reflexes were not delayed. The knife was already in his right hand. Voight went for the shotgun, and Quinn reached for the revolver with his left hand. Stevens was a step behind Quinn, bent like a bull and running at him.

The three men smashed awkwardly against the chair, upsetting it and sending the guns crashing to the floor. In the hellish light in the middle of the room, and still wielding the scissors, Lieutenant Martins swung slowly from the table, immediately going faint and dropping to both knees. Zebulon was kneeling beside his wife, pressing his palm to the wound and feeling its inexorable spread.

The three men, entangled like a tumbleweed, fought in the near dark. Quinn's skull burned painfully as

Voight and Stevens simultaneously wrestled him onto his back and tried to pin him.

"Hold him!" Voight shouted. "I'll get the shotgun!"

Quinn squeezed his eyes shut. He did not need to see, only to feel. By instinct, he rotated his wrist and snaked his right hand from under Stevens' forceful intentions, then slashed outward with the knife. The wide sweep cut skin to the bone and drew a wail from Stevens. Quinn opened his eyes, which felt like they were in a slowly closing vise. Through pulsing red circles, he looked into the flickering light from the lamp by the door. He saw the man's torso looming above him, felt blood dripping on his arm. Quinn had slashed the man in the left shoulder. The wounded private had lost some, but not all, of his grappling fury. Apparently unaware of his companion's injury, Voight continued his assault against Quinn, a palm pressing down on the man's left arm while the colonel gropingly sought a weapon.

Quinn had taken all of this in during the space of a heartbeat. Stevens hung there, still a potential threat; on the swift return swipe, Quinn's knife cut deeply through the man's throat. Blood poured down like a waterfall, Stevens dropping and Quinn rolling out from under him toward Voight. The dying man flopped to the floor, clutching at his throat, which bubbled as he exhaled and caused him to gag horribly when he inhaled.

Voight did not continue to struggle with Quinn but released him and rose, the shotgun in his hands. He pointed the weapon at Quinn and straddled his chest, simultaneously stepping on the man's right wrist, pinning it. Quinn could barely see through the sharp pain.

*"You bloody snake, where is Beaudine?"* the colo-

nel screamed as his companion writhed incongruously at his feet. Voight pointed the gun at Quinn's mouth. *"Talk!"*

Quinn could barely see through the pain, let alone speak. Moving images appeared in his memory, of night, of the man on the horse beside him, of the blond mane bucking from a sudden halt. Along with them came words, fragments of heated disagreement—

*"You haven't even told me why we're here!"*

*"Look, keeping secrets wasn't my choice. Those were orders."*

Quinn remembered hesitating, and then the other man came toward him, a man who must have been William Beaudine. A man he remembered as having a jaw like rock, eyes like a wolf's, hair the color of pitch. Beaudine held a metal box under one arm, the same arm that carried a six-shooter. The other hand held the reins. They were making their way through flat terrain lit by the moon.

He remembered more. Abstract things that had eluded him to this point. He knew that Beaudine had said if they rode hard, they could time the attack to coincide with the full moon.

Quinn remembered deeper. He saw them riding hard, the setting sun behind them. They had been farther west . . . at a boat.

And then, as quickly as the memories had returned, as quickly as they flashed by, the sights and sounds were gone. He was breathing heavily on his back, his chest aching from where it had hit the chair—

Quinn felt his scalp dampen with blood that was not his own. It belonged to Stevens, lying to his left. At forced rest now, his vision cleared. He saw Voight towering above him and his hard-breathing, scowling face loomed large—but only for a moment.

"Watch out!" Martins cried thinly.

A water basin flashed white as it crashed against the right side of Voight's skull, spraying ruddy water in all directions. Quinn rolled to his left, toward the inert Stevens, as the shotgun discharged, punching through the floorboards. Splinters, dust, and countless speckles of Stevens' pooling blood flew into the air. Voight staggered forward but did not fall.

The iron basin clattered to the ground and the man who had wielded it, Zebulon, raised it again and threw it down hard on Voight's face.

"You *killed* her, bastards! *You killed my wife!*"

The proprietor turned his angry eyes on the man who still wielded the scissors. Martins was struggling to rise. Noticing the fire, Zebulon stormed back and overturned the second basin on the flame.

"You won't have my home, too!" the grieving man cried.

Still wielding the scissors, Martins continued to use the edge of the table to pull himself up. Before Zebulon could charge him, the staggered but conscious Voight had revived somewhat. Quinn, still recovering from having ducked the shot, got halfway to his feet but was not quick enough to reach the shotgun. Voight still held it and spun on the other men.

Without thinking, Quinn threw the Bowie knife. It missed the man and struck wood somewhere. Quinn rolled over Stevens as the shotgun fired again, the blast missing him but hitting the twin-domed hanging lamp suspended above the center of the room. Glass, flames, and fuel rained down, tinkling and burning where they hit the floor or cushioned chairs.

Lieutenant Martins was on his feet in the near black room, wielding the scissors before him. Voight used the shotgun as a crutch to get to his feet. Snarling in pain and anger, he made ready to fire into the dark where he had last seen Quinn.

"Not this!" Martins said to him. "The *mission*! Let's go!"

Voight hesitated.

"Help me! *Now!*" Martins yelled.

Voight shoved his way through the dark, encountering Zebulon and driving the stock of the weapon into his gut. Zebulon cried out and doubled over. Voight pushed him aside and reached Martins, who was upright and shuffling toward the door. Voight tucked a shoulder under the man's arms and bared his teeth at the dark.

"You will both *die*, Quinn!" he cried as he yanked open the door. "You and Bloody Bill will both die!"

Quinn stayed where he was, flat on the floor, on his belly, shielded by the corpse, until the two men were out the door. Then he rose as fast as his aching head would permit and began stomping or swatting out the small fires that burned at the door. Before crushing the last, he picked up a piece of the chair back and set it ablaze for a torch.

The carnage he saw, that he had inadvertently brought on the Moores, made him physically ill.

Zebulon had not bothered to stand up after the blow. He had dropped to the floor, beside his wife, and held her, sobbing. The dog lay low, on his forepaws, still and quiet. Giving Zebulon his privacy, Quinn looked around for his knife. It was stuck in a wall about an inch above where Voight's head would have been. He went over and pulled it out. Then he went to the door.

There was muted sound in the barn, and Quinn was inclined to pick up one of the guns and finish this. Then he considered the odds. For all he knew, Martins was waiting for him to do just that while Voight saddled the horses. Quinn knew that a gun was not his natural weapon. Though he felt cowardly, he stayed where he was.

Quinn knew only a little more about himself than when he had been hiding behind the outhouse. But he had learned two things: Beaudine had left him to rot in the desert, and he hated Martins and Voight. His own odyssey was no longer just about finding William Beaudine and finishing whatever it was he had set out to do.

His new undertaking was to find and kill two, possibly three men.

# CHAPTER THIRTEEN

LIVING WHERE SHE did, Jane could always see potential trouble coming. That was the advantage of being on the borderline between a desert and a flat plain. People coming from one were sapped of energy, and from the other were visible a good half mile distant. There was no need for quick decisions.

But life was not a desert or a plain, and the life of her son could well hang on what Jane Smith decided in the next few seconds.

One of the men had obviously noticed that Douglas was not where he should have been, and there was a great and swelling commotion that was bound to crash against her here. If Douglas was to have a chance of getting away, there was only one thing to do.

She said to him quickly and aloud, "I want you to stay under the blanket, and when I tell you, start counting to fifty silently. Do it just like we do when counting how far away thunder is. You hear?"

"Yes—"

"At fifty, you run hard for the river. If they see you, just keep running. If anyone is there, hide. If they find you, bite, kick, punch, do whatever you have to, but you get in the water and let the current carry you away, hear?"

"Yes, Ma. Yes."

The boy was listening to her, to the soldiers, and he was fully alert. Soldiers were pointing toward her, and she struggled to rise.

"You can't help me," she told her son without looking down at the blanket. "You *must* save yourself!" She was nearly to her feet. "Start counting now!"

"One . . . two . . . three . . . like that?"

"Yes! To yourself!"

Men were moving all around the dark camp. Horses were being mounted bareback, in haste. From the sounds of the whinnies and the shouts the men were running in all directions. That was good. They could not be certain Douglas had made for the river. If he was careful, the men who went that way might be far along, in the wrong direction, before he arrived.

As the boy huddled low, the woman finally managed to get her feet under her. She showed herself moments before Captain Dupré finished circling the perimeter of the camp. He carried a pistol; the gun and his pale hand looked like ice in the moonlight. Her hands helpless behind her, Jane affected a posture and an expression of concern as she stepped from her bedding. She struggled to be free of her bonds, rending her skin.

"What's happening?" she asked, looking around frantically, like a roadrunner.

"Where is your son?"

"My son? What are you *talking* about!"

"Don't lie to me—"

"I don't know, Captain—you *took* him from me!" She shouted, "Douglas! Douglas, what are you doing? Answer me!"

The officer stopped abruptly before her, both of them silent and listening. He looked behind her at the clump of blanket. He aimed his gun.

*"No!"* Jane screamed, throwing herself in front of him.

The captain pushed her roughly aside, the woman stumbling and falling as he stepped past. Dupré bent by the blanket and pulled it away.

A cry, half shout, half growl, caused the officer to jump back. He reacted as if a bobcat and not a boy with a pointed stick had leapt up at him, snarling. Landing on his feet, Douglas ducked low, beneath the groping arms of the officer, and bolted past him. He kept running. Because his mother had been given a clearing in the name of modesty, it took a moment before the men nearest her crossed that buffer and mustered a pursuit.

The officer leveled his gun above the head of the fleeing boy. Watching with horror, Jane fell back on her knees. She hurled her shoulder at the officer's legs. The shot flew wide to the north, nearly cutting down one of his own men.

The captain yelled an order in French and then glared down at Jane. He did not raise his gun for fear of using it.

"When the boy is captured, this will cost him an ear!" he yelled.

*"Creature!"* Jane howled. She spit at the man and drove her shoulder into him again, this time at his waist. The captain staggered back and drew a knee up hard into her jaw. The woman fell back, stunned. As she landed on her tortured, bleeding wrists, one of the soldiers had arrived and grabbed her by her bound wrists.

"Tie her to a tree," Dupré ordered. "She can watch when we bring in the boy."

*"No!"* she half screamed, half sobbed. "Punish *me*! I told him to go! You would have killed him!"

"Whether or not that is true, madam, you have not improved his chances . . . or your own!"

"Devil!" she cried, her voice cracking. "Why are you doing this to us?"

"I? I am doing nothing! You are just an unfortunate figure in a larger maneuver."

The man's voice was cold and inhuman, as it had been when he spoke the last words Sheriff Russell would ever hear.

Jane screamed inarticulately but did not resist as she was dragged to the tree nearest the camp, a leafy young oak. The soldier thrust her there, hard, and left her when he went to get a rope from one of the few remaining horses.

Wriggling her fingers and palms, trying desperately to pull them through the leather strap, Jane whimpered and begged God and Nehemiah to protect her boy. Running blood wet her bonds, her flesh stung, and her heart both ached and burned. Tired and hungry, she felt this thing must have been a nightmare. She did not understand how an act of mercy shown to an injured man could have gone so murderously wrong.

Jane tried to rise and run but her strength fled quickly. She fell back as the soldier returned. He pulled her up by one arm, forcing her to stand, and wrapped her tightly to the rough bark, three turns around the chest with a knot in the back.

"My hands . . . please . . ." Jane wept. If she could have them free, she felt she could struggle against the ropes. Without that, her plight was hopeless.

The man did not understand, and without a word or a look of charity, he left to join his fellows in the hunt. Once again, now from a distance in all directions, Jane vaguely heard shouting as the men and half of their horses made their way through the dark.

Her ragged wrists dripped their wetness along the tree. She sobbed, she prayed, and despite her best efforts to stand, her trembling legs gave out, and she sagged against the restraint. Her insides hurt from where the rope pressed, but she simply could not rise.

As she hung there, crying, she heard something she had not been expecting. It was so soft that she thought, at first, it had been her imagination. Then it came again.

"Ma."

Jane was instantly alert.

"Don't be mad," Douglas said very, very quietly. "I couldn't make the river, so I climbed the tree."

Jane inhaled so sharply, it stood her erect. She had not thought the situation could become worse. It had. Until now her only hope had been that her son was busy ducking and dodging his way through the hunting party, as she had seen him do chasing wild turkeys. Instead, he was up a tree on the fringe of the camp.

"I'm not mad," Jane said exhaustedly.

"I didn't want to leave you either."

"Did you hear what the captain said?"

"I heard. But I'm not scared."

"Oh, Douglas—he's serious."

"I know," the boy said. "But I think I have an idea that can help us both."

"What kind of idea?"

"One that will bring us closer to getting away together."

# CHAPTER FOURTEEN

Q UINN WAS CERTAIN that he had felt deep grief in his life. He felt that in his bones, if not his memory. The experience was all too familiar.

In just the space of twenty-four hours, he had experienced the pain left by the parting of Nehemiah Smith, stepped fully into the void the man had left in his home, his family.

Now this.

The grief of Zebulon Moore was like a changing storm: now thundering, now raining, now fiercely destructive. After the men had placed the woman's body on the table, Zebulon cried, wailing vengeance, and kicked the parts of the broken chair against walls, against the bed, until they were little more than splinters and he could barely stand. The one torch became many, propped here and there as the men improvised a wake. The dog pulled himself up by his forepaws to sniff at the woman's cheek, then lowered himself to the floor and remained there.

As eager as Quinn was to get after the two men who had done this, he knew that he could not commit himself fully to pursuit while any part of him remained here. His mind, heart, and hands were bound to the service of Zebulon.

Since neither of them was destined to sleep, the two had left the woman's side only long enough to dig a pair of graves by moonlight. Quinn opened one up behind the outhouse for Stevens, while Zebulon dug one near a well on the western side of the way station, near the fertile vegetable garden, not far from the root of an old cedar tree. In case the two villains decided to double back, the men were in earshot, if not eyeshot, of each other.

Quinn also finally recovered the box Zebulon had buried. He did not look at it; helping the widower was more important.

The activity did not mute Zebulon Moore. As Elizabeth lay on the table, even as he crashed through the room, he talked to his wife about their courtship, her mother—"that white-quilled porcupine" was just one of the epithets he used—but mostly about the heyday of the way station. Zebulon was mourning two deaths: a life and a life together. Quinn was also concerned for a third life, if Zebulon's doleful moments were any indication.

"What am I gonna do without you?" the old man asked. "You did everything here, everything that mattered, all that people needed including me. Especially me. Hell, my bonny one, I'm just an old buffalo hunter."

Quinn did not intrude. But he had quietly taken the

guns and put them outside, behind the well. He must have seen men do impulsive, stupid things in his life.

It was the deepest black of night when the bodies were finally interred. Mrs. Moore had been wrapped in a bedsheet with the cushion of the broken chair beneath her head; Stevens had been placed in his grave without a shroud or a ceremony. Quinn had kicked dirt over the man's trail of blood to keep from attracting flies.

Zebulon used some of the broken chair to form a cross, marking the final resting place of Elizabeth Hopkins Moore.

"It's fitting, see," Zebulon said, weeping as he used a vine to fix the crosspiece and addressing Quinn directly for the first time since her death. "This was her favorite chair. She let guests sit in it, though she always took away the cushion her considerate head now rests on. It was the only selfish thing she ever in her life did."

"I don't think that's selfish."

"Me neither, but she did. It was a gift from her sister, who died as a pretty young girl. But it was my wife's only keepsake."

Quinn seemed to recall that words were spoken over graves, though he could not remember any. Zebulon did not seem of a mind to borrow phrases—or to linger. Once the cross was placed, the dog came out and lay there, and Zebulon walked toward the back door.

"I know how to make coffee and eggs," he said. "You want some?"

"Sure, but—"

"And there's blood." Zebulon stopped in the doorway and looked at the spots where his wife and Stevens had lain. "What did she used to do . . . ? Soak it in hot water, I think. I'll heat the water, pour it on, and then we'll eat." He sniffed. "Not much I can do about the smell of gunpowder. Winds will chase that out once the sun stirs them."

Quinn followed the man inside. Behind him, Zebulon trailed clouds of grief that Quinn could actually feel—empty, without joy or life or sound.

"Zebulon, let me take care of the stains," Quinn said.

The man stopped hard and turned. "Nobody touches where my wife"—he choked a little on the word—"where my wife fell. You take the other."

Quinn nodded and collected the two basins while Zebulon stirred the fireplace embers to life with a poker. He put the torches and the rest of the chair in, then fetched water from a cistern out back. While that boiled in a hearth kettle, he looked for the coffeepot. It was on a shelf, clean, the ground beans in a tin beside it. Only when he got there, with his back to the room—and to Quinn—did Zebulon Moore begin to sob as he had not to this point, his shoulders heaving so hard that he was forced to brace himself against the wall. The dog heard, came to the doorway, and flopped down there to be near both his masters.

Quinn went out front. The moon was behind the house and threw the shadow of the station across the fence. Beyond, to the south, was darkness. An owl hooted from somewhere in that blackness, the only creature he heard.

Standing there, Quinn could think of nothing to say or do that would help the other man. Especially not when he had been the cause of all this. If Quinn had chosen to go somewhere else, the woman would have still been alive—

"Where else could I have gone?" Quinn asked himself. It was a real question, without self-reproach.

It was expected, even *intended* that he be here, or his belongings would not have been left in the barn. And then maybe everything would have happened just as it had. Those men might have found the satchel when they went to get their horses in the morning. They might well have done who knew what to Zebulon and his wife to learn more about the man who had left it.

A man did not avoid his fate. That notion was in his head. He must have believed it.

The matter of William Beaudine was something Quinn had not gotten to broach with Zebulon—who the man was, what he had said. There was a strangeness about this man who had left him in the desert, then brought his belongings here.

"Why didn't he leave them with the Smiths?" Quinn wondered. Their home was on the way.

*The horse,* he decided. The Smiths had nowhere to keep one. It would have drawn trouble.

He would press the man later. Right now Zebulon needed to mourn. And Quinn had not decided what he was going to do next. Pursue those men, of course. But to where? To what end? Had Beaudine planned for those two to be caught between them, north and south?

*Did he* tell *me that was the plan?*

That might have worked if the enemies had followed recklessly into the dark, but they had not. They had waited until it was light. Clearly, they did not know this country the way Beaudine did.

The sky was still slate black but there was a sense that dawn was nigh. Bugs were headed home like ghosts to their graves. Night birds were falling silent as morning birds began their songs. The chickens were waking in their coop, gossiping in the way that poultry did.

*How is it that I remember all of that?* Quinn wondered. What things were chosen to survive a knock on the head and which ones got clubbed away?

Tired, dirty, and thirsty, he went to the cistern, filled a ladle, and used it to wash his hands of the dried blood that had once flowed through the veins of Private Paul Stevens.

"I made that fatal cut with some competence," he told himself as he thought back to the struggle. It was not a point of pride, cutting a man's throat. But it was also not something you did for the first time and felt it had no more significance than kicking a bad dog. Without question he had killed men before, most likely with that very knife.

That silent killing skill was likely why he was on a "mission." And yet, if the returned memory was correct, he had been told *not* to kill those men.

Quinn washed his face and thought back to the confrontation with Voight and Stevens. He dried his eyes with his sleeve, closed his eyes to enjoy the last cool sensation he was likely to feel for many hours. As he looked at the dark behind his eyelids, he turned inward, seeking details from his brain. He tried to visualize the face he had seen before. He tried to see and feel himself sitting on the back of—

*Snowcap.* That was the name of his blond stallion. *Keep going,* he thought.

"Snowcap," he said. "Whoa, Snowcap. Giddyap, Snowcap."

He said the words softly several times. He visualized the mane before him. The plains he had ridden today.

But it was all a creation, not memory. He recalled nothing. He opened his eyes, and they wandered, landing on the barn. He thought about the satchel, put his hand on his sheath.

Still, nothing came.

Quinn refilled the ladle, poured water over his injury, then filled it again, and drank slowly while he watched the sun begin to rise. And not just the sun glowed brilliantly: All the plain with its patches of trees, cacti, and scrub brightened from far to near, the rounded glow throwing light on the birds that had already taken flight. How could the same God who made all that make men like Martins?

Quinn turned when he heard shuffling footsteps behind him.

"Mr. Quinn? I want to go with you."

Zebulon Moore's voice was raw and quiet. His face was without life or luster. His head was bent forward, looking like it weighed a good ten pounds.

"Don't you have work here?"

"More important work lies out there," he said, pointing with his forehead. "Anyone comes, they can help themselves. I can't sit around here. Food's on the table. I only cleaned the blood from there. The rest of it can wait."

"Been a long night," Quinn said. "Let's get you sitting down, at least."

Quinn started toward the door. Zebulon grabbed his arm.

"I can help you. I *want* to help you. I used to hunt buffalo—a long time ago, but some skills don't leave you."

"No, they don't."

"I can hunt men if I have to."

"Zebulon, I appreciate your sentiments, but I'm not sure where my own search is going to take me. This may be bigger than those two."

The sun threw first light on the cowhide crags of Zebulon's face, the creases on his cheek still damp.

"Let me say this a different way," Zebulon said. "I'm going to put my dog in the barn, and also the chickens, and let them figure things out. I already packed some provisions, and I got my rifle and two six-shooters. Once we eat, I'm off after those two assassins, who I will see join John Wilkes Booth in hell. You can join me or not."

Quinn did not have to think about the proposal. Even if he were inclined to go on his own, it would not do to have both men bumping into each other as they pursued the same target.

Quinn extended his hand, which Zebulon enfolded in both of his own. The proprietor turned then, his eyes catching the light of the early sun as it fell on his wife's resting place.

"I was married to that girl for over forty years, Mr. Quinn. Except when I was hunting, we have never been apart."

"I expect she will always be at your side, Zebulon. I can't imagine that God would make any other kind of arrangement."

"No," Zebulon agreed. "If I was God, that's how I would set things up. With all the misfortunes that are the devil's doing, it *has* to be the plan. The reward for good and honest behavior."

Quinn gave the man a tight-lipped smile, and they walked inside to where the smells of the night had been replaced by the coffee, eggs, and warmed biscuits that sat on the table.

L IEUTENANT MARTINS AND Colonel Voight had ridden northwest without cease, trying to put as much distance as possible between themselves and Quinn before dawn. Martins had decided not to make a stand because, with two against two, in the dark, with himself weakened, dumb luck was as valuable as experience. As much as he wanted Quinn's blood, catching Beaudine was more important than stopping the knife fighter or Zebulon Moore.

It was also more important than mourning their lost member. They had not even collected Stevens' remains to give it a frontier burial. What the men had taken was his horse in case they needed a replacement. Out here that was always a possibility. It seemed to both men as though the moonlight would shine on the man or his spirit in that familiar saddle.

The men moved assertively though not recklessly through the dark. Martins felt well enough to ride, but the terrain was awkward and uneven in the dark. He had actually regained consciousness about the time of Quinn's arrival but felt it prudent to feign insensibility. That had been a common tactic during the War. Officers walking through medical tents tended to be taciturn. But once they got outside, they talked openly.

And it was outside that many casualties had been collected after great engagements, there being too many to keep under canvas. Lieutenant Martins had been taken prisoner with a leg wound inflicted by a charge into a Union picket at the siege of Petersburg. He was found by Southern troops and, in an overcrowded outdoor infirmary, heard their plans for retreat. Had he been mobile, he would have snuck away and communicated what he had learned to General Grant.

Lieutenant Martins did not feel in any way pleased about what had happened to Mrs. Moore. He was reminded of that every waking moment because of the expert nursing she had given to his head wound. He had not intended to kill her, only to stab her thigh and get the gun. But he could not see her well the way he had been spread on the table. He had lunged too high. Regrettably, the mission had to take priority. If they failed, other wives would die; others would mourn— the wives of Captain Dupré's men among them.

*Beside*s, he thought, *we paid for her life with the death of our own man*. Martins did not believe in heavenly scales, though they always seemed to balance in the end.

It was not until sunrise that the men were sure Quinn had not immediately pursued them. There was no sign of activity on the southeastern horizon. Martins was looking at maps in his head and considering options.

"You holding up okay, Lieutenant?" Voight asked. "You seem kinda distant."

"Physically? Yeah. I was just thinking about Stevens and Sergeant Pendleton. I think the sergeant would've been amused that a woman was wearing his uniform."

"Way he liked women? No doubt."

The late Nathan Pendleton had been with a woman shortly before he died, ambushed by the Mexicans whose sister it was. He should have known better, and his companions had no regrets. He died fighting, something he loved almost as much as what put him in the fight.

Martins looked at the other man. "How about you? You need to rest?"

Voight shook his head. "Even if I did, we have to make up time we lost in Oak Ridge. First we've got to find water for the horses, though."

The colonel took a map from the inside pocket of his jacket and studied it. Now that the sun was up, they could quicken the pace—as soon as they decided where they were going.

"What's it look like?" Martins asked.

"We got a small lake northwest or a river running to the northeast. The river's nearer—about two miles from here. But it's the wrong direction if we're making for San Francisco."

Martins was silent for a long moment, and he stared ahead. Voight looked over at him.

"Lieutenant?"

"We're not," Martins said.

"We're not what?"

"Going to the coast. At least, not directly."

Voight seemed confused. "Where are we going, then?"

"Truckee. It's closer and quicker."

"Truckee?" There was a heavy sound of consideration in the word.

"The train station. A chance."

Voight regarded the map and then the lieutenant.

"The captain would have expected a change of plans to be left at the way station, if such was our intent."

"We're not changing our plans, only our point and method of entrée," Martins said. He faced Voight. "The only way the original plan can succeed is with the letters. Beaudine has them now, along with the rest of what's rightly ours."

Martins was pleased he'd had the foresight to remove a gold coin and put it in his shoulder holster, under the Colt Lightning revolver, in case it was needed. He had, in fact, been melting it to a large nugget to disguise its origin when Beaudine and his partner had struck. The lieutenant was also pleased, and surprised, that the man who had clubbed him had not taken it.

"He may have destroyed the papers, for all we know. And hidden the gold," Voight said.

"Not a Pinkerton man," Martins said. "He'll give it all back. Besides, you know who this will expose. He'll want that evidence."

Voight was pensive. "That's even more reason to stop him, I think."

"Our chances of catching him out here, with the head start he has, make that unlikely," Martins replied. He was still mulling options, thinking aloud. "Zebulon said he has at least twelve, thirteen hours on us, and in territory he knows."

"We rested. Maybe he hasn't."

"I can't stake the mission on Beaudine being tired, which is why I'm thinking that pursuing him is not the best course of action. Put yourself in the position of Beaudine and Quinn. They may well have already hightailed it to what they think is the target in San Francisco.

Especially Quinn. That was a damn fine horse he had. Shoulda taken it. Or shot it."

"He said he didn't remember anything," Voight said. "He sounded convincing. You don't believe that?"

"Not if he's Pinkerton, too. That may be his speciality, playing stupid."

Voight was still processing all that had been said. "If it is, we got more trouble. He saw us at the campsite, saw you at that cabin. They'll be watching for an attempt on *el presidente* after Ensenada, especially if Quinn gets there and can describe us."

Martins nodded, half smiling. "I wasn't just lying on that table back there, thinking nothing. How's President Grant getting to San Francisco?"

"Train to San Francisco," Voight said. "It's been in the papers—big transcontinental landmark."

"Right. It goes through Truckee."

"What're you thinking—we derail it, kill Grant, and leave Juárez to the French, like we planned?"

"Nothing that dramatic. There's a town on the map—what is it?"

"Apple Town."

"We need a new wardrobe," Martins said. "Not sure the president's men will let a bunch of ex-Confederates near the train, in uniform."

"The president's men? Lieutenant, without the letters—"

"They're going to help us, Colonel." Martins regarded the other man. "We get the clothes, then meet the train in Truckee and tell the president's men about the plot against Juárez—"

"How are we even supposed to know about that?"

"We were doing business in Mexico City—you had a peach plantation once. We'll say we are growers *helping* the government. We'll say that we met the column in the desert, recognized the men as French soldiers."

Voight brightened. "I see what you're thinking. We take the train to the ship, and instead of pointing the French out, we let them on board."

Martins nodded. "The only change in the plan is that Maria won't be the one on the inside, killing Grant. We will be 'her.'"

"What about our pay? Beaudine has that."

"He'll be in San Francisco for sure. It'll still be on him when we kill him."

Smiling as though he'd just had a long shower, Voight looked at the map. "Then it's the Scouse River and on through Apple Town to Truckee."

Martins nodded. "Afterward, while two nations are in chaos and soldiers can be landed in Mexico—somewhere along the way, I kill Jason Quinn."

Voight replaced the map and passed jerky to his companion. As they ate, and with renewed enthusiasm, the men urged the three sluggish horses on in the rising heat of the new day.

# CHAPTER FIFTEEN

THE TOWN MAP looked like the letter "R" in Morse code: dot-dash-dot.

Apple Town had not been much of a place before the train came through the territory. William Beaudine felt it was not much of a place even after. It had been established before the Civil War for one bad reason only: as a place to go for men who did not want to serve in the Union or Confederate armies. Those in Truckee and other towns openly called it "Cowards' Roost," but the occupants did not pay much attention. They proudly called themselves the first settlers of a new movement, the Free States of America. All their attention went to growing apples to raise money so they could trade with but be independent of Washington and San Francisco. A town of sorts grew around the orchards. Mexicans and freed slaves stumbled onto the place and stayed as well, though in sections slightly separate from the main street.

That was how Apple Town got its odd shape. Almost at once there was a movement afoot among the two hundred residents to call it the more distinguished Morse Junction, to call attention to the telegraphy that had finally and truly linked California to the nation.

That topic was still being debated, always the first item on the agenda at town hall meetings.

Two years before, the Central Pacific Railroad had decided to bypass Apple Town because of its hermit-minded citizens, who still wanted to be the hub of the Free States of America. So the railroad put their stop in Truckee, where they were happy to take on shipments of apples from Apple Town to be delivered to the more contented inhabitants of the rest of California. That changed when the rail yards suffered a massive fire early the previous year. The railroad moved a few locomotives to a shed in Apple Town, and the settlement finally had a main street that was more than a "dash" with a few shops.

It was still called Cowards' Roost, especially by veterans of the wars.

William Beaudine had no use for men who ran from fights, except among one another. There was enough of that in Washington, and the West needed men. But if the men were bickering farmers, there was one thing that was true here as throughout his West Coast travels: Beaudine had been impressed by the industry of the women the peevish deserters and objectors had brought with them or married out here.

Aggie was impressive, though her story was her own. Born in El Paso, Augustina-Rose Sanchez had

never had it easy. Her father had been a Mexican jour-
nalist who had fled Santa Anna and stayed. Mrs. Sanchez had worked as a seamstress while her husband
had taught English to others who crossed the border.
Both had died of cholera when Aggie was fifteen, and
she fell in with a gambler who introduced her to a life
on the stage—first as a dancer, then as an actress. She
had left the stage because she had stabbed her leading
man in the side with a prop letter opener during a per-
formance of *The Death of Ivan the Terrible*, in which
the hand of the tsar was not quite as late as the rest of
him. The actor had declined to file charges, fearing a
trial would have sullied his growing international
name and reputation. That had happened in Denver
two years earlier. Beaudine had read of the incident
and sought her out. By then, Aggie was living in a Denver attic, trying to write plays to earn money as a play-
wright or actress.

"How would you like to act again?" Beaudine had
asked her over dinner. She had dressed for the event in
her Russian ball gown, the only fine clothes she owned.

The twenty-four-year-old with hair the color and
sheen of a raven's feathers was immediately interested.

He told her that the Pinkerton National Detective
Agency was always looking for women to work for
them in a variety of capacities in the field.

"Would that mean what I think it does?" she had
asked with a strange mix of suspicion and resignation.

"I won't say it might not come up," Beaudine had
answered honestly. "But mostly what I need is a spy.
Someone who can work as a maid or a waitress and
watch people, listen to what they say. The railroad is
opening up a lot of opportunity for anarchists and car-

petbaggers, and the federal government wants them stopped."

He had said that Pinkerton would move her west and subsidize her writing while she remained available for whatever jobs came up.

Aggie had agreed almost instantly. The two things that had appealed to her about acting were pretending to be other people and the ever-present chance that something might go wrong onstage, testing her resources and wits. The work Beaudine had described fit those criteria—and also solved her current financial plight.

The personal relationship that developed between her and Beaudine was secondary. It was convenient. Until Jason Quinn got involved with the Pinkertons a year later. The knife fighter had been reluctant at first. He had fought a war for the Union and hunted Indians for pay in the Montana Territory, and like a gambler who wanted to leave the table with his winnings, Quinn had his eye on San Francisco. He was nearly ready to make that move when Beaudine had sought him out. Under contract from the government, Pinkerton needed a man who could throw a knife to silently kill Indians who cut telegraph wires at night.

"The braves will think it's evil spirits, not a white man, because white men use guns," Beaudine had told him.

Quinn had come for the money and the challenge. He had stayed for Aggie. The man suspected that she and Beaudine were closer than they let on. He knew those looks, those private half smiles, the things they did not say or have to say. Quinn also knew that he himself was infatuated with the actress. It was she, in fact, who had convinced him to go on this mission with Beaudine. She had just returned from a month in Mexico, where she had lived at the presidential palace in Mexico City, working as a maid, watching and listening to confirm rumors of a plot. And being humbled in the process: She had spent more of Pinkerton's gold in the palace than she had expected. To most of the men she approached, it was more desirable than she was.

She was the one who had first heard about a potential attempt on the leader's life during the upcoming trip. The intelligence came from a spy, a palace secretary whose acquaintance she had made—a man who was in the employ of the French and subsequently arrested.

The city was a den of weasels ready to kill more than they could eat, she had told Beaudine. The assignment needed someone with Beaudine's single-mindedness and tactical skills and Quinn's tracking ability and his skill for silent attacks.

That was when Quinn got pig footed and made things messy. Realizing he might be gone for a month or more, he professed his affection, and she used her charm to convince him to go, to make her proud.

Quinn only learned about Beaudine and Aggie's relationship before he and Beaudine set out. He had seen them kissing when he was supposed to be getting his horse; he had sent a boy for his horse so that *he* could kiss Aggie goodbye.

Quinn did not know whether he or Beaudine was being used by the woman, but he did not like it in any case. He had said a hostile goodbye to Aggie. He had not spoken much with Beaudine during the hard ride to Ensenada or later on the hazardous chase that the Rebs led into the Nevada desert. It was not until that final showdown after the theft of the box—

*No,* Beaudine thought as he rode into Apple Town.

*You can't doubt what's done.* Whatever guilt he felt or
hurt he had caused was booted away like a crowd of
tumbleweeds. The mission mattered more. He had to
be clearheaded, and he needed Aggie. That meant
convincing her that he had done the necessary thing if
not the right thing.

Beaudine rode up to the small quadrangle block and
hitched his horse beside Aggie's roan. She made a point
of getting it from the stable every morning and going
riding at least once a day if it wasn't raining, which it
usually wasn't here. It was a reason to keep the animal
near and saddled, in case she needed it for work—or a
getaway. In this business, people made strong lifelong
enemies.

While his horse drank, Beaudine took his rifle and
the lockbox and walked up to the small cottage at the
eastern end of Main Street. He saw the familiar writing
desk in the window where it got the morning sun. The
locomotive shed had gone up a quarter mile farther,
and the street had been continued to there—with not
much on it. It was an eyesore, and Aggie kept threaten-
ing to move. But she was accustomed to the people and
more important the sounds. If something was off, if
people or animals were suddenly quiet, she would hear
it before she saw it.

That would serve him, too, especially now.

Aggie knew Beaudine was coming a full minute before he arrived. She hurried to the door, smiling from
her clear forehead to her chin, the morning sun striking her full as she stood there. Beaudine remembered
how and why he had responded to her the way he had.
She was confident but feminine, careful but unafraid,
and above all beautiful.

Her joy drained away quickly, replaced by a look of concern. It was so unguarded that Beaudine could see it when he was still a few strides distant.

"You look like you've been to another four-year war," she said.

"Feels like it," he said as he rode up, catching a glimpse of his worn, filthy self in the window ahead. "I could use some breakfast and coffee."

"Of course."

Aggie did not suggest that he get himself to Anna's Table down the street. She knew the man and saw that he was both tired and in a hurry. She also did not ask about the box he carried under his arm. He would tell her about it—if at all—in his own time.

The woman, fresh as a morning flower, went back inside, and Beaudine followed quickly. The coffee smelled strong and familiar, and she was busy setting out bread and the raspberry jam he liked. The scent of her was delicate in the air; he felt vulgar as he stomped his boots clean enough and entered. As he removed his hat and placed the lockbox on the table, he saw the papers stacked on the writing desk. As much as he disliked taking her from that work, there was more urgent business. And her quiet expression and following eyes told him she knew it.

"How—and where—is Quinn?" she asked.

"I'm going to need you with me," he said as he walked past her toward the small kitchen table.

"Where is he, Bill?"

Beaudine fell into a chair and looked at her across the small kitchen. "I had to leave him in the desert."

"'Leave him'?"

"He had his own ideas about how things should be

done. I had no options, Aggie. I hit him hard. He was breathing when I left. By rights I should've killed him."

"By what right? And what—," she began, stopped, calmed her rising anger. "What did you leave him *with*?"

"Nothing except his underclothes. I brought everything else to the way station at Oak Ridge, left it there."

Aggie knew how this business worked, and she knew that Quinn tended to be a loner and a firebrand. She also knew that Beaudine would never have sacrificed a member of his party unless time and events made it necessary. But she still could not believe he had done this to an ally.

The woman went about setting the table in silence, and the man offered no other details or narrative.

"You said you need me," Aggie said.

"Yeah. I do."

"All right. First I want to know what Quinn did. I wouldn't want to make the same mistake." She went to the iron stove. She did not want to look at Beaudine just then.

"He wanted to kill the men we'd been tracking. I told him that I needed them alive. The rest only myself, Pinkerton, and the president and his men knew."

"The assassins we foiled," she said. "Why didn't you kill them?"

It was not a question the way Aggie said it, but a challenge. She was asking if he trusted her.

He did not answer. He wasn't testing her loyalty, wasn't seeing whether she would trust him enough to go without knowing. He was protecting the mission.

Aggie brought over the warmed coffee, poured it. She was waiting for him to go on. He knew her actor's ways, how she drew other folks out with silence. Beaudine knew, of course, that whatever he said or did she would do what was needed. She would show him more trust than he was able—or willing—to show her. That was the difference in their relationship. She loved him more than the work. He . . . was not sure.

"Let's start with something simple," Aggie said. "Did you find out whether they intended to assassinate or merely kidnap President Juárez?"

"It's bigger than that. It always was."

Aggie was not surprised. "Tell me what you can, Bill. When you want to stop, stop."

"We were going to tail the Rebels. That's all. But then the Mexican marines in Ensenada sent them running."

"How? *Why?*"

"Some officer wanted to make a name for himself, tried to arrest them. Our contact, *Contraalmirante* Esteban Allende—I believe you met him."

She nodded.

"He told them they were only to watch the ship. They didn't even do that well. The Rebels got away—with the letter."

Aggie froze. "How did they get it?"

"Bribes to trusted dockhands," Beaudine said, spreading jam on the toast Aggie set before him. "That's how everything works there—you know that."

*The letter,* Aggie thought. It was a sentiment of gratitude from First Lady Margarita Maza de Juárez to President Grant, and it had gone ahead with her luggage. In itself, the article was nothing. But the official seal of the president on the back would get someone up the gangway for an audience with an officer on the ship. Once there, a fire, someone falling overboard, a stabbing—there were any number of ways to create a distraction to allow a separate plan to unfold unhindered.

"So the Confederates fled. Assassins should be made of sterner stuff." Aggie sat, refilled Beaudine's cup, and poured coffee for herself.

"That's not the end," Beaudine said. He took another bite, then sipped the hot coffee. "A rider arrived from the palace and informed me there was a second letter in the box, added before the baggage departed. Margarita felt that a woman should be the one to present it, a woman with ties to the government but who would not be a prize to assassins. That ruled out her daughter Felícitas. The bearer was to be Maria Allende, the daughter of *Contraalmirante* Esteban Allende. She was already in Ensenada."

"How do you know about that?"

"Love," he answered bluntly.

Aggie's expression changed from attentive to disapproving.

"Not mine," he assured her. "Felícitas Juárez was sweet on a man named Raoul Dupré. You mentioned him in a report."

"An agitator. The Mexicans say he is the head of a group of bandits in Zamora, but the French don't exactly wear the tricolors, and they pay the locals for anonymity. That would make sense, trying to woo a member of the presidential family."

"It backfired," Beaudine said. "Felícitas learned through a servant that he had been Maria Allende's lover since the days of Maximilian. Still was. Still *is*. Felícitas wanted to hurt them both and sent the information with the rider, that Allende's daughter was consorting with a French anarchist."

"Why to you? Why not to Maria's father?"

"And distract the man protecting her own father's life? Felícitas felt like she had been kicked by a mule, but not in the head. In her letter, she said her father had mentioned that the Pinkertons watching for assassins in Ensenada had his absolute trust."

Aggie shook her head sadly. "A traitor to Mexico and to her father. It's abhorrent."

"Well, a woman in love . . . ," Beaudine said. Realizing again that was its own swamp, he let his voice trail off. He finished one piece of toast and started on another. "What you did not know about the mission, and what Quinn was not told, was that the men who ran from Ensenada—who are still out there and may be after me—were only part of what we were after. Washington thinks the enemy may have *two* presidents in their sights. Maria was not with the Rebels at their camp. We think she must have gone to Dupré to tell him about the letters, that the Confederates might have to shift tactics. I'm guessing they each had a target president."

"You mentioned the Rebels may be chasing you. Why would Maria need the letter? Her father will be there. Her father's men would *know* her. She could admit the killers without being implicated, remain a source on the inside."

"Because Maria will still be compromised." Beaudine finally nodded at the lockbox. "That also contains the pay for the graybacks. Treasury gold."

"What has that to do with her?"

"Pay for the navy is kept in Mexicali. The letter of introduction, signed by the first lady, would have given Maria access to that as well. A paymaster, thinking she was on her father's business, would not have contested the withdrawal."

"She would have had to sign a voucher—"

"She did. It's in the box."

Aggie did not have to hear more. Maria must have slipped it away under his bedazzled eyes, or when he was asking to be personally remembered to the *contraalmirante*. For young women of a certain temperament and manner, this was a perfect and rewarding livelihood.

Aggie digested that while Beaudine digested his breakfast.

"I'm impressed that President Grant is letting himself be used as bait," she said.

"The man was a soldier before he was a politician," Beaudine said admiringly.

"What's your move?" she asked.

"San Francisco. Juárez should be safe until then."

"Will Quinn go there?"

He answered with reluctance, but honestly. "I don't know. Depends if the Rebels found him."

Aggie was absently stirring sugar into her coffee. Though she was accustomed to Beaudine's callous manner when it came to the job, she felt bad for Quinn. But as she herself had learned, in this business you were rarely told everything, and you followed orders just the same.

Beaudine looked at her as he finished his coffee. "I need eyes to replace Quinn. Will you be them?"

"Always. What are your immediate plans?"

"I haven't quite figured them out. I sent the rider back to the palace, suggested the Juárez coach travel alone and heavily guarded—the fewer people knowing its destination, the better."

"By land all the way to San Francisco?" Aggie asked.

"That was one plan, the other being by sea from San Diego. We were not told which, only that they would end up in San Francisco. They'd have been safer and more comfortable at sea, but the president's advisers seemed to feel it would be better to divide the enemy." He rubbed his face. "I figure that's four days' ride for them, with two of those days gone. A day's travel ahead for me—so I have time to rest here, rest the horse. We've been going without a stop since Ensenada."

"I'll get the horse to the stable."

"Thanks, Aggie."

"When do you want to leave?"

He rubbed his face with a palm. "Let me think."

"Well, you've eaten," she coaxed. "Maybe a wash?"

The woman's tone was playful, but for Beaudine on a mission, every act was judged with an administrative eye, a practical checklist from start to end.

"Yeah, that's overdue. Didn't have time to stop at the Scouse River. I'll do that, then take a bit of a rest if you don't mind."

"Of course I don't mind." Aggie had started toward the bedroom. "I'll turn down the—"

"The couch will be fine. Or the rug. I sorely need to lie down and close my eyes." He turned toward the window. "There's also the graybacks. I don't know if they're coming. I want to be able to hear anyone who approaches."

The woman's smile was more disappointed than before, but Aggie acknowledged his request with a nod and went to get a pillow and a sheet.

Beaudine thanked her, then went outside and around the side of the house with its garden and rosebushes.

There was a well out back, shared by the general store behind, a small church to the north, and a second cottage to the south, where the smell of apple pies was ever present. Those, too, went to Truckee for export. The owner, Frau Mack, was making quite a reputation throughout the region. She gave Beaudine a hearty wave from the open window of her kitchen. He took a moment to inhale, to clean his nose of the prairie.

The bucket was empty, and Beaudine hooked it on a line and cranked it down. He washed his face, went back inside, and happily removed his boots.

Aggie was clearing the table. "You want to be wakened?"

"Only if I sleep till this time tomorrow, which is possible," he said.

She walked over to him. "I didn't mean to judge you, Bill. I know that this job has big implications."

"Aggie, this has been tougher than anything I've done. It's not just missing Confederate gold or someone sabotaging the railroad because they're invested in the stage line. There are Pinkerton's expectations, which I will not fail to meet, but also what is actually at stake for two nations."

"Now that you say it—I regret more my tone. I also know that Quinn was probably hard on you."

Beaudine shook his head ruefully. "I wanted him to stand down. Son of a bitch would not. You hire a man for his qualities until you bump up against them."

Facing him from two feet away and one head smaller, she smiled up. "Put the burdens of the world and the road to rest for now. I'll draw the shades, take care of the horse, and make sure I am quiet as a cat."

"Except for the scratch of your pen," he said. "I like hearing that. Reminds me how clever my girl is."

Aggie put a hand on his chest, then turned toward the front door. Beaudine reached out and embraced her. The woman smelled as good as she felt. He did not end up sleeping on the couch.

# CHAPTER SIXTEEN

Douglas smith had been perched comfortably on the fattest lower limb of the tree for over a half hour. His mother was silent, save for twice whispering his name and contenting herself with the breathy response, "I'm fine." An Indian had once shown him how to make a sound like a whip-poor-will, but that was for signaling at a greater distance.

While he was up there, the boy briefly enjoyed the freedom that came from being invisible, like a mouse in its hole. He always thought that little creatures must be afraid all the time, but maybe that was not the case. He would get to know them better when they were home; there was no time to consider the matter now.

Douglas occupied himself by remembering back to every word Hank had said before he left, about all the things he could do with a sharp stick. He remembered that better than any of his lessons: *Flick. Stab. Dig. Cut a trench. Point. Write in the dirt.*

Using the stick like a knife, the boy did not have the gumption to think he could do more than scratch a single soldier, let alone a dozen of them. That would not stop the French officer from making good his ugly promise to cut off the boy's ear. Douglas had heard Dupré yell about that before they dragged his poor ma.

Hearing that voice again in his head was scary, coming from the mouth of the man who had let Sheriff Russell be shot to death. When he thought about it, Douglas's belly felt the way it had when that wild dog came to drink and snarled while he was bathing in the pond. Either you got a rock from the pond bottom or waited for your ma to shoot . . . or you talked calm and made friends, the way he had once seen his pa do with a bucking horse. That was what Douglas had done, and the dog had left without trying to bite him.

The jumble of thoughts somehow suggested something Douglas could do with the stick to help him and his mother. Something that— What were the words that man Martins had said to Hank? *Buy time.*

That was what Douglas needed to do now.

"I'm coming down," he said some time after last speaking to his mother.

"To do *what*?"

"To make friends with the captain."

The woman's horror temporarily froze her throat, and Douglas was already on the way down before she found her voice.

"You can't!" she wheezed. *"Douglas—"*

The boy hopped down nearly his full height from the lowest branch. He was facing the encampment.

"Mr. Captain!" he yelled, but then his voice cracked.

Douglas said nothing more, uncertain whether anything would come out. The boy from the fringes of the desert was not accustomed to a human hive, and the camp was immediately astir, no one more alert than Captain Dupré, who had not yet gone to bed but was studying a map by torchlight. The officer stood silhouetted against a torch, the paper dangling, its shadow twisting across the few horses and men, most of whom were still out looking for the boy.

"Mrs. Smith?" Dupré yelled.

She struggled to straighten herself. "Yes?"

"Is that your boy? Is he with you?"

"He is."

"I have something to show you!" Douglas yelled.

The captain drew his revolver and fired in the air before Jane could find the voice to scream in fear. She jumped against her bonds, then sunk back into them as the officer strode around the perimeter, folding the paper as he approached. Beyond the camp, on all sides, the pounding of hooves and the shouts of men could be heard as the searchers hurried back.

The officer stopped beside the mother and son, his dark features turned down at the boy. The young man stood with his legs slightly apart and bent at the knees. There was a sharp stick in his hand pointed toward the ground.

The captain noticed the boy's stance and looked up. "You were there."

"Yes, sir."

The dark face turned back down. "Why?"

"I was trying to see Hank."

Dupré stalked closer. "Why would he be here?"

"Do you remember, sir, when I asked to stop? Back when my ma changed horses?"

"Well?"

The boy raised the stick slowly. "That was because I saw this."

Captain Dupré looked at it. "A sharpened stick. Why did you want it?"

"I think it's from Hank, sir. He told me back at the house that if I ever wanted to find him, I should look for the pointers. I saw this, and it was pointing to the river."

"Was it?"

Douglas nodded.

His mother struggled to get free of her bonds. "Son, I don't think you should say any more." It was not for fear of him giving away secrets but of getting himself in trouble because he did not possess any.

The boy looked at her, then back at the captain. "Will you let her go, sir? Her hands are bleeding, and she is in pain."

The Frenchman regarded the woman. "I never argue when I am at a disadvantage," he said, looking at the stick. The officer turned and spoke to one of the men standing several feet away. The man pulled a knife from a sheath he wore on his cloth sash belt. He supported the woman with one arm while he cut her free with the other. She tried to stand but slumped into the man's elbow.

"*Ses mains?*" he asked the captain.

Dupré nodded once.

The man reached behind her and cut the leather strap. At once she tried to raise her hands to his shoulders for support; he stepped back from her bloody fingers, still supporting her at arm's length.

Douglas stuck the stick in his trousers and moved to help as the man set her on the ground, against the fat tree trunk. She eased down, her breath coming freely now that she was free of the rope.

"You want water?" Douglas asked as he supported her elbows. Her blood ran back onto his fingers.

"Later," she said. "I'm all right now."

Douglas wiped his hands on his trousers and turned back to the captain, whose eyes had not left the boy.

"Would you be lying to help her, boy?" Dupré asked.

"I'd do anything for my ma, but right now I'm telling the truth."

The captain extended a hand. It took a moment for Douglas to realize that he wanted the stick. Reluctantly, the boy passed it over. Dupré turned partway so there was torchlight on the stick. It had been rubbed to a point, from the stubble, most likely on a rock. It was possible that Hank had picked up both and worked on them clandestinely.

"Hank left this behind—for you? Why would he think that you would follow?"

"Not us. It was for Mr. Russell," Jane said quickly. "We told him the sheriff was coming."

"Then it's a good thing for us he is not," the captain said coldly. "Hank put this on the ground to indicate that he was going along the river. In which direction?"

"North, sir," Douglas said.

"To—?"

Douglas shrugged. "I have to guess Apple Town, sir. That's the only thing up there."

"Then why would he go?"

"I don't know, sir."

Maria had arrived and was standing beside the captain. While Dupré considered the testimony, she took him aside.

"There may be some truth in what the boy says," she told him softly in Spanish. "Before we separated, Martins and the others agreed to rendezvous at Oak Ridge. It was felt that coming from Mexico City, Juárez might choose a land route to San Francisco and avoid the sea altogether."

"I considered that, too," the captain said, "though they would be exposed on land, without the sea to protect them."

"We can anticipate that possibility without losing the ability of striking in San Francisco. Oak Ridge and the land route are northeast of here, same general direction as Apple Town."

"I know. I studied the map. They are both a half day from here. If we divert, we may not reach San Francisco before *el presidente*."

"Then maybe we have to change *our* plan. Perhaps we should go south, try and intercept him—taking care that my father comes to no harm."

"In that wilderness?" The captain shook his head. "Because of Ensenada, they are warned. They will avoid known routes. They will not travel in a caravan but in a single well-armed coach. We may miss him. No," the captain went on, "we must reach San Francisco in time to reconnoiter and carry out the execution. Once the Americans arrive, the forces will be formidable, success unlikely."

"Both have their risks."

"I will take the one that places us in proximity to Juárez. He is *my* target. What will *your* unit do if they cannot recover the box?"

"They will leave time to make the rendezvous, as planned. Lieutenant Martins is resourceful. He will come up with an alternate plan."

"Then there is no doubt he will achieve his target? You are sure?"

"Certain. I have spent enough time with them to know what kind of men he and his companions are. They will succeed even if it costs each one his life."

"That is the kind of risk I support," the captain said. "I will plan accordingly."

Faith was good, but plans were better. He would come up with something that still achieved every objective.

Dupré turned back to Douglas. "I do not know if you are telling the truth, but we will find out presently. Until then, I will not take action. If this hero of yours is looking for you, he may yet try to help you. And Hank, as you know, is all we ever wanted from both of you."

"May I have my stick back?" Douglas asked. "It's special."

The captain thought for a moment, then handed it over. Then he looked from the boy to his mother. "I will send the medic with bandages. You will not be bound, either of you. I will take no action against the boy." He stepped closer. "But if either of you does anything to impede our progress, you will be shot—like your friend Russell. Is that quite clear?"

Douglas nodded. Jane sat still, staring out at the camp. Dupré left then, trailing Maria and the others who had gathered like a centipede pulling its body.

The boy sat beside his mother.

"That was clever," she said. "Dangerous, but I know your pa and Hank would have been proud of how you conducted yourself."

"I hate him for what he did to Sheriff Russell and you," Douglas said. "I hate him more than I want to get away. I want to see him—"

"Don't," Jane said. "Don't think of using the stick. Don't speak what's in your heart. We are not the Lord God, and it is He and He alone who orders and allows the end of a human life in its time. Our soul is poisoned by such thoughts."

"I know, but I can't help it. Maybe if I pray to God, He will understand and forgive me."

A man arrived then with a canvas sack full of bandages and scissors, along with a bottle of alcohol to wash the wounds. He squatted beside the woman, and while he worked, Douglas folded his hands in prayer. His lips moved in silence as he prayed: first for his mother's quick recovery; second for the forgiveness of the black mark he had put on his soul; and third for the safety of Hank.

It occurred to him he need not ask for anything more.

The death of Captain Raoul Dupré would accomplish all three.

IT WAS A sad parting for Zebulon Moore, but a quick one.

As soon as the animals were in the barn, with meal for the chickens, raw meat for the dog, and pans of water for all—the door was shut. Zebulon bagged some fruit and vegetables for Quinn and himself, they filled their canteens, and then Quinn and the proprietor were out on the open range before morning was very old.

They did not talk, and Zebulon did not ask anything of Quinn. He just rode beside, a little behind, the man with no memory. Each man wished to be alone with his private thoughts and feelings.

Quinn was happy to give the man his privacy and was not especially happy to be alone with his own thoughts. A man whose past went back a little more than a day did not have much to chew on, except to think about Jane and Douglas and the mystery of the man who had abandoned him and the woman who seemed to have done the same. He wondered if he had been a happy man. It did not feel like it. Had he not recalled any of that, had he stayed with Jane—if she had wanted him to stay—he wondered if he would have been a happy man.

It was after an hour or so of riding, of sitting in a sun that exceeded the intensity of the day before, that Quinn began to feel dizzy. He drank water, ate an apple, removed his hat, and fanned himself. The bare wound throbbed hot where the sun glared at it. Quinn doubled the reins around his hands and held them tighter.

"You want to stop?" Zebulon asked.

"No. Maybe if we find some shade around noon—"

That was the last thought Quinn had before the heat on his scalp seemed to sear itself inward, like boiling water on snow. He bent over, crying out as pain flowed around the sides of his skull. He dropped the reins and grasped the sides of his head.

Zebulon rode closer on the right side. He took Snowcap's reins as the horse began to shy. He steadied the mount so Quinn did not slip off.

"I'm right here," Zebulon said softly. "You need to get off, you tell me."

If Quinn heard, he made no sign. His forehead was pressed to the horse's blond mane, and his eyes were tightly shut, though he vividly saw pulsing red swirls on both sides, like a whirlpool draining. "Zebulon—"

"Right beside you."

Quinn thrust out his right hand, gripped the other man's shirt. "He was my *friend*! We argued about the mission. He *clubbed* me."

"No one's hitting you now."

Quinn shook his head slowly, the movement causing the pain to explode.

*"Before that,"* he said through his teeth. "We were chasing . . . killers. Graybacks. They were sent . . . to assassinate . . . *Juárez*!"

The madness of the pain brought sudden, excellent clarity while making it difficult to speak. The mission rolled out backward from the confrontation with Beaudine in the desert to the hunt through the moorings and men in Ensenada to the departure from Apple Town . . . to Aggie-Rose.

"God! Jesus!" Quinn yelled as Zebulon pulled harder to steady Snowcap and now his own jumpy mount.

Deciding to dismount, Zebulon moved ahead a few paces to give himself room, then slid off without letting go of either set of reins. He felt like he had in his buffalo days, when veteran horses were suddenly panicked by proximity to the big herds.

Soothing Snowcap, which quieted his own horse, Zebulon helped Quinn from the saddle. The man could not stand on his own, so the onetime frontiersman took him in both arms and carried him several feet from the animals. The horses remained where they were, now that the apoplectic rider was gone.

The older man laid his companion on the hot sand, there being nothing else but scrub where, he knew from experience, biting bugs and lizards had a habit of dwelling. Zebulon went back and got Quinn's canteen and hat, wetting the other man's face with a little spill of water before laying the hat over his eyes. Quinn was breathing hard and heavy, his hands scratching at the dirt.

Zebulon knelt on one knee beside him. "What do you need, friend?"

Quinn shook his head and instantly regretted it. The fires burned fresh inside, causing him to gasp. "Have to . . . keep . . . still," he said. "Am I bleeding?"

"Nope. Whatever got cracked must've got jarred again."

"Yeah. Like it just happened . . . but with a different end."

"What do you mean?"

"Instead of forgetting, I'm remembering."

"That's what all that jabber was about," Zebulon said. "You some kind of ranger?"

"No. No, Bill is a Pinkerton . . . hires me from time to time. We fought about leaving those men alive, the Confederates. One of them took me prisoner after I woke. I escaped and . . . you know the rest."

"I do," Zebulon said mournfully.

Quinn's hand sought the man's arm. "I'm sorry for what happened and my part in it. If I had realized who we were dealing with—"

"But you didn't, and you bear no blame. Don't carry that."

Quinn nodded once, lowered his arm, and sunk back in the sand. It was strange that this was nearly how he started—only now he had clothes and memory and the pain of betrayal by two people who were close to him. He liked it better when he had been heedless and blundering.

"Listen," Zebulon went on, "we can't risk moving you till you're recovered somewhat. You keep having spells like that, you'll frighten the horses. And it won't do you no good."

"I know."

Zebulon looked around. "I can rig some kind of shade with scrub. Used to pile it close for warmth in winter when I was hunting and got snowed in. Mesh all the little vines, build a wall. No reason it shouldn't work to block the sun. Won't be much, but you won't fry."

"Thank you. I'll only need it—a short while, I think. Then we have to go."

"You know where to? You remember that?"

"I do."

"Is that where those grays are headed?"

Quinn nodded carefully.

"That's all I need to hear."

"Where are we now?"

Zebulon looked up, squinting. "Judging by how far we rode, and where the sun is, I'd say about a half day's ride north of Oak Ridge or southwest of Apple Town."

"That puts San Francisco due west . . . maybe a day's ride."

"It's about that, if you push."

"We'll have to," Quinn said.

"I been to San Francisco. There's not much there. Why do you want to go?"

"That's where Juárez is headed. The assassins, too, most likely. And Beaudine. He's going to be there."

"You got yourself a big roll call there. You gonna be up to it?"

"Yeah."

"I like your grit if not your common sense," Zebulon said. "But I'm that way, too."

Patting the man on the shoulder, the former buffalo hunter went off to collect tumbleweeds and pull brush from the few verdant patches.

When the older man was gone, Quinn grinned—at himself. As his life returned to him, he remembered being asked questions by every ranch foreman or cavalry officer he hired out to in Montana. Yes, he could sneak into a rival spread and cut their horses free the day before a drive. Yes, he could get into an Indian encampment and outstalk those famed stalkers to cut the throat of a shaman preaching war against the settlers. Yes, he could get behind Confederate lines and burn the command tent while everyone was inside— then wait and hamstring anyone who tried to put water on the blaze. He had grown up in Michigan, in wild timberland, where he lived with his parents and two younger sisters in a cabin. His father had been a lumberjack who was crippled by a falling tree. His mother nursed him until he died. If the boy had not learned to outwit wolverines for prey, they would not have survived. Quinn had learned to move so quietly, upwind, that he did not bother to kill his competitors: When quail or rabbits ran from those predators, he was waiting on the other side.

When the Quinn women moved to the Great Lakes region to work as bookkeepers for shipping and industry, the surviving man of the house took his heave and went west. He remembered now that it had always been his ambition to continue moving west until he reached the Pacific. It was ironic that he was on the verge of achieving that goal after forgetting he even had it.

*All I have to do is succeed here and head up the coast,* he told himself. He had sent his savings to a bank in San Francisco, and with his wages for this job, he would be set for whatever opportunities presented themselves on the infamous, bustling Barbary Coast. Perhaps a knife shop. He'd never want for business there.

And then it struck him, a welling of fullness and loss at the same time. One that pushed his old self back where it had been—in the past.

Jane.

She might not want him, he thought. Or San Francisco, however much it might help Douglas grow into a man who could get schooling and learn a trade. Would he give up his dream to stay with her?

*I'm forgetting I got some mountains to scale first,* he reminded himself. Assassins who had a mission and a reason for wanting Quinn as dead as their former cause. Something else he had learned in Michigan came back to him as well: *Don't eat the kill till the wolverine is beat.* They had a way, especially in winter, especially when cornered, of coming after you and your victory.

Shutting his eyes, Quinn welcomed the crinkling sound that was Zebulon building his little wall. It did not cool him worth a Richmond dollar, but it did push back the white light that had gotten inside his head and burned through his forgetfulness. He smiled as he remembered—as though reading them for the first time—the letters that told him how "little" Angel and Patricia Quinn were now Angel Wellington and Patricia Waters. He remembered his mother writing: *P.S. Your father was your age when we wed.*

Thomasina Quinn had not needed to write more than that.

The red circles had faded to an amber unity, and the pain in Quinn's head had subsided considerably. His breathing relaxed, and his heart took kindly to repose, and his thoughts blended into a dream.

Save for the last one, which clung like a burr. The fact that he had been right about one thing. It was easier to plan for tomorrow when he knew far, far less about his past. . . .

# CHAPTER SEVENTEEN

AUGUSTINA-ROSE SANCHEZ HAD left Beaudine asleep
in the bedroom and gone to her writing desk. It
was not to work on one of her plays but to write in her
diary. She had kept it since she went to work for Pinkerton, thinking the adventures of an actress-turned-spy
would make a delightful show.

It might have, had it not been her life. That kind of
play was like the military adventure that had enjoyed
a long run in Denver, *How General Grant Won the
War.* She had costarred as Grant's wife, Julia, mostly
sitting at home sewing or praying as the fortunes of a
sundered nation played out.

In her diary, she could confess to her sins and confusion. What did she feel toward Beaudine: gratitude
for this life or loathing for the price, even though she
did love him? What had she felt for Quinn? She had

persuaded him to take a job, but she did finally care for him. He was rough and wild and—

"A cutthroat murderer," she muttered.

But there was yet something innocent about him. She sat with the book open, the blank page bright with early-afternoon sunlight rather than with freshly inscribed thoughts, the ink dried on the tip of her pen as she did aught but reflect.

She went to the kitchen and had a slice of the apple bread she bought from Frau Mack. She peeled and ate a carrot. While she ate, she stopped thinking about the past and looked at the future. A bag was always packed for a quick departure, so all she had to do when Beaudine woke was change. She had not bothered to dress fully after leaving the bedroom; she was wearing only her white silk robe with lavender floral embroidery. The angle of the sun at this hour would prevent anyone on the street from seeing her. For all its diverse population, Apple Town still expected modesty from its women.

Not that there would be many people about at this time. The main street was burned from above by the sun and by roasting dirt from below, and only men going to the saloon for refreshment were out.

Except for the two who rode in in the late afternoon.

Aggie was sitting at her desk, rereading a portion of her play, with her guest still asleep, when she heard the *clop-clop* of a trio of horses—two full of rider, one empty by the lighter sound of it. She looked up by habit and saw, as the animals walked by, the passing of dirty gray fabric on two pants legs.

Former Rebels were not uncommon in an amnesty melting pot like Apple Town. But a pair of them riding slow from the plains, straight toward her, when two Rebels had been in pursuit of William Beaudine—that struck her as possibly unhealthy. Especially if they saw and recognized his horse settled out front. Fortunately, it was tied behind hers, from where they were coming. And their heads were down, like they were half drowsing or avoiding the sun, which was in their faces.

Rising, she went to the front door and pulled back the dainty lace curtain that hung on the glass panes at the top. Unless the men were just passing through, she saw the tail end of them heading toward one of the two things left on that side of the street: the general store or the rail yard.

They stopped in front of the general store just a dozen yards from where she stood.

Her heart pushing against her ribs, she let the fabric slip back and turned into the room to consider what she should do. If the men were after Beaudine, they could not know he was with her. Even if they asked Mr. Levey, the owner, he would not know Beaudine by name. Since joining the Pinkertons, Aggie did not use names when discussing her life or who her callers were.

*If they aren't here for Bill they're here for supplies,* she decided. She peeked out again. The men had not sought a stable but left their horses saddled. Either they were not intending to stay more than an hour or two, or they wanted to be prepared for a quick getaway.

With nothing on but her robe, Aggie went outside and walked Beaudine's horse from the hitching post to the fence along the side of her house. It was a narrow spot, but it was the side she shared with the church. Father Sherman was making rounds of the two outlying ranches near Truckee. Even if he was here, he might be puzzled but not argumentative about the animal.

Returning to the bedroom, where it was dark and filled with a sleeping man, Aggie grabbed her clothes and changed in the hallway. It was haphazard without a mirror, fixing the high neck of the v-shaped dress, but she would not be out for very long, and Mr. Levey had sad vision to begin with. She hoped that the other men were inattentive. They had seen her in Ensenada, and she them—albeit she had been dressed like a dockside flower vendor then, dirty and with cuttings in her unkempt hair. Before going outside, she took a parasol to shield her from the daylight—and from the men.

And a derringer from a drawer in her secretary. She kept the gun in her right palm at her side.

The cross breeze that kept the cottage tolerably warm was not present in the street. She opened the parasol and walked briskly to where the horses had been tethered. They were drinking greedily, and two of the animals were sweating. They had been traveling for quite some time.

She entered the store, and the bell jangled above the door. Mr. Levey was with the two men in the small dry goods section of the store. He squinted over with eyes dimmed from years of prospecting up and down California, and bowed courteously.

"Good afternoon, Miss Sanchez."

"Good afternoon, Mr. Levey."

"I'll be with you in a minute."

"No need," she replied. "I know where the books are. You can put a copy of Mr. Harte's opus on my account."

"Everyone's talking about *The Luck of Roaring*

*Camp and Other Sketches*," he said. "You'll get my last copy."

"I hope it is an inspiration to me," she replied.

The two men were busy poking through pants and shirts that were folded on a shelf. They did not look up. Aggie took a moment to study them. The uniforms, and the men, were definitely those she had seen at the docks.

She turned down the aisle that had a selection of books, secured the volume, and left.

Her walk back to the cottage had an urgency that had not been present during her stroll. Those two men were not looking for Beaudine—or, apparently, their purloined letter. If they were, their uniforms would have been a calling card. They would have left them on to draw the man out. The men were also not on their way to San Francisco. Apple Town was in the wrong direction.

There was something else afoot, and Aggie went back inside to watch out and see where they went.

She had her answer ten minutes later, even as she heard Beaudine stirring in the bedroom. The men were headed northwest, where there was only one possible destination.

The railroad station at Truckee.

THE FRENCH COLUMN was up with the sun and moving at a brisk pace to the west. Jane and Douglas had both managed to sleep, from exhaustion rather than from peace of mind. They resumed the ride in the same positions, Jane with Maria in the front and Douglas in the rear. The woman was limp with fear, and she had to force herself to eat the apple and biscuit that were provided. Dupré did not seem so much invigorated by the rest as eager to reach their destination. His expression did not change, but his posture went from upright to forward, his eagerness exposed by small tics and backward glances along the line. With each passing mile or hill, he seemed to become more infected with purpose.

For his part, Captain Dupré was impatient to engage, to fulfill the task that had been set him by General Marais in Paris: to organize a pair of assassinations that would allow a fleet to land in Mexico, a fleet that would already have left Clipperton Island to the south. The land had been annexed by Napoleon III a little over a decade earlier and had been a useful port of call during the war against the Juáristas.

Initially, of course, the column was not supposed to participate in the attack. It was to be done by the Confederates working alone. But when that plan faltered, the captain had had no choice but to execute the backup plan and move in. The risk, of course, was that he or his men would be captured and identified, causing an international incident. But there were no American troops permanently stationed in the narrow region through which they would be traveling. And the risk, ultimately, was worth it. The French had been shamed with the other European nations being driven from Mexico. The humiliation had affected their credibility and effectiveness as an international power. That must be restored by this bold counterattack.

But the captain was also a thoughtful, thorough man. Before they set out this morning, he had taken a look around with his binoculars. He saw no one from the rise, neither man nor horse. The Smith boy had probably lied the night before, probably to spare himself punishment. Perhaps he had heard that his ear was to be forfeited. But if Douglas had not lied, then the column was being dogged by a mongrel who was well hidden.

*Given the naïveté of a child, the truth could go one way or the other,* the captain thought as they rode. After all, Douglas had blurted Hank's name back at the cabin. That had been anything but subterfuge.

As he marched, he mentally reviewed the plans he had crafted in Mexico City—altered to accommodate the possible loss of the letters that would gain Maria access. She might believe in the three Confederates, but he had to *know* the expedition would not fail.

Juárez would reach San Francisco by frigate. That was certain. There was no way he could reach the city in time by coach. President Grant would reach San Francisco in his own vessel. The same reason applied: It was the only way to cover the ground between San Francisco and the meeting by the scheduled time. One man would have to cross from one ship to the other—whether by boat or by shore, it did not matter. The press would be there, the reporters and their cameras announcing the target. That was where the French, posing as cheering Juáristas, would strike.

It would be sudden and turbulent, and while half the unit was engaged there, the other half, if necessary, would go on board to strike at the other target. It would tax the men to be half here, half there instead of the boarding party that had originally been planned. But that required a person on the inside, and if Maria could not be that agent, incapacitating guards, then success had to come another way.

*Divide the targets and conquer.*

He had no doubt that Maria, with her great infatuation for him, would be able to kill. He had carefully nurtured her love in Mexico City. And on the farm outside Chihuahua where the rest of the French troops had lived raising animals for cover, the woman had successfully slaughtered chickens and pigs under their tutelage. And while there would be an advance ship of the French fleet to take her away after the raid, that was to ensure her silence. Captain Dupré would be remaining. He would work with the fallen aristocrats and the embittered churchmen to overthrow the soon-to-be-discredited Juáristas. He would rise on two continents: at home by restoring a French presence in North America; locally by restoring the influence and wealth of the nobility and the stolen lands of the clergy.

*Just three months in the planning, since the presidential meeting was announced, and finally here,* he thought with passions that were difficult to control.

No more harassing guerrilla skirmishes for the dozen French soldiers who had remained after the ousting of foreign powers. Here was a plan quickly but completely formed, down to the hiring of America's fallen, the Confederates. By surviving or more likely by dying, they would stir their own downtrodden brothers into action by destroying the man who had crushed them, Ulysses S. Grant. No one campaign had ever been so ambitious, the assassination of two leaders to sow two rebellions.

Whichever plan the captain ended up executing, there was one advantage that had been added to their side—a gift of providence suggesting that God was on their side. Whether the French attacked from the inside out or the other way round, anyone trying to stop them would be faced with a daunting, delaying impediment.

The boy and his mother would be at his side every step of the assault.

M ARTINS AND VOIGHT did not exactly feel like new men, but they felt less conspicuous than they had when they arrived in Apple Town.

They were spent to the marrow by their continuous movement, first their flight and now pursuit. They were glad that the settlement was every bit as isolated as they had heard. Save for the trees that filled well-tilled, distinctively manured plots before and behind every establishment, and in seven separate groves, Apple Town was as openly serene as any small Southern town the men had ever been in. There were not many pedestrians and no horses about, presumably due to the heat. People nodded in a polite but perfunctory way, but seemed as curiously uncurious as any townsfolk Martins and Voight had ever encountered. Even their uniforms caused no stir.

That was fine with them. They had been desirous of privacy and anonymity. They had been hoping for something else, too—that, as they had heard, the railroad ran late. Although this was a presidential cavalcade—as the newspapers had reported—it was still reliant on an expansive array of track subject to weather, geography, incident, and mechanical devices subject to failure. There would be, they hoped, an opportunity to rest in Truckee.

The men rode their horses back down Main Street for two of its four blocks and stopped in a place called Anna's Table for a meal, the first they had enjoyed in six or seven days; they could not tell exactly how long ago Ensenada had been. Even the flight from the desert in pursuit of Beaudine had been a blur of movement and tactics. And that was not even two days ago.

The slaying the previous day of Elizabeth Moore still clung like campfire smoke, slightly noxious but unavoidable.

Large, white-haired, grandmotherly Anna came over with a slate containing the menu. Martins deflected questions from Anna about where they were from and where they were headed.

"We're growers on a tour of the state," he said vaguely, "seeing how California raises their apples and oranges."

"Better than anywhere else in the U.S. of A.," she said, then, considering the men's Southern accents, added, "At least, those few states west of the Rockies where I have dwelt."

"Southern peaches would be a wonderful addition to your agriculture," Martins could not resist pointing out.

"I wish you luck. Frau Mack always said she wishes she had them and cherries." The woman glanced past them out the window. "Three horses—all yours?"

"That's right," Martins replied. Martins forced a smile. "About that—tell me. There do not seem to be many people out."

"They work in the morning and evening, by torch," she said. "Some hunters are out getting meats for us and Mr. Levey, but mostly we wait for the winds to come from the Pacific, late afternoon. Makes things bearable."

"Very wise. You don't get many visitors, then?"

"Some, on the way to the railroad in Truckee. A few engineers come to check their trains and tracks. They're all at the west end of town."

"We saw. Has anyone new come in today?"

"Here?" She shook her head. "You might check the hotel, though they have to come here to eat and no one has. You expecting someone?"

"Oh, a man—slender, long face, dark hair, would've been tired out—expressed an interest in buying that horse. We met him down at Oak Ridge. We thought he might have come through here."

"No one that I know of. But if you're looking to sell—"

"Not especially. We brought it to carry any fruit that we purchase. I was simply curious what happened to him."

The men ordered, and Anna took her slate and left. Martins and Voight found the woman banal and her eagerness to engage bordering on rude. Sovereignty was not all that had been lost when Robert E. Lee had surrendered. A bastion of good manners, too, had been trampled under.

It was a strange thought for a man to have after murdering a woman with scissors, Martins had to admit. The War had done that, too: a windstorm that turned everything on its side.

But the larger issues were too big for one man. Past those Rockies Anna had mentioned, life had been reduced to essentials. And right now the steaks were juicy, the potatoes filling, and the whiskey satisfying. That was all the men required. They paid with coins they had received at the general store in exchange for a gold nugget. Richard Levey had been only too happy to accept it as payment.

"Years of prospecting, this is the largest lump I ever held." He had cackled with delight after determining that the nugget was, in fact, gold.

It was late afternoon, with the day beginning to cool somewhat, when the men got back on their horses and once more headed toward the general store and past the railroad yards in the direction of Truckee.

They were unaware of the two sets of eyes that did not adhere to the casually welcoming pattern of the others: a man and a woman who followed the men's departure with sharp interest.

# CHAPTER EIGHTEEN

J ASON QUINN WAS instantly if dully awake. He was
lying still on his back but with his hand snaking to
his hip, like there was a brain in the palm and little
eyes in the fingertips. It was the "old" Quinn, the restored Quinn, and he knew it. His head had no more
than a headache, thumping a little but not significantly
painful. He was able to open his eyes.

The sun was just up and night was creeping behind
him quickly. The horses were tied to a rock a few paces
to the north where there was grass. They were still
saddled, which told him that Zebulon, at least, had not
ruled out the need for a quick escape . . . or attack.
Dark brown feathers swirled around him in the morning breeze. The smell of roasting meat came on every
breath. What had caused him to wake was the sudden,
sharp crackle of a fire that Zebulon was stoking. There
were two birds, on spits, cooking over the fire.

"Sorry for the disturbance," the older man said, turning toward him. "Fat dripping. Caught a pair of quails and thought you might want one. We ain't ate for a time."

"Thank you."

Quinn eased up on his elbows. The pain in his head had definitely subsided. He relaxed his knife hand and a warm, damp kerchief slid from the top of his head when he rose.

"Prairie doctoring," Zebulon said. "I figured you needed that more than your hat on your face, overheating things."

"Thank you again," Quinn said, rolling his shoulders and stretching stiff legs. "Did you rest any?"

"Some. Just to knock the fuzz from my eyes. Figured I could afford that. Horses is good alarms."

"Did something worry you especially?"

Zebulon handed Quinn one of the spitted birds, taking the other for himself. Sitting up fully and holding the bird on the stick, Quinn was reminded of Douglas and his rabbit. He would have given a great deal to be back there, rid of this quest.

"What concerned me is that we're only the rest of the morning's ride from Baker Road," Zebulon told him, pointing behind them, toward the southwest. "That's the flattest ground out here to go east and west."

"I'm assuming that's why we went this way?"

"It is," Zebulon said. "I figured if anyone was in a hurry to get to San Francisco, they'd eventually end up here."

"Beaudine would be ahead of us," Quinn said. "Maybe the Rebels, too."

"Not necessarily. I didn't see or smell any fresh horse

patties. Also, there's something else which speaks against what you said."

"What's that?"

Zebulon took a big bite of his bird and pointed northeast. "Been sitting here smelling horses since just before sunrise, coming from that direction. Likely someone was camped for the night and just set out."

Quinn was now sharply alert. Because he was trained for hills and mountains, for conifer and elk—and for smelling what Indians sweat, wore, or ate—this land was still somewhat foreign to him. He had not noticed anything. "Any idea how many horses?"

"You can't tell that from the smell. Could be a herd . . . or it could be two mounts that's being pushed hard. All I can say for sure is they ain't mules. Those smell different. Like camels I once saw at a show. Each of them is special."

Quinn took a bite of meat, then stabbed the stick into the ground and recovered his hat from where Zebulon had left it secured on the ground by a stone. He shook off the dust, put his hat on, and looked under the brim toward the rising sun. He saw no silhouettes, but the wind was coming from just to the north where there were hills. Riders might be in among them.

"It could be anyone," Quinn said.

"Or it could be one or more of those Rebels."

The man was not wrong. Martins might have been slowed by his injury, or he might have taken a longer route to avoid another confrontation before his mission was completed. He and the other Rebel could have fallen behind Quinn and Zebulon.

Quinn looked around slowly, careful not to rattle

his head. "If you're right, there's nowhere to hide the horses here."

"No reason to. I'm not moving until I see who it is. If it's the man who killed Elizabeth, one of us ain't getting to San Francisco."

Quinn continued to stare to the east as he retrieved the stick and ate more bird. He was as hungry as hell.

"We don't want to invite an attack if it's strangers," Quinn said.

Zebulon bit down on his own bird. "I don't intend to lay the horses down or be on them until I know what's coming. You want to ride on and put some distance—"

"Don't talk stupid."

Zebulon smiled through a mash of bird. "I cannot tell you how many times those same words came from the mouth of my Elizabeth." He glanced up. "You still with me, sweetheart? If you are, I'm willing to join you whenever the Lord says, though I ask you to look after my friend here. He's a good man."

Quinn was touched by the sentiment but had no time to consider it. Zebulon rose suddenly, his experienced eyes staring just north of the rising sun, his rawhide hand forming a salute to block it.

"There's dust," Zebulon announced. "Eat fast."

Both men finished their meal, and Zebulon fetched his rifle from the horse. He set it on the ground near the fire and sat beside it. He was already wearing his six-shooters.

"You want one of the Colts?" he asked Quinn.

"No, thank you." He filled his right hand with a Bowie knife and felt it, got on his knees, flipped it up.

"You were pretty sharp with that earlier," Zebulon said. "And you didn't even know who you was then."

"Some things you don't forget," Quinn said, and slipped the knife back into the sheath with easy precision. "And some things get a little better when you remember."

The men were seeming portraits of contentment by the time the rolling cloud became moving horsemen. Sitting out in the open like this, Quinn felt relief when he saw that they were not Martins and Voight. Zebulon felt disappointment, which he expressed with an oath. However, both men were quickly absorbed with trying to figure out who the riders were. They appeared to be a column of men, all in white, save for a woman riding up front with the leader.

*No, two women,* Quinn thought as they neared, two doubled up on a horse.

"Could be bandits or else Juáristas escorting a noble lady to the same place we're going," Zebulon said. "They make pilgrimages to the missions here on behalf of the churches the new boys busted up."

The dust, handkerchiefs, and shawl made it impossible to identify the features of the riders, even as they neared.

"Watch what happens," Zebulon said.

"What?"

"They ain't gonna stop. Once had a rogue wolf running toward me on the plains. A missus, which can be ferocious. I didn't want to shoot, case she had cubs, so I rode toward her, and she ran toward me, and we came closer and closer and closer until we met—and one just eyed the other and continued on, like clouds that looked like they were gonna crash and release lightning but didn't." Zebulon realized he still had slippery quail grease on his hands and wiped them dry on his pants. "They'll do the same. I feel it."

As the column approached, Quinn began to feel as if Zebulon was right. The riders were about a hundred feet to the north and showed no sign of slowing or veering toward the two men. The man on point, nearer to them than the woman, looked over and nodded, indicating he had no business with them and would pass by. Zebulon nodded back.

Sitting behind the campfire, Quinn watched as the riders swept past at a proud, steady pace. None of the others looked over.

"They're a well-trained group," Quinn hazarded.

"Yeah, especially for guerrilla fighters."

Quinn's hands were idle though it was a false posture; he yearned to have a knife in each hand, ready and strong instead of relaxed and vulnerable. He was about to try to get up, just to move, when his eyes caught a figure he knew, a face that looked toward him, a rider who was decidedly unlike the others. Their eyes locked for just a moment, but that was enough. Quinn saw the clothes, the hair—his gaze narrowed, he drew breath through his nose, and his lips opened soundlessly.

"Must be the lady's son or little brother or something," Zebulon said as the boy rode past.

Quinn remained on the ground until the column had passed. Then he rose slowly. "Zebulon, we have to mount. Now."

The frontiersman looked back at the knife fighter. "What is it?"

"I know that boy," Quinn said. "And he definitely does not belong out here."

Quinn was on his feet. Zebulon rose and offered a steadying hand, but Quinn motioned him off. The knife fighter remained as he was until he was steady, until he was sure his head would not throb him back to the ground. Then he walked toward his horse.

"Who is he?" Zebulon asked.

"He's a clever boy who, I pray, is clever enough not to say if he recognized me."

"Do you know how you know him?"

"You know him, too, I would think," Quinn said. "Douglas Smith, of the station outside the desert. And one of those women must have been his mother, Jane."

"They been to our place once, never range even to Apple Town. What would they be doing out here?"

"Exactly," Quinn replied. "I've got an unhappy feeling that what Bill Beaudine did not want to tell me about just rode past."

T HE SMALL HAND of Douglas Smith tightened on his sharpened stick. It sat on his thigh, pointing outward, directing his angry thoughts at the man leading the column. But his mind was not on Captain Dupré. It was on the man he had seen sitting on the prairie by the campfire.

It was Hank. Douglas had seen him—he had *felt* the man—and Hank had seen him. He knew it.

Douglas' heart swelled with joy and hope, not only because Hank was alive but because he knew that the man would rescue him. He knew that because in the fast glimpse he'd had he saw what looked like the glittering beads of a sheath.

Hank had his knife.

The boy did not know if his mother had seen Hank.

She was on the wrong side of the column, and because she was sitting up front, most of her face was bundled against the dirt. Being a man, Douglas could just spit it out like the French soldier holding him.

That was not all Douglas had seen. He had recognized the man who was with Hank. That was actually the figure he had seen first, standing with his familiar mustache and gray hair like a mane. It was Zebulon Moore, owner of the Oak Ridge way station. Lieutenant Martins and Hank had been headed northwest to the old coach stop. Maybe Zeb was the one who had rescued Hank, and he came west with the younger man to get him where he was going.

As his mother would have said, God looked after His own, and the Smiths, without a pa, were His own.

Douglas wished he could whoop for joy or ride up and share the news with his ma, but he had learned a good lesson back at the cabin: to keep his mouth closed like a barn door and his secrets inside. He would not even tell his mother. This was his special secret. His, as the man of the house, to guard.

No longer concerned about anything, not even the smell of the man who was holding him, Douglas looked toward the west with a psalm in the back of his throat, one of his mother's favorites. He did not know the number but he knew the words of thanksgiving: *God is a nurturing Shepherd who knows just what you need. . . .*

BEAUDINE WAS GLAD that Aggie was with him. When he had seen the two men riding by, his impulse was to go out, learn if they were the assassins, and shoot them from their saddles.

Except, as she reminded him, the two men had not done anything yet. Nothing for which he had any proof.

"A loose-fitting coat possibly concealing a shoulder holster—that is not a crime," she cautioned. "Even the letters you took implicate only one person, Maria Allende."

Beaudine had taught her well, and Aggie was right. With new clothes and a few days' growth of beard, the men could be someone else. He had not studied the horses closely enough to know if these steeds were the same.

"Thanks for moving my horse," Beaudine said as the men rode from view and he turned from the window. The Pinkerton man was moving quickly to finish dressing, having come from the bedroom with just his trousers and bare feet. He was also thinking out loud.

"There's nothing up here but Truckee, and that's the direction they headed," he said as he pulled on his shirt. "If they meant to make San Francisco, they were being a mite leisurely about it."

"Very true," Aggie said. "But since we don't know, we're going to have to track them from a distance, and carefully."

"At night," Beaudine said.

"You still want me to go?"

"If you're game. I'd've slept through their visit and missed them entirely if not for you." He kissed her once his boots were on.

"Get your horse," she said. "I'll pack food, meet you out front."

Beaudine was angry at himself for having slept so long, however much he had needed it. He had trained himself to do without sleep, but then he had been on the flatlands or in the mountains, not with Aggie. Being with her made him feel for Quinn and the loss he must have experienced. She was a remarkable woman.

Thinking about Quinn made Beaudine wonder how and where the man was. He was also unhappy that he had no idea where the third and fourth members of the Confederate party might be. One of them might have dropped one off behind to protect their rear. Or to link up with the fourth member of the unit and the French soldiers who were supposed to support the mission, if needed.

*Follow the men. That's my only play,* he told himself. *That, and pray that they are Martins and Voight.*

Retrieving the lockbox and slipping from his pocket to his lapel his badge—a silver shield that read PINKERTON NATIONAL DETECTIVE AGENCY—he put those concerns from his mind as he went around to the side of the cottage.

The townsfolk were out doing their gardening in the cooler late afternoon, and there were smiles and flung salutes from people Beaudine did not know. They might have been mostly deserters and traitors, but they were sociable.

Aggie returned, wearing a high-crowned hat with a wide brim to keep the setting sun from her eyes and the wind from her long hair. She was mounted moments after he had walked his horse to the street. There were a canvas bag of food and two full deerskins swinging from the saddle. She handed one to Beaudine as he rode up beside her.

"You got more than your derringer?" he asked.

She nodded toward his horse, where there was a rifle in the scabbard and a .44 in his holster. "Whichever one of those you're not using."

Beaudine grinned, then urged his horse ahead. Aggie was right with him, her tawny riding skirt and matching blouse fluttering around her, a shawl tied to her waist for the cooler mountain passage. The two men were already well clear of the town. If they turned and saw a man and a woman, they'd have no reason to suspect they were being followed. And if the men *were* concerned, that meant they were those Beaudine was looking for.

And it occurred to him then that maybe this was not a good plan at all.

He reared up.

"What's wrong?" Aggie asked, stopping.

"Our intelligence said the French soldiers were on hand to attack in force if force was needed," Beaudine said. "What if these boys cooked up something else? They lost the letters, but they still might have a plan for getting on board the train, not the boat. And the train goes through Truckee on the way to San Francisco."

Aggie looked ahead. "The way they're going will get them there by midnight," she said.

"We have to get there before them," he said. "We'll have to go through the foothills of the Sierra Nevadas."

"At night?"

"Even Pinkerton can't make the sun stand still."

Aggie was neither surprised nor afraid, just challenged. She understood the business the same as he did.

"That'll be the other direction," she said, turning her horse around and starting out. "You coming?"

A moment later, Beaudine was galloping toward her, loving the woman all the more.

# CHAPTER NINETEEN

THE TRAIN, WHICH had been due at one a.m., was late by several hours. It was now closing in on dawn, and there was not a hint of rumbling along the tracks or a headlight and steam around the bend.

Goodman Martins sat on a bench and closed his eyes on the track side of the long wood depot. He was kept company by another gentleman who, he said, was awaiting the arrival of the president, whose armies had saved the nation. That was not something Martins cared to hear.

Every now and then, Martins would get up, look, and listen for the train. Voight was watching for anyone who might have been looking for them. It was more tedious than the prairie crossing from Apple Town, and that had been dull.

But the quiet ride, partly in the late-summer dark, had given Martins time to rehearse what he was going to say to the guards on the train. He was convinced it would get him and Voight inside, and that was all he needed. His wartime training would do the rest.

Franklin Voight was on the other side of the building, pacing. The light of two large lanterns showed the dark storefronts of what little of Truckee there was to see. It was not much: two homes, their windows lit; an occasional child and a dog; a pedestrian now and then. The small white-haired trainman James Grand—excited for the impending arrival of the Civil War hero and American president Ulysses Grant—could not stop practicing what he would say if his eminence got off to stretch his legs.

"The town has only been in existence since eighteen sixty-three, when it was called Gray's Station after Joseph Gray, who had a roadhouse on the old Trans-Sierra wagon trail," he said, fast and sure. "Our blacksmith, Sam Coburn—who would be honored to meet you, Mr. President, sir—is still around, which is why our town was renamed Coburn's Station after three years. When the Central Pacific Railroad came through, they renamed us Truckee to pacify the local Paiute, whose chief was Tru-ki-zo."

Unlike Martins, Voight listened to the man; it was something to do.

There were a few people inside the depot, all seated, eager to meet the president. Some were eating picnic basket food they had brought, expecting the delay. Buggies sat outside, horses were hitched to a rail, and there was a general quiet upon the place. On the opposite side of the tracks were the water tower and the train works for repairs. It had been busier earlier when

a two-man crew was making ready to water the locomotive. Now there was nothing to do but wait.

The sun and the train arrived at almost the same
time.

Almost at once, the trainman rang a bell to alert the
sleeping town that Mr. Grant was finally arriving. The
people in the depot rose up from their torpor, the man
awaiting Grant jumped to his feet, and the citizens of
Truckee began slowly to arrive like pigeons to seed.

Voight took a last look through the crowd, saw nothing suspicious, and went to join Martins.

The wooden platform shook as the headlight came
round a turn. The whistle blew shrill but proud, ivory-
colored steam poured into the sky, and the crew on the
other side of the tracks was up and ready. The president was not scheduled to stay very long, and they did
not want to be responsible for any delay.

The trainman came around back, fixing his hat and
tie, his heart thumping. He smiled broadly when blacksmith Coburn arrived with his wife and apprentice.
Red, white, and blue banners were draped beneath the
windows of the two cars, and they danced in the bursts
of steam from below. Military guards were stationed at
the front doors of the two cars, on both sides, with two
men in the caboose.

The train slowed with a grating cry, sparks leaping,
the engineer leaning out the window with a tired smile.

"Ya made it!" the trainman shouted.

"Rocks on the tracks back at the tunnel," the engineer shouted back as they pulled in. "That was the
whole of our problems."

"I'm sure the president understood!"

"I hear he was asleep most of it."

The engineer made a tipping motion with his left hand. Grand thought it disrespectful and wagged a finger at the man.

The giant black engine groaned to a stop as more citizens arrived at the station. Grand urged them to keep back, since the president—if he was awake—would need room to breathe.

Martins stood near the locomotive, where Voight joined him.

"This is going to be easier than I anticipated," Martins said. "If he comes out, we address him directly. If not, we'll wait until they are ready to go and then confront the guard. He can't afford to turn us away . . . and there won't be time to take it up the chain of command."

There were at least two dozen people clustered in a semicircle around the first car. There was a sense of import, there were the buzz of voices and the slosh of water pouring into the water compartment behind the locomotive, and finally one guard, then another, with stoic expressions and searching eyes, stepped from the railcar, armed with rifles, and gently urged the crowd not to press forward.

Martins and Voight stood on the periphery as the trainman and Coburn wormed their way to the front of the throng. When the stocky figure of Ulysses Grant appeared on the steps, smiling and waving a thick hand with a thick cigar, general applause rose along with cheers from people grateful for his achievements, which, by extension, included this great railroad.

"Good citizens," he said, "I am humbled by your reception and grateful that I can actually see you, since all the reporters and their blamed flash powder are in San Francisco."

There was general laughter as the trainman presented the blacksmith and his guests and the crowd moved in a little against the unyielding guards and droplets of water splashed upon those at the fringes of the growing multitude.

"We had better get to the guard," Martins told Voight as more people arrived behind them.

While the president shook a few nearby hands and smiled at the ladies and children, the two men shouldered their way through the crush. They drew annoyed looks from those they pushed aside, and they made quiet apologies.

"Excuse me. This is important," Martins droned softly but firmly. "The president may be at risk."

The two men finally reached one of the sentries, a man of some thirty years who scowled at them from beneath his thick mustache, and his rifle held diagonally across his chest, he used it as a barricade to keep the men from breaking through.

"Officer, I bring news for the president," Martins said. "From the Pinkerton men."

The guard's gray eyes looked at the man, who was lit only by the light spilling from the inside of the train, the new sun being on the other side of the depot. The soldier was quietly sniffing; his second responsibility as a sentry, after first stopping a man, was to determine whether the person was drunk. This one was not.

"Your hands, sir," the officer said. "Let me see them."

Martins raised them, as did Voight his own. The eyes of the two Confederates were looking past the sentry.

The spray had stopped, the water chute having been swung from the train, and there was no doubt that the train's departure was imminent.

The sentry turned to call his superior, a major who was standing behind the president. His about-face was met instead by the wife of Mr. Coburn and the blacksmith's apprentice.

The eyes of Bill Beaudine and Aggie-Rose Sanchez looked past the officer and met those of Goodman Martins and Franklin Voight. The certainty of recognition fell first across the face of the Pinkerton man, then tightened the expression of the Confederate lieutenant. From the bottom of his eye, Martins saw the man flip back the label of his jacket, which had been turned over, to reveal his badge.

The people, the train, the platform seemed to soften from view, leaving only the agent and the president behind. Martins knew, at that moment, what John Wilkes Booth had had to feel five years before, in the president's box at Ford's Theatre: the weight and glory of history, a point of light that obliterated everything that came before and might come after. All that existed was the task, the honor of his forebears on his shoulders.

Even as he felt this, thought this, his hand was reaching into his new coat for the Colt Lightning revolver. Two, maybe three shots and the Pinkerton, the guard, the president would fall in quick succession.

"Cover me!" Martins heard himself say, half turning to Voight as the gun cleared his coat.

A small flash from the direction of the lady, from a derringer, and a sharp pinch in his waist caused Martins to freeze momentarily. The crowd went silent and motionless at the pop. They scattered and screamed as a louder sound put a hole in the man's stomach and doubled him over.

Behind Martins, fully exposed as he fell, Voight stood with his own revolver in his hand. He turned, like a buck fleeing from a springing mountain cat, but even the thinning crowd slowed him.

The confused soldier turned toward Beaudine, backed off, and pointed the rifle in his direction.

"Get out of my way!" Beaudine shouted as he pushed past, following the fleeing Confederate.

Behind them, Aggie grabbed the soldier's rifle and pushed the barrel toward the ground. "He just saved the president, man!" she shouted.

The confused soldier turned toward the two running men, joined by another officer while the remaining men circled the president and hustled him back on board the train.

His legs churning, Beaudine overtook the panicked Rebel. He grabbed him by a fistful of left shoulder with one hand and jammed the gun to his spine with the other.

"Stop or die!" Beaudine shouted.

Voight scraped the soles of his boots into the ground and raised his hands. Beaudine seized the six-shooter that was in one of them and jammed it in his belt. Still holding the man's shoulder, he yanked him around as Aggie and the two guards came up behind him.

Frowning at the face that was lit now by the orange rays of the new day, the Pinkerton man put the barrel of his Colt up under the man's nostrils and cocked the hammer.

"Where're the other two men? And the French column?"

Voight was surprised by what the man knew. He blurted, "Stevens is dead, killed by Quinn at the way station. Maria, the French—I don't know. I swear."

"Who is their target?"

Voight had recovered himself somewhat and did not answer. Beaudine rolled his lips together as though that would keep him from firing.

"Bill," Aggie said. She did not touch him for fear of releasing what was inside of him—weeks of planning, days of pursuit and flight. But her voice alone had a calming effect.

He lowered the gun, and the soldiers took Voight between them. The major in charge of the detachment had walked over and faced Beaudine. He was an older man with one eye. He knew battle fatigue when he saw it, and the unsought, unintended responses it caused. He pushed Beaudine's Colt farther toward the ground. His good eye briefly lit on the Pinkerton badge.

"The lady tells me you have a story to tell."

Beaudine looked up at the creased orange face and proud eye patch. "Yes, Major. But first I have a request."

The officer drew his shoulders back, tacitly asserting command but showing a willingness to listen. "And that is?"

"We have to get this train to San Francisco," Beaudine told him. "Other lives are in danger."

# CHAPTER TWENTY

QUINN'S PLAN, SUCH as it was, had been simple and elegant.

Throughout the daylight, the two men had kept a considerable distance from the column, two travelers on the same well-established road and nothing more. At night, the plan had been for Zebulon to move off to the north, where there were hills, while Quinn slipped into the camp to try to free the Smiths. It was as good a plan as any, Quinn had felt, as long as the men stopped.

They did not.

Quinn was not sure why the line pressed on, though the road was flat and relatively free of gullies and sand pits—a hazard on the plains.

"We only have about a half hour of darkness," Quinn finally said to Zebulon. "I don't think they'll be stopping until they get where they're going, probably San Francisco."

"Seems likely. You think they're part of this plot?"

"I don't know. I was not the best informed of men." Quinn studied the slow-moving line. "Yeah, I'm going to go in. I'll try for the boy first, bring him to you, then go back for his mother. You take off and get the boy to safety."

"That's a suicidal errand, friend Quinn. Even if you get yourself out, which is unlikely, as you'll be shielding the boy from gunfire, they'll have the woman surrounded. You sure they been abducted, those two?"

"They would never have up and left, and they definitely wouldn't have been separated. Or riding under the restraint of someone larger."

"Okay, all that's fair. In that case, I say we ride in and take them. Just grab them off their horses before it gets light. I'm guessing those boys are about as tired as I am, so they won't be too fast or too sure with their guns or pursuit."

Quinn considered the plan. He could not think of another one.

"Of course, we could just wait and see where they end up," Zebulon suggested. "It might not be something bad."

"The way Douglas looked at me didn't suggest he was going someplace he wanted to be."

"Then we have our plan. 'Let the hooves and bullets fall as they may,' I used to say when bison got itchy and stampeded the way they are prone to."

Quinn was still thinking. He did not like Zebulon riding into a situation like that or the Smiths riding out of it.

"Tell you what," Quinn suggested. "Why don't we just ride in and ask to join them? Worst they can say is no, in which case we grab the boy and his mother and ride."

"I have no way of knowing if that's a better plan, only a different one," Zebulon said. "I'll go where you do."

"Makes sense to try and find out more before we charge in," Quinn said.

The two kicked their horses to a quicker pace. The column had slowed, and they overtook it before the horses had worked much. The men took opposite sides of the column, Quinn on the north side, where Jane Smith would be. The moon would be enough to show her face, if her shawl was down.

The riders looked back as the men galloped toward them, Jane turning with them and seeing Zebulon for the first time. Her eyes reflected the moon in their round fullness, and her exposed mouth was wide, still, and surprised. He smiled at the woman, pointed to the south, and fell in beside her. Quinn arrived simultaneously, riding beside Captain Dupré but looking past him at Jane. Their eyes met. Maria, still behind Jane, had to feel the fire.

"Speak English?" Quinn asked the man, who, up close, did not look Mexican.

"I do."

"Mr. Moore and I were wondering if you had a map," Quinn said. "We're trying to get to San Francisco, but he says this is the road to the capital."

"I'm afraid we cannot help you," Dupré replied with a stern French accent.

"I see. Well, then, how about just allowing us the company of fellow human beings? Moore and I, we've been out here—"

"I'm sorry, but we are engaged in a private matter that does not admit outside participation. If you will—"

Quinn leaned to his right, reached across with his left hand, and grabbed the man's reins. Steadying Dupré's horse, Quinn swung onto the man's stallion, simultaneously drawing his knife, reaching around, and putting it under Dupré's soft chin. Quinn held the reins tightly and kept the horse calm. His head pounded, but he refused to let that distract him.

"Jane!" he shouted. "You here by your own choice?"

"No," she said. "Hank, be careful—"

"Name's Quinn. Jason Quinn. And I want you to take my horse, with the boy on it, and get clear of these folks. Zebulon will go with you."

"What about you?"

"Let's go," Zebulon urged, extending a hand that wasn't holding his six-shooter. "It won't pay to argue." He looked past her at Quinn. "Not exactly the plan, you know."

"You're not the first person to tell me that on this mission."

Dupré was sitting very still, more for clarity than from fear. Certain that these men were likely with Beaudine, he shouted back, "Kill the boy!"

Jane screamed, and Zebulon spun his horse around, firing into the air in the hope of panicking the horses. He succeeded somewhat: Jane fell to the ground, and three of the men were reared off as well. The one riding with Douglas still had his seat and reached for his gun.

His heart drumming, Douglas dragged his stick across the horse's neck. The animal bolted now, with Douglas remaining on its back while the man behind him was tossed hard to the dirt. The boy managed to stay seated while the horse ran off, Zebulon charging after him. The sun was just coming up, and he could see the boy clearly, the horse racing and leaping not far off.

Jane's fall and the sudden departure of Zebulon caused the captain's mount to kick as well. The animal's first buck caused Quinn's head to explode, and he lowered the knife, lost his hold on the horse, and fell onto his back. Dupré still had the reins and seized control of the animal.

Snarling, the captain reached for his holster and drew his revolver.

Jane recovered and threw herself across Quinn, feeling the tension in his body as he gripped his head. She held him, her cheek to his, expecting to die there, and that way. Except for Douglas, it was all right. It was good.

The shots she heard were from farther off than she had expected, and from behind. Dupré and several men shouted at once, and without releasing Quinn, she looked back across the plain.

There was a white coach with six armed men on or around it firing at the column. None of the Frenchmen fell but that was because, she presumed, the others had fired high. If the column dared to go for their rifles—

"*Arrêtez-vous!*" Dupré shouted at his men, apparently having deduced the same thing as Jane. The men in the distance wore the uniforms of the Mexican navy. They were accustomed to firing on rolling decks and did not miss unless they intended to.

The Frenchmen, or at least the few who had maintained control of their horses after the volley, did not return fire. The rest took a few moments to quiet their animals. And then, suddenly, save for the rolling, thinning cloud from the distant shots, the field was still and silent.

Jane turned her attention to the man now called Quinn. With gentle hands, she turned him onto his back and cradled his head.

"What happened just now?" he asked.

"The French surrendered to Spanish soldiers," Jane said.

Quinn laughed through his pain. "Another army invading us?"

"Just a coach," she said. "An ornate one. Don't talk—rest your head."

Quinn did as she suggested, though he knew at once who it was that had just saved them: no less than the president of Mexico, Benito Juárez. One Spanish officer and then another came to check on them. Jane assured both men that they were all right, that she was familiar with treating Quinn's wound.

When the officers were gone, Quinn said, "You speak—"

"Spanish, yes," she said. "Funny how that surprises Northerners. Out here, we deal with more Mexicans than we do Americans. Now *hush*."

He lay back, obedient and spent.

Zebulon came riding back with Douglas, followed by the coach and its armed guards. Douglas flew from the saddle more than dismounted, stumbling as he knit his way through the unhorsed French with their arms raised. He dropped to his knees beside his mother and Quinn.

Jane released Quinn long enough to hug her son for the first time since before the adventure had begun.

Quinn was well enough now to see the two, if not to smile.

The hug was tight but quick, the boy breaking it to bend over Quinn.

"Are you okay, Hank?" he asked.

"He has his memory back," his mother told him. "His name is Jason Quinn."

"Jason." The boy smiled, then scrunched his face critically. "Which do you like better, Hank?"

The man was about to answer when Jane put a hand on his mouth, encouraging him to rally before saying any more. It was just as well, Quinn thought. He was going to say "Pa."

The Mexican contingent disarmed the French, and Zebulon took lariats from several horses to cut them into bonds. The former frontiersman took a bayonet from one of the French saddles to cut it.

As Zebulon stood apart from the prisoners, not far from the coach, *Capitán* Donato Ortega strode over, his white breeches gleaming in the sun. He was an imposing figure, younger than Zebulon by about a score of years, but poised beyond his age. He had swapped his rifle for a pair of pistols that swung freely at his sides. The men introduced themselves.

"Probably feels good to stretch," Zebulon said in passable Spanish.

"Yes, but especially to take on the enemy," the officer replied. "We had heard the French might be pursuing us, intelligence from American agents." He pointed one of the revolvers ahead. "That man I just checked on—who is he?"

"One of those intelligence folk. Name's Quinn. He

and a Pinkerton named Beaudine blew up a thing against your president in Ensenada, he told me."

"What happened to those men?"

"Quinn killed one of them at my way station in Oak Ridge. The other two fled after they killed my wife. Don't know where they are."

"I am deeply grieved and grateful to you."

Ortega swept off his bicorne and maintained a moment of respectful silence as he looked toward the front of the line, where *Contraalmirante* Allende had discovered his daughter among the French. After a moment of initial shock, the officer had put duty before family and left her with the French before joining Ortega to check on Quinn and Jane. Though his posture was formal and his expression stoic, his eyes showed loss and bewilderment.

*It will be sorted out,* Ortega thought, then looked back at the coach. The president had remained there, reluctantly, with the footmen. Juárez had wanted to come and see his rescuers, but Allende and Ortega feared his presence might incite the captives to new spirit.

And as Ortega had pointed out, there were still assassins afoot.

Ortega returned his hat to his head after Zebulon had finished cutting the ropes. Then the officer bowed to the man. "I thank you again for your industry and sacrifice. I go to bring your intelligence to his excellency."

Zebulon wasn't sure what many of the Spanish words meant, those last in particular, but he returned the bow, and when Ortega had left, he began tying the hands of the Frenchmen to the pommels of their horses.

When he was finished, he went and collected Snowcap, who had stood where his master had left him.

Zebulon turned the horse around and walked him the few paces to where Quinn had fallen.

"Brought you a friend," he said, leading the big brown animal toward its reclining master. "Seemed a little lost."

Quinn smiled. "Thanks, Zebulon. For everything."

*"Shhh,"* Jane told him.

"I'm okay now," he assured her, turning slightly to his side and causing her to frown. "I am. My memory stayed put, the pain is behaving better, and I'm surrounded by all that's dear to me."

He was looking at Jane, who smiled.

"Is that your real horse?" Douglas asked.

"Ever since he was a colt," Quinn replied, still looking at Jane.

"So beautiful," the boy said.

His eyes still fixed on the woman, Quinn replied, "Quite beautiful."

# CHAPTER TWENTY-ONE

Their prows facing toward the shore, hulls rocking serenely out of synchronization, the two warships were an imposing backdrop for the two presidents and the governor of California. With the verdant hills of San Francisco spread before them, the men stood still and full of purpose as photographers took their pictures and reporters shouted questions, which all three men ignored.

"They will have a statement after they meet," the American president's secretary assured the nearly three dozen men who had gathered, some of them having journeyed from Washington with the president.

Benito Juárez and his party had ridden into San Francisco along the western spur of the Baker Road with the French prisoners in tow, hands bound and horses tied reins to tails to the coach. Those were the first photographs that had been taken, both Grant and Juárez posing tall and proud before the fallen French captain.

"That will sober those lunatic imperialists in Europe," Grant boasted confidently.

The Mexican president was pleased and grateful when Grant extended a thick arm toward the building where the other surviving assassins were under guard.

"Let the anarchists try as they might, they will never pull our nations asunder," Grant said, more to the reporters than to his fellow leader.

When the leaders had finally, jointly, and publicly expressed their gratitude to the "hidden men and lady of Pinkerton who averted a foreign plot," as Grant put it, the two leaders departed for their meeting on board the USS *Resaca*.

Before the men departed, Beaudine took the opportunity to return the letters to *Capitán* Donato Ortega, who had ridden in with Juárez. The officer received them gratefully and, sharply saluting the American, promised to deliver them at once. The gold was given, with less ceremony, to *Contraalmirante* Esteban Allende. The desolate man received it with a father's genuine gratitude. Maria had already been turned over to him, having committed no crime in the United States. With her only sin in Mexico having been robbing the exchequer—and with the French captain likely to be hanged for the murder of Sheriff Russell—her rehabilitation was likely.

The French and both Confederates were in the custody of J. T. Clark and his local constabulary, who had escorted them to the hospital. Martins would be charged with the murder of Elizabeth Moore, Voight with sedition and the attempted assassination of the president of the United States.

Amidst the hubbub and the crowds, Beaudine sought, but did not see, Jason Quinn. He was directed to Chief Clark, who watched with the eyes of a seabird for any other criminal acts.

"He'll be out shortly," the tall, clean-shaven man said, the brass buttons of his uniform near blinding. He nodded his head upon stately shoulders toward a telegraph office behind him. "It's already been determined that every act he committed was in self-defense. My men are arranging for him to provide statements about the other two. We'll want one from you, too, sir."

"I will furnish that with pleasure."

Aggie was off seeing to Jane and her son, making sure they had medical attention from the president's own surgeon, who was treating them in the carriage that had brought the president from the railroad station. Zebulon Moore made sure they had food and drink from Barbary Bea's. He charged it to the governor of California, feeling that if Henry Huntley Haight could advocate for the rights of the defeated South, he could treat loyal members of the Union to lunch.

When Quinn finally emerged from his interview, hat in hand and turning it round thoughtfully, he found Beaudine waiting for him. He was holding a bottle of Scotch the president had given him on the train. It had not yet been opened.

"Walk with me?" Beaudine said, extending a hand toward the cobbled lane that went along the docks.

"All right," Quinn said.

The men turned to where the crowds were thinner and people went about their personal business.

"I'm sorry about what I did," Beaudine said sincerely. "I most truly am."

"I believe that," Quinn said.

"That from me?" Beaudine asked, indicating Quinn's head.

"Yeah."

"Damn."

"Yeah."

Quinn did not bother telling him about his lost memory or anything else that had transpired. He was done with this business, this life, and every part of it.

"Did you prove what you had to prove?" Quinn asked.

"With your help, I did," Beaudine replied. "I couldn't tell you about the French. Mr. Pinkerton and President Grant did not want them turning back. We want their *fleet* to turn back, and now it will."

"I understand. It's a stinking business, but there you have it. I notice Aggie came back in."

"I didn't know where you were or what you were doing," Beaudine said. "I needed backup."

Quinn nodded. "I'm glad it all worked out."

Beaudine stopped, offered the bottle. "Drink?"

"I don't think so, Bill. I said I understood—not that I forgave."

Beaudine looked at his companion with a trace of sadness in his eyes and smiled. He nodded, then cocked his head toward the carriage. "New friends?" he asked.

He looked over, felt nothing when he saw Aggie. "They're the best things to come out of this. If you'll excuse me, I'll be joining them now."

"Sure." Beaudine extended his hand. "Will you take that, at least? In gratitude if not friendship."

Quinn clasped it. "For that, I will."

After turning, Quinn walked toward Zebulon and the Smiths. Aggie saw him coming and, with a smile and a respectful tip of the head, swept away to join Beaudine. Against his own wishes, he watched her go with a sideward glance, saw her embrace her Pinkerton man as she had done the last time they had been together. Only this time, it meant nothing to Quinn.

Reaching the coach, he was introduced to Dr. Orville Soderbergh.

"Save for a few cuts and bruises, they are fine," the portly surgeon said. "I'll leave you to them, unless there's anything you need." The physician squinted. "That bump on your head?"

"No, thanks, Doc," Quinn said. "I'm afraid you fiddle with it, you may cause me to forget things."

"A scalp wound is a tricky thing," the doctor agreed. "Make sure *you* don't do anything to hurt it. Amnesia can come sudden and deep, like a dust storm."

The others just smiled as he took his bag.

"If you need anything, I'll be seeing to the prisoners at the hospital," Soderbergh said as he left.

Zebulon watched him go, pressing his lips together firmly. For the first time in memory, he did not say what was on his mind: *Hurt the one named Martins for me, Doc.*

"I'll trust in my president to see that justice is served," Zebulon said, unprompted and grave.

Quinn regarded the man, his own expression somber. "The man will hang. I guarantee it."

"I expect he will. It won't bring my darling Liz back, but she and I will rest better." The frontiersman sighed and looked at Quinn. Then his eyes rose toward the south and squinted generally homeward. "I've got a dog and chickens to check on—or at least a well-fed dog, unless the birds pecked him to death. I'll be taking leave of you all." He extended his hand to Quinn. "I can't say I'm glad we met, but I will state before God that I am honored to know you."

"I feel the same," Quinn said, shaking the man's big hand. It felt better, richer than Beaudine's.

Zebulon made his farewells to Jane and Douglas in turn, then went to find out where whoever had taken the horses had put his.

"The Mexicans have it," Jane told him. "I saw them move them with the coach."

He thanked her and set off across the crowded wharf.

"He's a good man," Quinn said. "I'll miss him."

"He's going to miss that woman something terrible," Jane said. "They were quite a team."

Sitting inside the shaded coach, with Douglas beside her and the driver feeding the horses up front, Jane cast soulful eyes on Quinn. "Where are you bound, Jason?"

Douglas chuckled behind her. "It still sounds funny. Mind if I call you Hank?"

"You can call me whatever you like, Mr. Douglas Smith," Quinn said before he turned his eyes toward Jane, then toward the gleaming city spreading across terrain that was blessedly not flat. He inhaled deeply the salt air of the bay. "San Francisco is where I always intended to go, except I was constantly getting sidetracked with earning enough money to do something when I got there."

"What would that be?"

"I rightly do not know," he admitted. "Look at it, all full of opportunities . . . and civilization. I figured I'd settle that when I got here and found out what was needed."

"I see," Jane said, eyes downcast.

"First, though, I was thinking. We should probably go back to your cabin and collect your goods, get a wagon. I mean, that is if you and the boy are intending to come with me."

Jane's eyes snapped up at the same time as the boy's smile split both cheeks. He raised his sharpened stick in triumph, nearly piercing the red velvet ceiling of the coach.

"I think I would have withered right here if you hadn't asked," Jane said.

After she stepped from the carriage and put her arms around Quinn, the two embraced as the world buzzed around them and the future loomed as big and bright as the Pacific.

Ready to find
your next great read?

Let us help.

**Visit prh.com/nextread**